THAT'S MY BABY

ALSO BY FRANCES ITANI

FICTION
Tell
Listen!
Requiem
Missing
Remembering the Bones
Poached Egg on Toast
Deafening
Leaning, Leaning Over Water
Man Without Face
Pack Ice
Truth or Lies

POETRY
A Season of Mourning
Rentee Bay
No Other Lodgings

CHILDREN'S BOOKS
Best Friend Trouble
Linger by the Sea

THAT'S MY BABY

A NOVEL

FRANCES ITANI

HarperCollins Publishers Ltd

Published by HarperCollins Publishers Ltd

First edition

The lines from Florence Treadwell's poem "Recalled" from *Cleaving*
(© 1999) are reprinted with permission of the publisher, Ronsdale Press.

HarperCollins books may be purchased for educational, business or
sales promotional use through our Special Markets Department.

HarperCollins Publishers Ltd
2 Bloor Street East, 20th Floor
Toronto, Ontario, Canada
M4W 1A8

www.harpercollins.ca

Library and Archives Canada Cataloguing in Publication
information is available upon request.

ISBN 978-1-44344-780-5

Printed and bound in the United States

LSC/H 9 8 7 6 5 4 3 2 1

For Phyllis Bruce

Ah! now
in the twilight
I'm catching something of you
(a relenting in your absence),
an outline, a quickening: shoulders
half turned, head in profile,
you're swinging round
towards the camera
as if recalled.

—"Recalled," Florence Treadwell

THAT'S MY BABY

"THE 'C' JAM BLUES"

W HEN SHE THINKS OF DUKE'S MUSIC, A favourite comes to mind.

"The 'C' Jam Blues," an early recording. Every note, every nuance, in the vein, in the tapping heel, in the heart, in the bone.

This is what it says to her; this is how it goes. Duke on piano, basic start, plain enough, two notes, steady beat. A touch of bass, a tap of drum.

> *This is what I say, say, say*
> *Do you hear, do you hear?*
> *We hear, all ears, we hear, we hear*
> *Let's have the news, the news*

Sax next, piano riffs off this, theme pursued. Talk gets fast and spicy. Violin strolls in with confidence, sure of the information. Cornet adds joy, voices light, voices deep, echoes, reminders, two cents' worth. The news is spreading, get it, love it, wallow in it. Someone adds an unexpected detail. Ah, we knew that all along. Listen to this, then; I know something, too. "Tricky Sam" Nanton mellow on trombone, then talk, talk, talk; Bigard, clarinet; Sonny Greer, drums; they're all here, partaking of the news.

Just under three minutes, that's all it takes. Each becomes a part, owns a part of the whole.

Belongs. Settles in. Stretches the news until the topic changes. Owns the news, even after moving on.

Owns. Belongs. Belonging. Longing to belong. Must she do this to herself?

She's the one who turns on the music, adjusts the volume, sits there and listens.

She's the one who yearns to be part of the conversation.

1998

LOST LUGGAGE

HANORA'S DREAM HAS RETURNED. SHE HAS left her luggage on a train and the train has departed. The luggage is on a high rack. Elusive, invisible, sometimes seen but not reached, sometimes narrowly out of sight. She searches frantically before thinking to look up, but by then it's too late. She wakes in sadness. It is truly gone.

Wake up, she tells herself. I am not travelling, I'm home.

And remains in bed awhile longer. Dream luggage makes her uneasy. She is uncertain of ownership. Does the luggage belong to her or to someone else? The real concern is that the dream returns when loss threatens.

Loss of something or someone. She's been around long enough to know the signs.

The worry stays with her all morning, so she pays

attention, later, when she takes the elevator to the lobby to retrieve the mail and finds an envelope containing five photos of Billie's newly painted kitchen.

Why would her cousin send photos of her kitchen? Is this, too, a sign? She lives three blocks away. Because of Billie's problems, Hanora visits almost every day.

Billie is losing her mind. Her memory is perforated with holes. Blanks. Synapses won't work.

Prends garde.

Hanora thinks of the book she is trying to work on and wants to weep. Billie's problems have taken over her life. Gradually, at first. As weeks and months have passed, demands have increased hour by hour. There is always a new crisis looming, an unexpected event landing on her door-step—or, more realistically, shrilling through her phone.

Once upon a time, Hanora called herself a writer, a journalist. Hasn't she travelled the world and written about those travels? Hasn't she covered elections, coups, celebrations, invasions, wars—and once, peace? Hasn't she written a shelf full of books, two of which were awarded international honours? Well, not a full shelf—six. But months have passed since she's written anything. Seven months, exactly. Which makes her feel as if she isn't a writer at all. When a writer isn't writing, uncertainties bubble to the surface, uncertainties expand.

The research she has been doing is about a painter and

diarist, Mariah Bindle, whose memory also began to fail, but at a younger age. The book will focus not on memory or memory loss, but on the artist's life and work. For a time, between wars, Mariah was celebrated in art circles. After the Second World War, interest faded and her art was overlooked. Most traces of her disappeared. Half a century later, her paintings have begun to attract attention once again. They are turning up in galleries and at private sales. The National Gallery recently announced the purchase of two of her larger oils.

Hanora became interested and began to make inquiries. What draws her to the art is Mariah's sense of inclusivity, her soothing juxtaposition of colours, especially when the colours are stark and bright. The earliest drawings depict the rugged beauty of the Canadian Shield. The land early settlers loved and hated: its stubborn resistance to being tamed; its formidable presence invading spirit and memory and bone.

After much tracking, after many phone calls and several blind leads, Hanora met with Mariah's family—great-grandchildren of an older brother—and was permitted access to the artist's papers. Diaries, journals and sketchbooks had at one time been shelved in an upstairs closet in the original homestead south of Madoc, Ontario. When the house and adjoining land were sold while Mariah lived abroad, the closet was cleared, and at least some of the diaries and papers were stuffed into boxes and passed on to her brother's family, forty miles away. For many years they were stored in a shed, and it was there that they were later discovered. Storage arrangements were less than ideal, but somehow, two bulging cardboard boxes survived, though not in the best condition. No value was ever placed on these by generations of family. Mariah had been the spinster artist, the eccentric relative who disappeared for years at a time and wandered about the world. No one knew what to do with the material. The boxes were kept but ignored.

How much has been destroyed or thrown away can only be guessed at, but Hanora believes that what remains is of value to the country. When she interviewed the present members of the Bindle family, they greeted her with what she recognized as modest relief. They were unsure of how to dispose of the papers that were in their possession. Hanora was a writer, a researcher, someone who was interested. She knew what to do and where the documents should eventually be housed. They could not conceal their pleasure.

When Hanora first came across the paintings and learned that the artist had spent her childhood years an hour's drive, more or less, to the north of her own hometown of Deseronto, she knew with certainty that Mariah would be the subject of her next book. The attraction became more intimate after she riffled through some of the letters and diaries, and began to understand Mariah's experience as a female artist travelling alone in the world during important eras. Mariah's personality is captured by the recording of her own activities—the details intimate and conversational, at times.

So far, Hanora has read only a portion of the contents of the boxes. Apart from working with oils, Mariah created hundreds of drawings in pencil, pen and ink, wax crayon, coloured pencil, and charcoal, in diaries, journals and sketchpads, over a period of almost half a century. The body of work amounts to a visually recorded history. Not only of the rural area south of Madoc, where she began to draw people and places around her, but of the larger world between the wars, and during the Second World War in Coventry. Hanora is the first researcher to examine the boxes. These are safely stowed in her apartment, and the contents await inspection. The family is eager for the book, as is Hanora's publisher. She'll get the work done, but she has to read every one of the documents. She also wants to examine the drawings carefully. She has access to many of the oils, because she has tracked these to various galleries and has been permitted to photograph them for research purposes.

Her deadline has not changed. What has changed is that she's had to put the project on hold while she attempts to solve her cousin's problems. She doesn't have the energy for both. Not today, not yesterday, probably not tomorrow. Rather than be completely frustrated by her inability to work, she has set everything aside until she can get to it, at least part of the time.

But a writer writes, she tells herself, determination rising. And this is the moment when she decides that she will remember, record, get facts on paper. Not everything, but items of importance only—to Billie and to her. She may not be able to get to her own project, but she can still pick up a pen and tap at a keyboard.

𝄢

INSTEAD of Mariah's story, Hanora will tap memories of another kind: her own, and Billie's, too, whatever her cousin has left. This used to be a joke between them. One rapped a finger against the side of the other's head. Anybody home?

A joke no longer. Billie has first-hand experience with nobody being home. Problem is, she doesn't realize how scrambled things are; or she does, but only partly. Hanora finds herself in the position of having to make decisions for her. Not all, but many, most. Some days she curses the moment she agreed (eight years ago, after Billie's husband, Whitby, died) to take on the responsibilities as executor and power of attorney for her cousin's affairs. This now means power of attorney for Billie's *life*. At the time, the request seemed sane enough. Billie has no children. She and Hanora both live in Ottawa. Billie's older brother, Ned, who is a widower, has lived in Rochester, New York, his entire life. Ned has a daughter, also in Rochester. Both believe that Billie, up there in Canada, is just fine. Both complain, sometimes rudely—even crudely—to Hanora. Both are far away and talk to Billie by phone. (Billie's half of the conversation: "Oh, hello. Everything's good. I'm fine. I'm sitting here watching TV. Hanora is with me. How are you?")

Neither Ned nor his daughter is helpful, and neither is realistic; neither understands the immensity of the problems presented by quotidian tasks or has offered to lend a hand. Ned retired years ago, and Hanora wonders if he is suffering from memory losses of his own. The nursing coordinator asked, earlier in the week: "Do you think Billie's brother also suffers from dementia? From what she's told me, he seems to have an insight problem."

What Hanora knows is that criticism from the sidelines is not helpful. But she has no time to waste on Ned's problems or his daughter's grudges.

"Medicate me, Hanora," Billie said, the day she signed over power of attorney. "If I lose my mind, don't hold back." The witnesses laughed. Everyone laughed. Billie laughed.

Billie lives alone in a two-storey house with three upstairs bedrooms, all of them unused. In 1953, she and her husband, Whitby—everyone called him Whit—bought the place on a street dense with old maples. They paid $12,000 for the property, then painted hardwood floors red, walls and furniture white. The house remains red and white, accented with greys and blacks. They converted a back-yard shed into a studio for Whit. Given the severity of winter, the studio was insulated after the first year. Whit painted in his studio and taught art at the local high school in the evenings, as part of a continuing education program for adults.

Shortly after the war, Billie decided to train as a teacher of the English language. She moved to Canada from New York, and for decades taught English to new arrivals to the country. When she was thirty-one, she met and married Whit, who had served in the war as a stretcher-bearer. As fast as postwar camps in Europe emptied out, immigrants and refugees arrived in the country and filled the city's language classes to capacity. Many students, if not most, were traumatized by their experiences. Billie was determined that her students would find work, would be capable of buying streetcar and bus tickets, reading grocery labels, receiving medical attention, getting their children to school. She fought for their right to be part of society. She was the first person her students phoned in emergencies. She attended their ceremonies when they became citizens. The extra bedrooms upstairs were sometimes full for weeks while alternative accommodation was found. Some students moved to other towns and cities after learning English. Billie and Whit wanted to have children, but Billie never became pregnant. They turned their energies toward community; they helped everyone around them.

All of that changed in 1990, when Whit died. He had stopped teaching entirely by then, and was preparing a solo exhibit for a new gallery in the west end. He was standing by a chair in his studio when he slumped to the floor. Billie, at home and also retired, sensed that something was wrong and called out from the side door. There was no reply. Neither knew he had a heart condition. Whit had avoided doctors, evaded checkups. Perhaps he knew something after all.

Billie managed well in her home until memory problems started, about a year ago. Perhaps a year and a half. She abruptly stopped using the second storey of her house because she said she could no longer manage the stairs. Some of her furniture was cleared from the room she loved best, the red-and-white living room, and banished to the basement. On her orders, a bed was carried downstairs by two workmen hired from a shrinking list of people she had taught, the students of her past. Many were old themselves, or had moved away or lost touch.

There is a full bathroom on the main floor. Billie sometimes uses a cane to move from bed to bathroom to armchair. She sits, mummified, all day and evening, before a large TV, her phone at her side. She wanders into the kitchen, a land of hazards. She pretends to prepare food, though a volunteer from Meals on Wheels arrives daily to deliver a main meal. Billie does not leave the house, though she could. Occasionally, she makes a list and has groceries delivered. Carrots and turnips rot in the fridge. Half-eaten meals have to be thrown out. Bread is coated with mould. Hanora has seen more than a few wine bottles in the recycling box at the back door.

During the past four weeks, Billie has melted the inside of her microwave (now replaced and used only by caregivers to heat meals), placed newspapers on top of the electric range (now unplugged) and flooded the cupboards beneath the sink (nothing to be done except mop the water after another increasingly grim phone call—*Hanora, come right now. I need you! I left the tap on and there's a flood. I think I forgot!*).

Every step Billie takes is a step into panic, depression, paranoia, anger. Especially anger. Each of these emotions has its companion, sorrow. Hanora can no longer manoeuvre her way through the obstacles Billie erects. Solving her problems has become exhausting. The interaction is wearing them both down. The phone rings night and day.

If Hanora hadn't known what Billie was like before her mind began to slip away, she'd now believe that her cousin's lifelong ambition has been to thwart her.

Hanora has never owned a house. She has travelled about the world so many years while writing for newspapers and journals and while researching her books, she hasn't settled long enough to consider buying a house. Nor has she any desire to look after roof repairs, eavestroughs, grass cutting, leaf raking, snow removal, leaking basements, window washing, replacement of garage doors, general upkeep. Because she lives alone, apartments suit her well, and she has lived in many. In her present building, she has created an office where she loves to work. From her apartment, she can move about, travel, return, work, travel again.

She tells herself that she has choices. She can carry on until she resolves Billie's issues, or she can return to her book about Mariah and abandon responsibility. But how can she abandon Billie? Her own history, intertwined with her cousin's, stretches back too far. Ties cannot be disregarded, which means there is no choice after all. How does one desert someone who is loved? If a younger relative were to appear from miracle-land—if Billie's niece were to move to the city—she would gratefully hand over responsibility. But no miracle takes place; no one appears. The real decision is about providing safety, about finding a place where Billie can live out her days while receiving care and support. But Billie does not want to leave her house. She refuses to make decisions. Or rather, her decision is to do nothing and hope for the best.

These are the consequences of her refusal: she has waited so long to make plans—there was never any intention of making a plan—she is now incapable of looking after herself. She has become dependent, and the person she depends upon is Hanora. *Hanora! Come quick! I need you!*

When Hanora lies in bed before falling asleep, she wonders about her own strength and how long it can last. Billie's problems scroll through her mind. Did her cousin truly believe that by taking no action, she would die peacefully in her bed at home? Surely not. That is not part of reality.

When Billie is upset, the scene is piteous. She thrusts out her arms like a child, wailing, weeping, imploring. "What's wrong with me?" she cries. "I'm all mixed up. Why do I feel so lost?"

What is lost is her mind. She gropes for reason, for recent memory. Without memory, she truly is lost. The more she panics, the more confused she becomes. When she remains calm, she is capable of carrying on an almost normal conversation. "Thank heavens I still have my marbles," she tells Hanora, and she believes this, absolutely. There is a disconnect between her actual behaviour and what she understands and remembers about that behaviour. But her worsening situation won't be resolved until action is taken. She stubbornly stares out the window when the topic of moving is introduced. Her doctor, the visiting nurses and Hanora are the ones who have seen her in her worst state. They are trying to create a plan, having agreed that she can no longer stay alone in her home.

The administrative workload is Hanora's. She has toured four residences in the city. Each has an assisted-living floor. She has found a place she believes to be suitable.

Details of the move lie ahead.

BILLIE'S PHOTOS

———

HANORA WALKS BACK THROUGH THE LOBBY and steps into the elevator. She greets Mr. Filmore, who has come up to the main floor from the storage room below. As always, he is dressed for safari: belted khaki jacket, four patch pockets. The hat has to be imagined, net drooping over the nape of the neck. At least he wears long trousers in winter. She thinks of him as Filament because he's long-legged and thread-like. He never stoops. His safari suit is impeccably clean. One morning, she heard her own voice greet him as Filament and her cheeks reddened in embarrassment. If he heard, he didn't let on. She is pretty certain his hearing has worsened since he moved to the building more than a year ago. He lives alone; his wife died. That's as much as she knows about him. He slaps his newspaper against a trouser leg, memories of a swagger stick. Demeanour and carriage point to him having stories to tell, but Hanora can't muster the energy to inquire. He raises a hand as if to tip his imaginary hat—she has always loved the gesture—and steps out onto the nineteenth floor.

She glances down at her opened mail and sends a silent message: *Oh, Billie, is this what we've come to? We amount to more than this.* But she sees that this is also a message to herself: *We amount to more than sending and receiving photos of a painted kitchen. We have outlived people. We, too, have stories to tell.*

It occurs to her that Billie might have mailed the photos in a moment of clarity.

In her apartment office, Hanora spreads the photos over her desk and reaches for a fresh notebook. If Billie thinks the photos are important enough to send, she will grant that they are important enough to document. If there is a better place to start, Hanora has no idea what it is. The effort might amount to nothing more than a few pages of written memories that help Billie connect to her past. At the very least, Hanora will be writing.

Before moving to her present apartment, Hanora donated cartons of books to the city library. She kept those she has yet to read and those she might reread. Shelves line the walls in the room designated as office. She has retained her reference books, even though the new computer is a help when she needs information.

She sees that the phone light is flashing. Billie again. She'll listen to the message in a moment. Everything and nothing is an emergency these days. She humours herself by thinking, *Maybe I'll find my lost luggage in Billie's kitchen photos.* And laughs aloud. She knows the difference between dream and reality. As much as anyone does. She also knows there might be no difference at all.

𝄢

BILLIE's photos:

Photo one: Pine table in corner, lace curtain, unstreaked window. Aunt Zel, honorary aunt and family friend, told her when she was a child: "Clean windows in shade, Hanora, never in sunlight." Aunt Zel owned a rooming house in Deseronto and had many windows to clean. Hanora would pitch in and help if she walked up the road to visit on a day when windows were being scrubbed.

Photo two: Four pears arranged unnaturally on countertop, one with sunken brown spot.

Photo three: Braided rug in reds, whites and greys, created by Billie long ago. A Polish woman who arrived in Canada from a postwar refugee camp on the outskirts of Nairobi helped Billie make this.

Photo four: Two pressback chairs with red cushions. As Billie lives alone, one chair in the kitchen is enough; the extra is for company. Apart from Hanora, who visits? A line of individuals shuffling ever forward, people who convince Billie that she is capable of managing her own house. She calls them "the strangers." Collectively she needs the strangers, especially as her personal hygiene has lapsed, but at times she forgets her needs and threatens to bar the door. The strangers amount to fifteen people, most of whom have had police checks, and all of whom Hanora has hired, checked, confirmed. She receives reports by phone, accepts frequent changes to schedules. Four caregivers come and go at different times. Meals on Wheels delivers food. A physiotherapist arrives occasionally, as does a home-care supervisor, house cleaner, snow remover in winter, grass cutter in summer, the student who painted her kitchen, footcare provider, public health nurse, doctor. As Billie no longer goes downstairs to the basement, the house cleaner does the laundry. All these activities are coordinated by Hanora. It was the doctor who phoned to say that the move must go ahead, and soon. Billie must be moved to a residence that provides assisted living. City agencies are now involved. The area nurse followed up with her own phone call. "Your cousin has to be in a place where she will have round-the-clock care. Safety has become the primary concern because her dementia is going to worsen over time. We've also noted that she has begun to be non-compliant with the caregivers."

Hanora leaned into the wall, phone to ear, and thought about non-compliance. She was certain the nurse was reading from the pamphlet she'd placed in Hanora's hand several weeks earlier. The next thing she'll say is that the disease takes its own course. "This disease, you know," said the nurse, "takes its own course." Hanora stared out the window and imagined the nurse's face, the harsh red patch of skin above her right cheekbone, the fixed expression of weary but professional intensity. *Worsening condition noted*, she replied to the nurse, but silently. *I can document every step of my cousin's worsening condition, to the minute. And if you want to talk jargon, here's something else from your pamphlet: caregiver compassion fatigue. Please consider, and offer realistic suggestions.*

What she wanted at this moment was to sleep for a week, but she could not. She was supposed to be the strong one; she was in charge.

Photo five: And now here it is, in the last of the photos, the sign she's been watching for. The tiniest detail, a corner of a piece of luggage shown within a framed 1939 photograph of Duke, which now hangs in a prominent place on Billie's freshly painted white wall.

After the student finished painting the kitchen, Billie must have had him go to the storage space beneath the stairs and drag out the seaman's chest she'd purchased at a market stall during her 1939 trip to England. She'd have dug the photo out of the chest, or maybe the student did on her behalf. Before Billie met and married Whit, she had been escorted to the Portobello Road area by a man they both knew as Blue Socks, or just Socks. In a shop that sold old items from seafarers, Socks helped her find the antique chest and then haul it to the hotel where he and Billie were staying. Later that day, he took her to a pub for a drink of shandy. She recounted the details on a postcard of Godrevy Lighthouse. Hanora has kept the card ever since, and now it is taped to a shelf of Virginia Woolf books. Billie ended her note on the card with: *A curl of lemon peel floated in a glass offered tenderly by Socks. I miss you. I miss life aboard ship. Love you everly, your cousin Billie.*

𝄢

THE framed 1939 photo is black and white, taken by no other than the singer Ivie Anderson, with a camera bought by Hanora and paid for with money she'd earned by writing three articles about cheese. Hanora had a copy of the photo made after the war and sent it to Billie.

The cousins are standing on either side of the gifted composer, the three smiling broadly. And there's the luggage, the suitcase she remembers as hickory brown, borrowed in March 1939 from her dear friend, her great love, Tobe. A corner of the luggage with its leather strap-buckle has been caught by the camera in the same frame that holds Duke Ellington. Hanora remembers setting the bag down moments after disembarking at Le Havre. And while goodbyes were flung about, while passengers hurried toward the special boat train to Paris, while Duke greeted musicians and cheering fans, she dared to ask Ivie if she would take the photo. Ivie grinned, shoved her purse strap farther along her arm and called to Duke, "C'mon over here, Governor. These young ladies want a photo." Duke obliged. And Ivie—as they used to say in those days—"took the snap."

So, Hanora thinks. Dream luggage is not lost after all. It arrives in the mail and appears in a photo taken so many decades ago, I will make no effort to subtract the years.

Her memory cells take up the challenge. The scene at Le Havre comes alive. Sounds, too. Music awaited Duke wherever he appeared in Europe: on station platforms, in streets outside clubs, on the quay at Le Havre. A chaotic mix of jazz lovers, musicians, photographers with bulbs snapping, press shouting for his attention and a quick interview, fans hoping for a few words, a glimpse, an autograph.

In the photo within the photo, Duke stands between them, all six feet of him, or rather, slightly more than six feet. How could anyone look at that amazing smile and not think *grace*? He was dignified, private, preoccupied, friendly at every encounter. The three are looking directly at Ivie, who, behind the camera, is dressed to kill in a close-fitting button-down coat with flared bottom. A flash of red, a crimson stripe encircling her black hat, a hint of lapel beneath the coat.

For almost eight days, they have been passengers on the SS *Champlain*, sounds of music escaping day and night from beneath cabin doors (ah, how the music beckoned, like soothing conversation, like seductive voices). Duke, wearing old slippers and a thick white bathrobe lined with royal blue, was glimpsed in corridors in various parts of the ship, a clutch of sheet music in hand, sometimes aware of others, sometimes not. Any time he and Hanora were face to face, he spoke to her, always allowed a grin, his moustache a careful shadow over the shape of his smile. And Ivie, with her pencilled, wide-arced eyebrows, invited the cousins, not once but twice, to join her for afternoon coffee upstairs, in the café lounge. Sometimes the other musicians were around. Like most passengers on board, especially at first, they were exploring the ship affectionately referred to as the *Lady Champlain*.

One morning, Ivie beckoned Hanora and Billie into her cabin. Seashells were strewn across the top of her dresser. She saw Hanora looking and said, "These travel with me everywhere. They remind me of places I like to be." When she learned that this was Hanora's first time at sea, she said, "Oh, my dear, have you never walked a beach at sunset? Never dug a half-buried shell out of wet sand?" She reached into her collection, pulled forth a sand dollar and held it out. Perfect and five-petalled, its colour a mixture of sand and cream. Like other keepsakes, it sits on a bookshelf in Hanora's office. Kept these many years.

She calls up the singer's voice with ease. The way Ivie controlled lyrics, the way she slipped into a song with style and kept its energy going, letting everyone know that the spark she brought to the room would remain long after the song came to an end. Her songs were charged with seduction, the promise of dusk and starlight. They could have been set in carnival alleys at night, lights glittering, rides circling in the background. If you were in the room when Ivie was singing, you felt she was grabbing your hands and pulling you up. You wanted to dance while you listened. "It Don't Mean a Thing" . . . the song lodged in the brain for weeks on end. Others, too. So many others. "I Got It Bad (and That Ain't Good)." The slower songs compelled you to . . . well, no matter where you were when you heard Ivie's voice, you stopped what you were doing; you listened to every word. Hanora did. Listen.

In their shared cabin, Billie put on her own show, imitating Ivie. She swung herself in circles between the two berths, skirt raised to her thighs, hips wiggling, arms weaving. That sight, too, lodged in Hanora's brain. Billie laughing—always laughing—Tangee lipstick coating what she called her "glowing lips," red hair swaying, head back, eyes closed, freckles sprinkled across nose and cheeks, throat exposed. And then, collapsing onto her bed, kicking off the ultra-high heels she wore in the evenings when the two of them "fancied up" and headed to the main foyer on the promenade deck, or to the dance floor to check out the entertainment.

𝄢:

BILLIE isn't laughing these days; nor is Hanora, for that matter. If either could find something to laugh about, that would be celebration indeed.

Hanora returns to Billie's kitchen photos and wonders if there is a second sign, apart from lost luggage. Something she has missed. She shuts her eyes, opens again, stares hard. Not for a moment has she forgotten the dream.

Loss approaches.

Memories have been stirred. Plenty to think about for one day. So many people aboard ship are now gone. Ivie, in 1949. Tragically, an early death in her forties. Smoky clubs and bars, her places of work, did not help the asthma, the chronic lung condition.

Duke, who was thirty-nine the year they were at sea (and turned forty a few weeks later in Sweden, to great fanfare), died in 1974, leaving more than two thousand pieces of music as his legacy. As tastes changed over the decades, he invented and reinvented himself. Hanora has never tired of reading about him or listening to the body of work: records, tapes, CDs. When he was alive, she followed every turn of his long career. She met him; they talked. He had charmed. He offered encouragement at the outset of her career. She has only to think of Duke's name and she hears the resonance of his voice. Without playing his music, she can drift into the mood, toes and heels tapping.

As for the ship, in the fall of 1939 it was painted wartime grey and survived to sail only a few more times. The last crossing in the direction of the States, May 1940, was used to evacuate some of the desperate who, at the last minute, had succeeded in escaping the deadly chaos under way in Europe. Nabokov, for one. Hanora tries to imagine him aboard with his wife and son, one year after she'd sailed in the opposite direction. If she had met Nabokov, what would she have said? *I'm determined to be a writer. That is how I plan to make my living. I would like to interview you and your wife. Learn the conditions that have forced you to leave.*

When she sailed in 1939 she wouldn't have called herself anything. She had remained in Deseronto after finishing high school and found work by writing regularly for the town's weekly newspaper. Two articles had been accepted by the *Star* in Toronto. Nothing in *Maclean's* or *Life* or the *Washington Post* or *Collier's*. No awards. Not then, not yet. No book in sight, or even in her imagination. She knew meaningless facts about cheese because she'd reported on National Cheese Week. The rest would come later. And though she has celebrated her rewards, the celebrations have been short-lived. She knows, as every writer knows, that for the next assignment, the next book, she must start at the beginning again.

She conjures the giant ship the way she came upon it when she stood at the pier in New York in March 1939. A young woman preparing to board, ready for anything life set before her. The luggage she'd borrowed from Tobe had been checked and delivered to her cabin. She made her way through a warehouse-like building and out into the air again. The March wind grabbed at the ends of her scarf and blew wildly at her hair. She gathered her coat around her and gaped at the great ship that loomed in front of her. In memory, the anchor was the height of a building. Could that be possible? What is certain is that she came to a halt. "Keep moving, Hanora," Billie said from behind, and Hanora felt her cousin's hand on her back. "If you stand here gawking, we'll freeze before we get on board."

In June 1940, one year and three months later, after the SS *Champlain*'s final voyage from New York to France, that palatial vessel, one of the luxury liners of the world, a wonder of its time and in service only eight years, met with destruction near La Pallice, on the Atlantic coast of France, when it struck an air-laid German mine. A dozen people were killed and many others were injured. Days after the ship was damaged by the mine, its still-elegant remains were torpedoed by a U-boat. The Germans had decided to finish the job.

Hanora, by then living and working in England, wept when she heard the news.

𝄢

OTHER memories work their way into consciousness and will not be suppressed. Hanora braces herself, sinks to her chair. Opens her notebook to the first—dreaded—blank page. Removes the cap from her pen.

And now, in a kind of spirit dance of its own, the page, like music, beckons. Here rise the friendly demons. She will write what she can, when she can. She will try her best to involve Billie. Perhaps her cousin's failing memory will be awakened. Hanora has learned how capably Billie can blurt out surprising details. Maybe she will illuminate the thirties and forties for them both, but from her own perspective.

Sadly, it is Billie's present existence that moves forward unremembered and unrecorded by her brain. She asks a question, listens to Hanora's reply and asks the same question a moment later. She looks at an object she has owned for decades (a nightgown, a pair of glasses, a silver bracelet) and declares: "I have never seen this before in my entire life!" She always adds "in my entire life," and this causes concern because she is so adamant. There is no point arguing because Billie is so sure of her ground. Sometimes, Hanora questions her own reality in light of Billie's certainty.

Billie has no trouble recognizing people she knows well, but she does not know the year, the day of the week, her address, her age or what she ate for her last meal. People new to her are repeatedly asked who they are. Sometimes she is hostile to "the strangers" and shouts at them when they come to her house. The changes are frightening—not only for her but for Hanora, too. As for the strangers, most take Billie's behaviour in stride. They assure Hanora that they are used to working with clients who have varying degrees of dementia.

Despite Billie's memory loss, sparks of truth erupt. The detail she is capable of bringing forward from the past is sometimes astonishing.

Hanora thinks about her own memory and wonders if it will fail at some future time. And how she will know if it does start to fail. For the most part, Billie is not aware of memory deserting her, at all.

For now, Hanora will get things down the best way she can. Mariah Bindle's diaries and journals beckon, partially read, from a corner of her office. A reminder of work to be done, a deadline to meet. A reminder that Hanora has a profession. That she is a writer whose work is on hold.

During her second visit to the Bindle relatives, a family member, a triple-great-niece, retrieved a musty folder of papers that had been flattened under the lid of an old school desk in a spare bedroom upstairs, a discovery separate from that of the boxes stored in the shed. The desk, too, had been passed on to the family from the original homestead, which Hanora has not yet visited. In the folder, four drawings were loosely tucked inside a sketchpad. The family urged Hanora to select one for herself.

After carefully examining the four, she chose a drawing of a mother with a small girl who is crouching over sand at the seashore. The girl has discovered a shell and is looking intently at her specimen. What Hanora loves about the drawing is the way the girl's mother watches over her from behind. The drawing speaks to Hanora because of the look of love on the mother's face, the look of wonder on the child's. She had it simply framed, with a narrow border matching the colour of the sand. It hangs on her office wall. Sometimes, she feels a pang—regret? longing?—when she examines the drawing. Even so, she wants it nearby; she wants it in her space. She has never completed her own private search, but she has not given up, either. The search was set aside long ago, but never put to rest completely.

Hanora has no intention of abandoning Mariah Bindle and the book she promised to her publisher. One way or another, she will stay with the written word. But first, Billie's problems must be solved.

LOST IDENTITY

———

FRIDAY, HANORA'S BIRTHDAY, DEADLINE DAY. She was at the *Post* by noon and had the typed article in Calhoun's hands before he could complain. He stood over his desk and carried on a running conversation with himself while he rummaged through the pages. She wondered if he believed he was communicating and decided that, in his own way, he was. One eyebrow, the left, was shaped like an arrowhead in flight, and this made him appear to be on the verge of asking a question, which kept her on her toes. She focused on a spot over his shoulder, the mostly pink world map he'd tacked to the notice board. Ivory-coloured shelves were in disarray along one side of the office. A wooden filing cabinet with locked drawers leaned into the back wall.

Calhoun looked up. The arrow aimed higher.

"National Cheese Week is coming up, Hanora. Kicks off the seventh of November. Cheese people will be coming into the area from all over hell's half acre—pardon the language, glad your good mother isn't present to hear. Hand over top writing and you'll be paid top dollar. The Belleville paper and ours will run three articles, and we'll share the payment—they'll cover the lion's share because their readership is so much larger. We need length, thousand words minimum, that's for each article. Cheese is a million-dollar industry, and ads—I'm talking full-page—will be run in both papers over a three-week period. That's saying something considering we're coming out of a Depression, so get yourself to Belleville, start doing your homework. This county will be known someday as the cheese capital of the entire nation, so give the industry its due. You have a few weeks—I'm giving you plenty of time. Go out and interview workers in the cheese factories. Talk to . . . well, use your imagination, get into homes, talk to buyers, talk to dairy farmers. You know what to do. Do you have a friend with a car who can take you to a couple of factories?"

He knew she would ask Tobe. There weren't many cars in town. Anyone who owned a vehicle had to have money for gasoline. Nineteen thirty-eight wasn't as desperate as the earlier years of the Depression, when more than a few families in town had suffered from real hunger, but gasoline was still a luxury.

"One more thing, Hanora."

"What's that?"

"When you visit the factories, wear your clothes right side out, will you?"

She looked down, mortified. Her skirt was inside out, seams showing, hem showing. She told herself she didn't care.

On the way home, she kicked at clumps of dried mud along the edge of the sidewalk. A week earlier, there had been rain; now there was nothing but heat. She was thinking over her assignment. As usual, Calhoun had left no room for interruption. Hanora had accepted, as he'd known she would.

She carried on past Bogart's, where brooms were tied together, bristles up. A washboard and mangle were stacked on the sidewalk outside the storefront windows. Her inside-out skirt clung to her thighs. The heat and humidity were unusual so late in September; not a wisp of breeze wafted in from the bay.

I want the work, she told herself. I need the work. But why must I write about cheese?

She could take the train to Belleville. Buses also travelled to some of the rural areas. Tobe would drive her to a cheese factory. He was the town's nice guy, a favourite with the girls, though Hanora was the one who treated him—or pretended to treat him—like a brother. But he was more than a brother; she admitted that to herself. Much more.

Tobe's family owned two businesses, both under the Staunford name. In the middle of the Depression, despite the shrinking population of the town, Tobe's father had offered temporary jobs to some of the unemployed men. That gesture had kept hungry families from starvation. Some said it was the Staunfords who kept the town going during the harshest years.

In winter, families in need supplemented their food supplies by ice fishing out on the bay and trapping small game in the local woods; they earned extra quarters here and there by sawing wood and doing odd jobs around town. Anything helped. One man in town half-soled his children's shoes, using a sheet of leather and a shoemaker's last he had in his workshop. He did this for neighbours as well, charging ten cents. New shoes cost $1.99 at Eaton's, and few families could afford the expense. Everyone compensated, substituted, made do. If an alien had dropped from above and asked about the expression "making do," there'd have been as many explanations as there were citizens in the town.

In summer, children and adults picked raspberries on berry farms and were paid a cent and a half per quart. Gooseberries, the same. Hanora could call up hours under the hot sun, an aching back, a stillness falling over the field as each berry picker withdrew into silence.

A pound of hamburg cost twelve cents, and that was expensive. Boiled up in a pot of water, the pound of meat stretched a long way. Turnips, gnarled and shrunken, were boiled and made into soup. Farmers shared eggs, cream and butter, and traded at the stores for clothing. In late summer the previous year, Hanora's uncle Jim and aunt Grania had brought in a bushel basket of greengage plums. She and her mother, Tress, worked two straight days putting up plums for winter.

Tobe's father, also the previous year, had purchased a second-hand '34 McLaughlin Buick. The day the sport coupe made its debut along Main Street, several young people in town went to Tobe, begging for a ride. Tobe worked in his father's office but had use of the car only after his father was satisfied that he could drive safely. Once past that hurdle, Tobe invited Hanora to sit in the place of honour next to the driver's seat. Most evenings, they pointed the car in the direction of the nearest dance hall. Hanora had also taken her turn squashed into the rumble seat, flattened between bodies, wind whistling in her ears, legs stretched down into the cavernous, sheltered space. The car was designed for two passengers but could take four because of the rumble seat. Never more than five. Tobe's father's rule.

Hanora paused in front of Naylor's Theatre and crossed the street. People in town were faring better now. Calhoun wrote optimistically about "recovery from the tough years" in his columns. But how many facts would Hanora be able to find out about cheese? More to the point, what did cheese have to do with the life she was trying to create for herself? For some time, she'd been attempting to convince herself that she was on the threshold of change. Details were vague. She desired travel, wanted to move to a city, go abroad; she craved adventure. She wanted everything her small town could not offer, but she wasn't sure what that might be.

During the summer, she had secluded herself in her room for days and worked on an article about the Spanish Civil War. She wrote the story of a young man from town, Julian—handsome, gentlemanly Julian—who in 1935 had chipped a front tooth in a crash during a cycle race and had an awkward smile ever after. She'd been attracted to him from afar when she was a student, but he was several years ahead, a senior, a leader. He was also editor of the school paper. Hanora would never know if, like her, he had ambitions of being a writer. He left town quietly, travelling to France and then to Spain to work as a medic for one of the International Brigades. He did not live to come home. He'd been killed in the Civil War, which was still under way. His parents had not yet learned the details of his death; they'd been informed only that he had died.

Hanora's story of Julian was published by the *Star* in Toronto, and she was paid enough to start a savings account. Two days after the article was printed, Julian's parents came to thank her, a copy of the *Star* in hand. The father hung his hat on a chairback in the parlour. Hanora looked at him and thought of Julian's handsome face, his chipped tooth. The mother, wearing black, picked at a thread in her sleeve and began to sob. When they left, her husband had to support her to keep her upright. The two were slumped, defeated by war, by death.

Hanora wished she had known Julian better. Now there was talk of pulling the International Brigades back from the front lines in Spain. Her uncle Bernard, who ran her grandparents' hotel at the other end of Main Street, had installed a table-model tombstone radio in the lobby, and she sometimes went there to listen to the news. People from town dropped in to see the new compact radio. A few owned floor models at home, if they had radios at all. Hanora also carried home extra papers and magazines from the hotel. She read everything she could find. She wanted to write more about people her age who had travelled to Spain. She wanted to write about what the decision meant to families left behind. Her own father had left Deseronto in 1914 to join up at the age of twenty, and he'd lived to return, though he was badly wounded in the war that swallowed his generation. She had stopped asking what he'd seen and done because he refused to reply. He read the same papers she did, every one that came to the house, but he would not enter a discussion about war.

𝄢

HER parents were standing at the front door when she arrived home. Had they been watching for her? Voices were tense as she stepped in.

"Can you come to the veranda, Hanora? There's something we want to discuss."

Come to the veranda to discuss what?

Tress and Kenan went ahead while she kicked off her sandals and walked barefoot from the front of the house to the back. The floorboards cooled the soles of her feet. Sweat trickled down her arms. Her left palm was itchy. Her writing arm, her writing hand. Aunt Grania, her mother's sister, would say, "Left palm itchy, promise of money." If the itch was in the left foot, she'd say, "You'll soon be walking in a foreign land."

Thursday's child, Hanora reminded herself, and wondered what her parents wanted to tell her. *I'm Thursday's child and have far to go.*

Her parents had seated themselves side by side in the enclosed veranda. She plunked down in the one empty chair, which meant that the three of them sat in a row, looking out over the still waters of the bay. Was this something to do with a birthday surprise? If so, why did she suddenly feel trapped? Tress was speaking as if her words were being sucked into an undertow. Her hands were trembling. Kenan's good eye studied the tiles of the veranda floor.

A mumble, a declaration.

"I'm what?" Hanora watched her mother's face as she stumbled over the words.

"We're trying to tell you. We adopted you when you were a baby, two months old. Well, six weeks. We know your exact birthdate. You were born in Toronto, and that's where you were adopted. We brought you home on the train the day we signed the papers. We were thankful, grateful to have you come to us. Our chosen child. We chose you. We chose you because you're special."

Hanora stared.

"What are you saying? Sometimes I look like you, sometimes I look like Father. How can I be adopted? I was born in Toronto because you went into labour while you were visiting your aunt. Don't you remember?" She was aware of speaking wildly, of being on the verge of insisting that she could report the event of her own birth.

Her parents exchanged a quick glance. More silence. Tress made a harsh movement, shoved her hair behind her ears. Hanora knew the signs. For eighteen years she had watched her mother push at her hair, tuck it back, the signal that she planned to avoid unpleasantness. But her mother was the storyteller of the family; she could spin stories from a slim thread, pull them out of air, alter details as needed, change endings. Surely this was one more story, spun out to entertain and amuse.

Hanora tried again. Brazen. Daring. Demanding that Tress change the ending.

"If I'm adopted, why didn't you tell me before?"

No answer.

Kenan had begun to fidget, his own particular sign of discomfort. He tucked his dead hand into his dead-hand pocket. With his good hand, his expert hand, he lifted a brass paperweight from the side table and used its edge to trace invisible shapes onto the wicker armrest. He set it back on the table and drew a long breath.

"From the time I was a young boy, I was told that I looked like Uncle Oak, who raised me. I was adopted, too. You know that. I was lucky to have an uncle who was so kind. He was good to you, too, when he was alive. He took damned good care of me when I was a child."

All of this was true.

"No need to swear," said Tress. She pushed her hair back again. "We have loved you," she said. "Loved you so much." She added, weakly, "That's why we couldn't tell you. We meant to . . . planned to—earlier, years earlier. When you were seven, or eight, or twelve. We'd look at each other and say, 'Now.' But there never seemed to be a good time. The right time."

At that moment, she saw that her parents had been afraid. Afraid that she would turn on them in some vile way, not being their real child. But she was their real child.

They were about to celebrate her birthday. She was an adult. Several of her friends and classmates were already married. Two of her friends had children, babies.

Their own babies, not adopted.

Not given-away babies.

She had a fleeting thought while her parents looked to each other for support once more. *Perhaps at seven or eight, I might have found the news exotic.*

"Who are my real parents?"

"We are your real parents." Tress paused. "We don't know who your other parents are."

"Which means I'll never know?"

"Adoption documents are sealed. That was one of the conditions. No one is permitted to see them once a child has been . . ." Tress stumbled. "Once the mother puts the child up for adoption."

Thrown away. Once the child has been thrown out.

Hanora had begun to listen as if she were a fourth presence in the room. Was she angry? If so, she was aware of experiencing something beyond anger. A collapse of self, a collapse of identity. She might be someone "other" entirely.

She was instantly depressed by the thought of being someone other.

How dare you? she wanted to shout. She aimed a hard look at her parents. How dare you tell me I'm adopted? What about my hair? It's like Aunt Grania's, the same shade of red. I belong to this family and I belong to both of you, and you belong to me. That's the way it's always been. I grew up in this town. We are all from this town.

But she did not shout. She sat in the silence that had begun to settle over the room.

Were her parents telling everything, or were they holding something back? Something she could not, at that precise moment, imagine?

They must be speaking the truth. Why would they sit her down on her eighteenth birthday and blurt this out if it was not true? Not her parents, no. They loved her. She was sure of that. She did not know how to process the information. She wanted to leave the room. She wanted to leave the house.

𝄢

SHE waited until she was in her bedroom upstairs before daring to trace her fingers over the locket with the engraved letter, the cursive letter *H*, newly suspended from a sturdy chain. Before Hanora left the veranda, Tress had fastened the locket and chain around her neck.

Her birth mother, she was told, had provided instructions that the gold locket be given to Hanora on her eighteenth birthday. Tress had hidden the locket away all this time. Hanora pressed it to her palm. Her birth mother had owned this, had worn it when she held her tightly.

And frantically?

Sorrowfully?

She would have gazed into Hanora's face. Beheld her, loved her.

If she loved her when she was born, did she love her still? Was she alive? Did she give her away and move on? Was she forced to give her away? Who forced her? The letter *H*—did it stand for Hanora?

The locket was oval, had a rich, warm lustre. Hanora opened the clasp: no photo. If photos had once been placed there—there was space for two—they had been removed. The back of the locket revealed age, wear. Had it belonged to her birth mother and to someone else? Someone before her mother?

She resolved to find out.

And what of her father? Who was he?

Where?

She sat on the edge of her bed. She knew that Tress and Kenan had not moved from the veranda since she'd come upstairs. She knew that Tress had noticed the inside-out skirt, and had not said a word. The skirt was not the concern. For the first time, Hanora wondered if Tress and Kenan were unable to have children. She wondered if they felt shame because of that. If that was why they adopted her.

There has to be a memory, she told herself. Something stored from infancy, something gathered into the cells. She closed her eyes and willed such a memory to surface. Tried to conjure a mother's face she would never fail to recognize. A voice, a tone, the singing of a nursery rhyme, a lullaby. A voice that had accompanied her through life so far. One to which she had not yet paid attention.

She went to the bureau and scrutinized herself in the central bevelled mirror. Adjusted the wing mirror on either side and looked into three versions of herself. Features fell away one by one: broad forehead, rounded chin, green eyes, pale skin, a few freckles, red hair. She'd been told that her Irish ancestors had bestowed the red hair. There were redheads in the extended family. Aunts, uncles, her cousin Billie in New York. Thinking of New York, she wondered if she should leave town and move there to share an apartment with Billie. As cousins, they'd always been compatible, conspiratorial, even though Hanora was several years younger. Billie had come to Canada many times to visit; Hanora had never been out of the province, not even to cross Lake Ontario. They'd exchanged letters ever since they could print. Every summer during Billie's childhood, her mother had escorted her across the Great Lake by steamer to visit. Billie assumed the role of leader, took charge, counted on Hanora to look up to her. Hanora was happy to take on the role of adoring cousin.

She stared into the mirror again. She saw someone with a slender figure, long legs, long stride. A not-too-bad singing voice. She had participated in school musical productions, but she planned to be a writer, not a singer. No one in the family had been either. Now she was not so certain.

Whose hands did she have? Facial expressions? Temperament, personality traits? Were her birth parents clever, practical, hard-working, intellectual? Were they like her? Was she like them?

Were they alive?

She understood with sudden clarity that she no longer had anyone to resemble. No outside definition of herself. Her story, the story of herself, had altered. Her known past had been wiped away.

She breathed deeply, lined up her thoughts.

She had a gold locket, no photo inside. She had a birth-date, a city, information that she'd been adopted at six weeks of age. A trail was beginning and would have to lead somewhere.

Where had she lived, and with whom, during the first six weeks of her life? What was she to do with this partial information when the key people were unknown?

I am Hanora Oak, she told herself. Hanora Oak and someone else. Someone who lives in the imaginations of a mother and a father I do not know. A shadow of myself.

No, she was the shadow of the other Hanora, the real Hanora, who had existed before her. The one whose existence had begun with a different set of parents.

She would follow the trail she'd been given, faint though it might be. She would find the other Hanora and make her real. She would merge the two. She would not stop looking, even if the trail disappeared. She vowed that she would never stop looking.

IN THE ROWBOAT

Y OU NEED TIME TO THINK," SAID BREEDA.
"You're in shock. I'm in shock hearing this. It's so
dramatic."

Hanora hadn't stormed out of the house, but she had
left quietly. Breeda was a close friend, the only daughter of
Calhoun, the editor Hanora worked for. Breeda was born
on New Year's Day 1920, shortly after midnight; Hanora
was born September 23 of the same year. They had attended
school together, same rooms, same teachers. They'd shared
the same stretch of Main Street, same shore of the bay,
same excitements, miseries, books, parties, and many of
the same friends. Breeda had never tried to come between
Hanora and Tobe. She understood, from the beginning,
that those two had a different kind of friendship, special in
its own ways.

The two young women were in Calhoun's rowboat out on the bay. Hanora was at the oars, barefoot, rowing fiercely. She welcomed the resistance, the pull of the boat as it sliced through water. When they were far enough from shore, they tugged their skirts high above their knees and stretched their legs to the sun. There were puddles at their feet, and Hanora splashed her toes against the floorboards and watched the droplets settle back. She raised the oars and allowed the boat to drift while she repeated, again and again, the conversation she'd had with her parents.

"I'm sorry, Breeda. I need to keep talking." She did not try to hold back the tears.

"Keep talking, then. What are you going to do?"

"What can I do? There's nothing *to* do. This is something that happened when I was six weeks old. I was given away."

"I'll ask my dad. After all, he was editor of the *Post* the year you and I were born. He's known everyone's business for decades. His memory is remarkable."

"Your dad wouldn't tell us anything. This place keeps secrets. It always has. You and I both know that. Anyway, what would anyone here know? I was born in the city. I would have appeared on the scene, suddenly, to a mother who wasn't pregnant. Or maybe she told people she was pregnant and travelled for months before going to Toronto to adopt me. Whatever transpired, people have kept quiet since that day."

"Or minded their own business. That's the line I'm always given at home. 'We mind our own business.'"

"Despite your father putting out the news. Well, I don't want him becoming a sleuth on my behalf."

"All right, then. I won't say anything. But you're in shock. And now you have this wonderful old locket. Let me look at it again. Too bad there isn't a picture inside."

"A picture of someone who could tell me who I am."

"We need to get out and do something. It's Friday. The new dance hall in Belleville, the Trianon, has just opened. We could go there."

"Not far enough."

"What about Tweed? There'll be a dance at the Pavilion. It's all jitney dancing Friday nights. You haven't been there yet. Canoes and rowboats glide in at the back, just below the dance floor. Some couples go out onto the lake in the afternoon and come in to dance in the evening. If we're lucky there'll be moonlight. We can ask Tobe to drive us."

"I don't know if he's available." But the thought of driving with Tobe made her feel better. At this moment she wanted nothing more than his calm presence beside her.

"He'll make himself available. He'll do anything for you, and you know it. You need to get away from home to think this through, Hanora. You and I could stay the weekend at my aunt's house. You remember Aunt Marlo;

you've met her at my place. Maybe Tobe will come back to pick us up on Sunday."

"I won't ask him to drive there twice."

"We'll take the train back, then. We have to change in Yarker and Napanee. That's easily done."

"And your aunt? On such short notice?"

"She'll be overjoyed to see us. She loves to have me visit. Her house is across the road from the Pavilion, right across from Stoco Lake. We can stay out as late as we like and no one will be listening when we come through the front door. When I was ten, I used to sit on the wooden dock behind the Pavilion and swing my legs over the water. At my aunt's, I slept upstairs on the open veranda and held my eyelids open so I could stay awake to listen to the music. If the weather stays warm, we can drag a mattress out there. We can talk all night if we want to. After we dance. We'll dance first."

Hanora laughed, but through her tears. "Dancing will be good. I could run fifteen miles without being tired. And I'm not going to hang around to see if my mother has planned a birthday supper."

"Of course she'll have something planned. She'll be making your cake right now."

"I'll ask if we can eat early. I'll tell her I'm going away for the weekend. I need to get away from here so I can think. Why am I not grateful, Breeda? My parents gave me a home. Well, I am grateful. I'm in shock. What if my other mother lives right here in town?"

"That's hardly likely. You were born in Toronto, remember? Row us back," said Breeda. "I'll start making phone calls to Tweed. You call Tobe. And wear your locket tonight. Are you sure there was no photo inside?"

"There isn't a single clue," said Hanora. But there has to be a clue, she told herself.

She pulled sharply at the left oar and pointed the bow toward shore. As she did, she became aware of a steady buzz in the sky, directly overhead. She paid little attention. She glanced down over the side of the boat and into her own image. Beneath the surface of the bay, her face was misshapen, the oar bent. She chopped at the water all the way back.

1998

NIGHTMARE

TWENTY STOREYS UP, HANORA'S OFFICE LOOKS
over the river that flows through the middle of the
city. Plants are lined up along the sill. A murder
of crows spreads across the sky. A scattering of crows.
How can so many marauding birds insert themselves into
the sightlines of one window? From the kitchen, a radio
voice explains windchill factor. On this March day, the
temperature is minus thirty degrees Celsius. With windchill, the voice continues, the temperature feels like minus
forty-one.

Every winter she tries to convince herself to move
to a warmer climate. Especially during the first months
of the year. So far, she has stayed. People in the building complain of brutal weather; she's not the only one. A
few travel south and stay there half the year. She thinks

of Penelope Fitzgerald's *The Beginning of Spring*, set in Russia, where everyone waits and longs for the unsealing of windows, the announcement of spring. Ah, for the unsealing of windows!

She thinks of her own travels—alone and unofficial—to Leningrad and Moscow in 1965 during the Cold War, how she sailed at the end of April, driven by curiosity. She'd been a journalist for two decades by then, living out of hotel rooms, learning languages, making contacts in different parts of the world. But she had never before visited the Soviet Union. Readers west of the Iron Curtain were interested; the *Sunday Times* was interested, and paid an advance to fund her trip.

That was the time of spacewalks, the ongoing race for space travel, but no one, to that point, on the moon. Her job was to record her observations of ordinary men and women on the street, of social conditions, of the May Day celebrations, of the astonishing parade of military might. This was less than a year after the forced "retirement" of Nikita Khrushchev. From afar, Hanora had long been fascinated by the history and literature of Russia. As far back as 1938, when she was living in Deseronto, she'd read about one million people marching past Joseph Stalin through Red Square, in celebration of the twenty-first anniversary of what was called, by the reporter at the time, the Bolshevist Revolution. It wasn't easy to envisage one million marchers across the same square in the same day, especially as her own country's population at the time was only eleven million.

After making arrangements, she travelled by train from London to Tilbury, where she boarded the Soviet liner *Baltika*. She did her best to blend into the diverse but small group of passengers—Brits and Australians, a few French. Together, they were treated as a touring group, with few choices as individuals. The ship stopped briefly in Copenhagen along the way. An icebreaker cleared a channel through pack ice as the *Baltika* neared Leningrad, their final port.

Her passport was confiscated by Intourist as she stepped off the ship. Intourist, founded by Stalin, controlled every activity on the ship and off. When Hanora argued to keep her passport, she was told, brusquely, that it would be returned when she arrived in Moscow. Passengers hadn't been told that their passports would be forfeited before they were permitted to step onto Soviet soil. Hanora had no choice but to follow the dictates of power.

On board, she had been assigned to a cabin as deeply buried as one could be below deck, a destination she had difficulty finding any time she tried to return. In that labyrinthine ship, where specific areas were barred to passengers and heavy steel doors were locked, she circled and circled, up and down short flights of stairs, ending at the doctor's quarters every time. The doctor, a heavy, jolly man often reeling from drink, opened his door, patiently checked the number on her key, laughed and spoke to her in Russian—she knew only a dozen words—and no matter what time of day or night, escorted her through passageways available only to staff and into the corridor that led to her own section.

Because of the cheap passage she'd signed up for, she shared a cabin with three other women, two upper and two lower berths, metal frames, everything white. The room was cramped and narrow, overcrowded when all four were there at the same time. Exposed pipes that criss-crossed the ceiling were painted white to match the bed frames. Hanora banged her head on a pipe more than once while climbing the ladder to her upper berth.

While the ship proceeded at the slowest possible speed through heavy fog up through the Skagerrak and down into the Kattegat, while foghorns made eerie tunnelling sounds from their own ship and others that passed menacingly close, while the band performed in the lounge until midnight—large Soviet women playing tuba, French horn, trumpet, trombone and double bass—while all this was going on, one of the pipes in the cabin ceiling leaked, causing slow but serious seepage into Hanora's mattress.

She had to be relocated to another cabin. The three women with whom she'd been sharing were uncommunicative from the outset, after learning that she was not committed to their cause. They attended talks on Communism every morning in the main lounge, and did not pretend to be sorry to have her gone. Hanora, cast out, was delighted to rise in status by two classes, from fourth to second, up out of the bowels of the ship, a distinct improvement in comfort. From then on, she shared a room with a woman with hacked-off iron-grey hair, narrow face, lean, muscular body. Her roommate identified herself as Flor. After a night sharing the same room, Flor confided that she intended to disappear inside the Soviet Union because she wanted to live there permanently. She was secretive but told Hanora she was certain that she would be able to merge into Soviet society. She did not disclose her plan. She was, however, genuinely glad to have company, because she'd been alone in her two-berth cabin until Hanora was unceremoniously deposited there. Hanora wondered, meanwhile, if she was the only non-Communist on board, and why she had undertaken such a trip. She reminded herself to do her job.

Flor was happy to share bitter coffee or strong tea any time of day. She had a habit of gnawing at her lower lip, her upper teeth scraping away, especially while in conversation. At night, she ground her teeth. Listening to the gnawing and grinding, Hanora wondered if Flor was as confident as she let on.

Any time Hanora tried to talk to cleaning women,

stewards, women who changed linens, sailors on deck, she received the same answer: "No English." Sometimes, a frightened shaking of the head. Cool response from everyone. It was apparent that the entire staff, whether able to speak English or not, had been forbidden to interact with passengers. Only the Intourist leader, a tall and efficient peroxide blonde named Anya, could and would answer questions. Anya was much in demand and not easy to find because problems erupted from one moment to the next on the *Baltika*. Hanora had no illusions about Anya's awareness of her profession, but she kept her notebook in her handbag, her handbag at her side. At night, she pushed the notebook under her pillow.

After disembarking in Leningrad, passengers were taken about in controlled groups and then travelled, sans passports, by train to Moscow. Between Leningrad and Moscow, Hanora stared through the train window at a landscape rushing past, all birch and withering snow. The scene could have been late spring in her own country. She felt naked without her passport and decided she didn't want to leave the train.

In the capital, finally reunited with their documents, the passengers were taken to see the enormous red banners that covered the buildings enclosing Red Square. Lenin's image presided. During the impressive May Day parade, Brezhnev and Alexei Kosygin, bundled in greatcoats, stood high upon the reviewing stand above Lenin's tomb, surrounded by an entourage of uniforms. For hours, the armed might of the Soviet world rumbled past.

Hanora managed the best way she could during her time in Moscow. She toured a hospital, where she met and wrote about the entirely female physician population. She noted the terrible scarcity of men, the older women working as street sweepers, the absence of automobiles, the enthusiasm of Communist youth and their refusal to believe that travel to other parts of the world might be a good experience. (*We have everything here in our great country. Why would we want to leave? Here, let us give you a postcard of our brave cosmonaut, Yuri Gagarin.*) She wrote about the sparsity of goods in the GUM department store, the uncurbed drunkenness of men in the streets. She wrote about elderly women bundled against the cold, sitting beside barrels and dispensing beer by the glass in the streets. She wrote about her tour bus being attacked one evening—police were on the scene in moments, before anyone was hurt—by several drunken, hostile men outside the Tchaikovsky Concert Hall, the hostility aimed at the unwelcome and more prosperous westerners. She wrote of the feeling, the constant feeling, of looking over her shoulder.

The passengers had been assigned rooms in a large apartment-like hotel outside Moscow, which meant that no one could wander around the city without being bussed back and forth at designated times—that is, without being monitored. Hanora was again assigned to share a room with Flor. One afternoon, a number of their fellow travellers purchased cheap sparkling wine and stowed the bottles on windowsills in their rooms. A bottle burst in the middle of the night, wine and glass flying high. People ran into the halls because everyone was certain they'd wakened to gunshots. For the rest of the night, bottles were heard exploding, one after another, up and down the hall.

The next day, or rather the next night, Flor vanished. She was asleep when Hanora retired to her own bed; in the morning, she was gone. Perhaps she really did have friends or relatives who could hide her away until the group, under Anya's tight control, returned to Leningrad and boarded the waiting *Baltika* to sail back to Britain.

Hanora wrote about the tight control, even while chafing under the restraints. The guiding hand was one of steel. When she returned to England, she was aware of that country's astonishing recovery two decades after the end of the war, especially compared with the slower pace of recovery in Russia. Her article was well received, and earned her a prestigious award and several new commissions. But she wondered about Flor. Wondered if the woman with the iron-grey hair and the gnawed lower lip had been discovered without papers, or if she'd been welcomed, as she'd hoped. Flor was not seen again, certainly not by Hanora.

The Soviet Union during the spring of 1965 was a lifetime ago.

𝄢:

Now Hanora longs to move her plants outside to the balcony to expose them to sun. Spring will come, as will other May Days. Dictators will install themselves and be overthrown. Buffoons and thugs will seize power in different parts of the world. Walls will fall. New walls will be erected. Warmer days will arrive because they must, because one season has always followed another.

She turns away from the window and glances at Mariah's drawing of the child with the seashell, the mother looking on with love. She wraps her hands around her coffee mug to feel the heat. Outside, along the horizon, crows continue to fly past. On and on, they fill the raw city sky.

𝄢:

In the afternoon, she drives to Billie's house. Snow has begun to fall, the snowflakes so large, so distinct, the scene might have been created for the cover of a children's book. Hanora lowers the car window and stretches out her palm.

At the end of the week, Billie will be given the MoCA test. According to Billie's doctor, this quick screening method is designed to aid in the assessment of cognitive dysfunction and is fairly new—having arrived on the scene a couple of years ago. Hopefully, the results will provide insight into what's going on inside Billie's brain. The doctor has invited Hanora to be present; the test will take ten or fifteen minutes to administer. Afterward, he will send the results, along with Billie's medical file, to the residence Hanora has chosen. First, however, Billie must be convinced to move.

Hanora has tried several times to discuss with Billie the need for more care. Her cousin cannot afford to have someone move into her house, not full time, not over the long term. Even if she could, the workload is too much for one person; the coordination alone is an all-consuming job. Hanora has done the managing up to now, but—she steels herself—she already has a job.

Billie is evasive, crafty. She dismisses the care issue as soon as it is raised. She changes the subject, stubbornly stares out the window, has a sudden pain or declares herself too tired to concentrate. "Oh," she wails, "I feel sick to my stomach." And that ends the discussion. But her personal hygiene continues to go downhill; she refuses to let the caregivers wash her hair, and she doesn't care if she has a bath. She is content to sit in her chair without changing her clothes. She stares at the TV screen until she falls asleep.

After Billie's doctor administers the test, the home-care supervisor will visit and reinforce the reasons for the move. Hanora has phoned a real estate agent, but she does not want to think about how she will dispose of an entire household of goods. The enormous task of emptying the place will be set aside for another day. The agent assured Hanora that a house in the area would sell for about $170,000. A large leap forward from the $12,000 Billie and Whit paid in 1953. Billie will need every penny from the sale to pay for an assisted-living suite in a residence. She has a small government pension, along with a pension from the city classes she taught to refugees. Her income isn't huge, but it will cover moving expenses until the house is sold. Hanora and Billie's bank manager have worked out a plan together.

$\mathrel{\clubsuit}$

HANORA lets herself in through the side door, removes her boots and shakes her coat. The snow has stopped as quickly as it started. An odour of new paint permeates the kitchen. Billie must have asked the student painter to develop the photos of her kitchen and put them in the overnight mail. The framed 1939 photo taken in Le Havre with Duke Ellington is hanging on the newly white wall.

The furnace thermostat is turned up high. Condensation fogs the windows; surely moisture can't be good for new paint. Through the doorway, she sees Billie slumped in her TV armchair, a blanket over her legs.

Hanora scoops up Monday and Tuesday's unopened mail from the kitchen table and slips it into her purse. Billie has no interest in the paperwork that moves in and out of the house. She stopped paying bills months ago, cannot manage a chequebook or a bank account. Every detail of household management has been turned over to Hanora: banking, phone, hydro, heating, water and sewage bills, taxes, insurance premiums, health premiums, investment updates, pension information, payment of supplementary caregivers, responses to government organizations asking for information. Next to come will be changes of address. Billie's will was drawn up at the time of Whit's death, and Hanora is thankful for that.

Billie's request to be medicated turns out to have been prophetic. To keep her anxiety and depression in check, her physician recently prescribed a mild dose of medication. Hanora has devised a straightforward chart, a sheet of paper with squares. Billie is to make a check mark each time she takes a pill from her daily dispenser. She keeps the medication sheet on a small table beside her armchair, insisting that she can do this by herself. But the task is proving to be a challenge. Pills have been scrambled, taken at incorrect times, refills ordered improperly. Now Hanora is the one who orders refills.

Billie has heard the door open, and Hanora sees her scramble to pick up a pen and scratch something onto her medication sheet.

This isn't working. Because Billie's caregivers do not administer medications, Hanora will have to take over that job, too.

The TV screen in the living room is alive with images of a Vegas circus show, the sound muted. The bed, which takes up most of the room, has been made. Music is blaring from the CD player across the room: Artie Shaw playing "Nightmare." Billie still has vinyl and a turntable, but over the years she has replaced some of the records with tapes and, now, CDs. She has all the equipment, old and new—even a VCR. She still watches movies using videocassettes.

"Is that you, Whit?"

"It's Hanora."

"Oh," she says, and looks up. "I heard the car and thought Whitby had come home."

"Whitby is gone, Billie. He died eight years ago."

"I know that," she says, irritated. "The car sounded like the one we used to have, that's all." She does not hide her disappointment. "Why didn't you walk? Whit went out for a walk. He wandered away and I haven't seen him since."

"I drove because it's cold outside."

"What day is it?"

"Tuesday."

"The music," she says. "It's Artie Shaw playing 'Nightmare.' Did you know he played saxophone before he took up clarinet? He composed this piece himself. There's something deathly about the sound. It wasn't deathly when we danced to it, was it? More of a shuffle around the floor. Seems deathly now. I'd never have thought that in the thirties."

Billie knows her music. Nothing has interfered with those memories. The piece comes to an end and switches to "Copenhagen"—as fast as "Nightmare" is slow.

"We could dance to anything, fast or slow," says Billie, intuiting. "We could keep up. We had energy. Vigour. We were good."

"We were."

"I was thinking of the ship," she says. "That man."

"Duke Ellington."

"Not Duke. Did you get the photos of my kitchen? The stranger developed them. The pianist was playing 'Solitude' when Duke wandered into the salon one evening. You were on your way up from the cabin. I had gone on ahead. Duke laughed, and waved his hand at the pianist. He was pleased. He sat for a while with Ivie. Hodges and Carney were at Ivie's table, too. No," she adds, "I was thinking of the other man, the older one."

"Were you thinking of Foxy? Narrow face. Long, thin

nose, but huge body. He had the most even teeth of anyone
I've ever met."

"I didn't like Foxy's eyes. They were small and set
close together. I couldn't see the colour, only darkness
between slits. He looked as if he'd wiggled inside layers of
thick coats. He paraded around deck as briskly as a large
man could. How many coats did he wear, one on top of
another?" Billie laughs, recalling.

"You and I sat in deck chairs on those brisk days,"
Hanora says, thinking how good it is to see Billie laugh.
"Twice. The weather permitted that bit of insanity. We paid
two dollars for rugs the steward wrapped around us, an extra
over our feet. What luxury! Duke was out there one day,
too, even more wrapped up than we were. I loved talking to
him. He listened as if every word spoken to him mattered."

"Musicians know how to listen," says Billie. "They're
born that way. Or maybe train themselves to hear. And I do
remember how cold it was before we were wrapped up."

"It was late March on the North Atlantic, Billie. It's
March now. I came by because I want to talk to you."

"March," she says. "How can it be March? How did
the time whiz by? Today feels like Sunday. What day is it?"

"Tuesday."

"It feels like Sunday. I can't think what that man's
name was. The older one. Older then. Not as old as you
and I are now."

"I'm not sure who you mean. The ship wasn't full, but there were plenty of people around. And I haven't forgotten Foxy. He was on the make. Especially with younger women."

"We were young," says Billie. "But he didn't get far with us. Given a full passenger list, he would have made a conquest. But not many people were heading in the direction of war. The effort those days was to get people out of Europe. Still, Foxy was a great dancer. We both danced with him. His tactic was to ask someone to dance and then invite the woman out to the promenade deck. Wasn't my name Hanora?"

All of this has come out in one breath. The music switches again. This time it's Ella, another voice that compels Hanora to stop and listen. Billy Strayhorn called Ella "the boss lady." She's singing "Please Be Kind."

THE TEST

THEY SIT AROUND THE KITCHEN TABLE. An extra chair has been dragged in from the unused dining room. Billie is calm at the outset. Relaxed, assured.

"Are you checking to see if I have all my marbles?" she asks. She and the doctor laugh.

She opens the top drawer of a kitchen cabinet and reaches into a jumble of paper, loose pages filled with scribbles and columns of words, writing pads. She sees Hanora looking, tries to hide the contents, shuts the drawer quickly.

Ah, Billie. You should have taken up acting, not teaching.

She places a pristine notepad on her table, along with several pens and a pencil. She picks up a pencil and doodles aimlessly on the blank page while the doctor explains what he wants her to do.

"No problem," she says with confidence. Her smile is benign.

She watches the doctor's face, pays close attention now. She is in a rush to draw the cube, and leaves out two lines. Becomes hopelessly confused when asked to join lines and follow a sequence. Recognizes animals correctly. Draws the clock.

She is given five words that she'll be asked to recall later. She repeats them to the doctor and commits them to memory. She begins to doodle again, frantically now, on the paper in front of her, which is filling up with squiggles and marks, dots and numbers. Hanora can see, from across the table, that she has written, in the tiniest script, three of the five words she is supposed to remember. She covers them with one hand. The doctor does not seem to notice. Or maybe he does.

She's cheating.

She's afraid.

Now Hanora is afraid. She wants to leave the room. She wants to leave the house. The responsibility is overwhelming. This is more than she bargained for. Someone she loves is sitting at this table, desperate to fool her and the doctor. But Billie doesn't realize how easy it is to see through her attempts to distract. This is the part that is heartbreaking.

Several questions later, she is asked to repeat to the doctor the five words she has committed to memory. She panics, moves her hand away, bends over the paper, looks down to see what she has written. Even with three of the words mixed into her page of doodles, she can find only one. She invents the other four and seems satisfied.

The doctor does not show surprise. He provides clues. Billie cannot recall the other four, not after hearing the clues, not even with prompting.

The final result, which Hanora is able to see, is totalled at the bottom of the sheet: a score of sixteen of a possible thirty.

"How did I do?" Billie says, beaming. She sits up straight and adds, "You may go home now. Both of you."

THERE ONCE WAS A CHILD

ILLIE'S BASEMENT HAS TO BE TACKLED. A JOB of clearing out. Billie never goes downstairs, hasn't been down there for more than a year. Because the basement is underground, out of sight, that's where Hanora will begin. But before going to her cousin's house, she'll clear her head, walk to a nearby park that borders a wooded area. She'll take the winding trail that leads to a bit of a hill. The trail circles the hill and descends to rejoin the main path at the bottom.

The temperature is kind this day, and as Hanora walks she imagines spring turning to summer. She's glad she has made the effort to stay fit and active. She walks almost every day. She goes cross-country skiing at the Mer Bleue Bog, a ten-minute drive from her apartment. She is thankful for sturdy hiking boots, given the somewhat slippery ground today. Three women ahead, all using hiking poles, turn and greet her with energy. It's that kind of day. Sun shines through the clouds and anything is possible. The women are her age or slightly younger; they set a good pace and she is content to follow behind. She passes a bike frame emerging from the snow, half-rusted, the other parts missing. Stolen and abandoned, probably. Last fall's debris working its way through the dregs of winter. She hikes past a garbage bin with a slanted lid, latched to keep out raccoons and other small animals that live along the river. Despite the latch, food wrappers are strewn around the base of the bin, as if humans couldn't figure out how to use the mechanism. Soon, a city crew will come along and clear the trail completely.

As she ascends the hill, she allows memories of Deseronto, her childhood town. The bay out back of the narrow house, seen through veranda windows in all weathers. Coal shed on the left, climbing maple on the right, the shinny to the almost-tip worth the scraping of knees and palms. One time, high in the tree, she had a glimpse into the neighbour's bedroom, spotted old Mr. Fielding undressing, pulling off his pants. She saw his bare white bum and slid down the trunk, worried she'd get into trouble. She stopped worrying when she realized he couldn't have seen her; his vision was so poor he often steered his bicycle into the ditch on the way to and from the funerals he attended around the countryside, as a pastime.

Tobe, who grew up two houses away, came to the yard to keep Hanora company. He, too, was an only child. She told him about Fielding's white bum, and he climbed the maple but had no sightings. Tobe was attractive from the time he was a boy. Large, wide-set eyes, intelligent face, lean body, hands with long fingers, a thick mop of brown hair. He was extraordinarily calm; she learned to rely on that. He was a year older, but they got on from the beginning. Tobe also had a sense of justice. As did Hanora. Play was fair play. And the two loved absurdities. They invented games, laughed uproariously, shouted and sang, trekked around the backyard, always under the watchful eye of one set of parents or the other. Beyond the flat stones, the yard tipped into dark waters that groped at the shore. The shore was danger, off limits unless an adult was present. Hanora and Tobe climbed the maple together and sat on the thickest branch, side by side, partially hidden by leaves, hoping that if they were still, birds would settle around them.

"Life is treacherous," Kenan had taught Hanora. He'd heard the words often enough from his uncle Oak, who'd raised him. Hanora wondered, as she grew older, if Kenan truly believed those words. Perhaps so, after his war. But she refused to believe in the treachery of life. For her, life was a wonder, an adventure, a story, one story after another. For Tobe, life inspired awe. He wanted to find out, learn, see, understand what was around him. The difference between them, Hanora thinks, was that Tobe was decisive, immediate. He didn't falter, even if a decision turned out not to be a good one. Whereas Hanora weighed everything, delayed decisions, was bound by some unswayable inner dictate to consider all sides.

Outside the house, wind whipped up a spray at the edge of the bay on the blackest nights. She heard and stored the sounds of lashing waves. In summer, in fall, the water stilled. From her bedroom window she could see small inlet, large inlet, curve of shore, jut of land, the wide stretch of Long Reach. So much water, Lake Ontario's opposite shore could not be imagined. Another country, she was told, another country is far off in the distance, where the large boats and steamers head after they leave the wharf. Where your cousin Billie lives with her mother and father and her older brother, Ned. Hanora tried to believe but didn't really, because the other country did not allow itself to be seen.

In winter, the frozen bay beyond her yard became the town rink. Ankles collapsed inside skates. She was two when she learned to pursue Kenan, who carved figure eights on the ice while she turned this way and that, laughing, chasing, trying to follow. No one could catch him; her father could outrace any father, brother, uncle or grandfather she knew. His cap was pulled over his left eye, the sealed eye. A half face of scars. She'd known no other face, though she'd seen an early photo in her aunt Grania's black-covered album and decided that the younger man in the picture, the one with the plain face, could not be her own loving father, the one who could pick her up with one arm and solemnly waltz her around the parlour. In all seasons, before stepping outside, he reached one-handed for the cap that hung on a nail beside the door. The act of lifting, the flipping of cap to head, so much a part of his fluid movement that he had no need to pause. Only inside the house did anyone get to see the entire face, the curls in his dark hair.

Tress gathered up her own dark hair, allowing Hanora to slip long hairpins into the thickness of rolls or the figure eight, the pins disappearing like magic. Once in a while, at bedtime, Tress put Hanora's red hair up in rags. The next morning, she untied the rags and pulled them free and shaped ringlets with the tail of the comb. She told one story after another while Hanora tugged and twisted and tried to wiggle out from between her knees. The hair was too fine, too straight, didn't take to ringlets; any curl would be gone by lunchtime. Tress declared she would not make ringlets again; they never lasted. And forgot, and a month or two later plunked down in the curly-birch chair and said, "Let's put your hair up in rags tonight. I'll tell a story if you'll stand still." Her mother could pull stories from a current of air, from a wisp of suggestion.

There once was a child, a girl with red hair, who loved to be outside. One morning, she was in so much of a hurry to get out to play, she paid no attention to her clothes and wore her dress inside out. This girl sat on a branch in the maple tree behind her house and whistled to the birds. She put her right hand to her mouth and imitated their calls until they sang back to her. She waggled her fingers as if playing an invisible wind instrument; she cupped a hand to her ear to listen. She created exact tones, exact pitch. She fooled the birds into believing she knew their language, and perhaps she did, because they answered her every call. She was patient; she was a listener. She could sit still for a long, long time in the tree. Perhaps she was collecting stories the birds told about their flights over the deep waters and the great forests.

And Hanora would say, "Now it's my turn."

This is the story of the adventures of the baby hawk. She was born in a stick nest and was timid until she first learned how to fly. After that, her eyes could see so clearly, she could look inside the thoughts of others.

In 1932, Hanora's parents purchased the house they had rented since 1918, the year Kenan came home from the war. He'd returned wounded, two and a half years before Hanora was born. Her parents paid $119 for the house because the postmaster who owned it, Jack Conlin, had died and his widow wanted to sell. The price was low— 1932 was a Depression year. Kenan had work and he had a pension from the war and a few dollars saved; he kept the books for two businesses in town. Tress worked three days a week in the dining room of her family's hotel, which her parents had owned for decades. She and Kenan counted their purchase money and laid it on the lawyer's desk, and from that day had a house of their own. They had taxes to pay, but no more rent.

From the age of six, Hanora was permitted to walk along the boardwalk by herself to visit her grandparents at the hotel at the other end of Main Street. She passed Tobe's house along the way, before crossing the street at the corner. Tobe's mother displayed objects on an inner windowsill that fronted Main Street, two feet back from the boardwalk. The displays changed frequently: a collection of stones, smooth and rounded, gathered from the shore of the bay; a miniature toy train made of wood, engine to caboose; a collection of thimbles; a row of teacups in varying shapes and patterns; a lineup of fancy soaps Mrs. Staunton had made; a trail of glass elephants, the trunk of each raised as if to grasp the tail of the animal in front; a selection of whistles Tobe carved with his staghorn-handled pocket knife, a knife that Hanora was permitted to use. There were surprises on the sill. The contents kept changing. Townspeople sometimes walked out of their way to see what Mrs. Staunford had on display.

The family hotel was directly across the street from the train station and the steamboat wharf, and sometimes passengers climbed down off one and boarded the other. Hanora's grandmother, Mamo Agnes, was in charge of the territory called kitchen, because she was a cook like no other. She had an assistant who could take over in a minute, but Mamo Agnes still put on her apron, rolled up her sleeves and created a thick stew, three dozen tea biscuits and six layer cakes in a morning. Between meals, in good weather, Mamo Agnes and Grampa Dermot sat on the veranda of their house next to the hotel. They dragged out two Morris chairs—one of the chairs a rocker—and kept an eye on their end of town, and on the coming and going of boats at the wharf and trains at the station. Before Hanora was born, the day-to-day management of the hotel had been given over to Tress's older brother, Bernard, and his wife, Kay. Uncle Bernard kept the books through the years of layoffs and low salaries and rum-running and even more years of gambling on steamers that criss-crossed the lake, the boats discharging passengers on the wharf late at night. Bedraggled gamblers stumbled across the street to dollar-a-night hotel beds, keeping the place alive during the lean years of the thirties. Al Capone was a guest more than once after crossing the Great Lake in his own small craft. The family protected his identity, knowing that he registered under another name.

When Hanora visited, she ate in the hotel dining room with grandparents, aunts, uncles, cousins and any other visiting relatives who were there at mealtime. A special table in the corner was reserved for family use. The dining room was noisy with the clatter of cutlery and the conversation of travellers touring their samples, factory owners who dropped in for a quick meal, an eccentric doctor who'd put together his own medicine show, and once, a stunt pilot accompanied by his female assistant, who was also his wife and whose job it was to stand on the wing of the plane while it was aloft. The woman's name was Johanna; Hanora never forgot. Johanna had beautiful soft blonde curls that seemed to be pinned to her head; she wore a pilot's cap over her curls when she performed.

Every meal Hanora ate at the corner table presented a new adventure. She listened to conversations and strained to understand. She watched and imagined the lives of diners who were seated about the room.

Best of all, she liked to hover in the background when her aunts gathered in her grandparents' house beside the hotel, or at her own home, or at Zel's boarding house. Six or seven women: her mother, Aunt Grania, Aunt Kay, honorary aunt Zel, other aunts who arrived in town from their farms north of town to shop, or for no other reason than to drop in and visit over an endless pot of tea.

Laughing and storytelling went on for hours, until the women remembered they had other duties: meals to cook, chores to complete. Still, they wanted to hear each other. They gossiped, passed on family news, farm and town news. One afternoon, the normally quiet Aunt Kay spoke up. She began to tell the tale of an ancestor whose sad epitaph had been printed on a mourning card after her funeral in England. In soft and melancholy tones, Kay recited the verse for the others:

Twas in the blooming time of youth
When death to me was sent
For all my husband's done to me
Dear Lord make him repent.

The women were shocked to silence. Shook their heads and looked to each other's faces. Kay repeated the verse and told them that the story had passed through generations with no details of what the husband had actually done. Those had to be imagined. After that, everyone who'd been in the parlour that day (including cousins who'd crept back in after tiring of playing outside) could repeat the lines of the verse about the unfortunate woman whose bones and sad story were sealed forever in her English grave.

The best stories were told and retold. Old Fielding, his face and bald head brown from the sun (Hanora remained silent about his white bum, though she was certain the women would laugh if she told), cycled from town to town, attending funerals, visiting homes and churches and graveyards, any and all within his bicycle's reach. Because of his bad eyesight, he fell into ditches on the way to funerals, and more often on the way back, if he'd found plenty to drink. He attended whether or not he'd been familiar with the deceased. He stayed for liquor and eats and conversation, and he was never lonely. Asked on the street one afternoon why he had turned back so soon after starting out on his bicycle, he replied sadly and politely that he hadn't had a movement yet that day; he'd have to miss the funeral. Tress and the women hooted over that. Mamo Agnes laughed with her face scrunched until her eyes appeared to be closed, but they were not. Mamo Agnes, the others said, didn't miss a thing. The same was said of Aunt Grania, who was Deaf but could lip-read any one of them. If she did miss something, especially when the topic of conversation changed without warning, she looked to Tress for explanation. Since childhood, the two sisters had owned a private language of hands they'd invented. Tress always kept her younger sister inside the conversation.

Hanora hovered in the background, grinning to herself, listening hard, stowing stories to share later with Tobe and Breeda. One afternoon, Aunt Zel took her aside and said, "You're the one with the memory, Hanora. Someone in the room is always the silent recorder, and I'm pretty certain it's you. It's good that stories are remembered and passed on. Stories give us a sense of belonging."

Days and months and years run together. Did Hanora start school before or after her father's friend Hugh visited for the first time from Prince Edward Island? She was surprised to learn that her father had a friend who'd journeyed to the same place called War. She watched from her bedroom window while the two former soldiers walked out along the shore of the bay in the evenings. When they sat in the veranda, their conversation could not be heard because they kept their voices low.

Her mother cooked special meals and made the place fancy with flowers and set out good linens when Hugh visited. One summer, he brought a radio of a size he could carry in his arms. They sat in a semicircle in the parlour after supper and listened to big band music while the tubes glowed from the back of the radio. When the program finished, Hanora felt that she was floating on remembered melody. After a late snack of bacon and cheese and tea biscuits and a pot of tea, a cot was made up in the parlour and the parlour doors closed to provide privacy for Hugh. In the morning, the bedding was folded and put away until nighttime again.

Kenan was the one who made breakfast. He cooked eggs several times a week because he'd been allowed only one egg per year when he was a child being raised by Uncle Oak.

There was a boy who grew up in this town. He had long legs like yours, and curly hair. He lived with his uncle and a bulldog named Jowls. On Easter Sunday, the boy was permitted to eat a single egg—the only egg he was permitted all year—and this was served in a special dish rimmed with gold. If you look on cupboard shelves around the room, you might find this special dish, which has its own gold-rimmed lid. The uncle who served the egg was not mean or stingy. He raised hens and sold the eggs to support the child. Every egg was precious and brought in money to purchase milk, or bread, or a new pair of britches, or a copybook or slate to be used at school.

On another visit, Hugh brought piano rolls and they walked along Main Street to Hanora's grandparents' hotel, where there was a player piano in the lounge. She invited

Tobe to come along and they listened to "Dizzy Fingers" while a crowd gathered round. Hanora thought surely it was not possible for piano keys to move so quickly. That night, the melody rippled through her sleep while long, wavering keyboards with black-and-white keys rose and fell through the air on their own, no player in sight.

Hugh told Hanora stories about Prince Edward Island. About wind that blew for days on end, about gulls that made brave attempts to lift, land, settle on the sea. He told her about two points of land that jutted into the sea a mile apart. At night, seaweed was gathered, as if the points of land reached through the dark waves while everyone was sleeping and tugged and twisted the weed into a long, thick cord. By early morning, there it was, arranged along the beach in a continuous loop, stretched out the entire mile between points.

One regular visitor to Deseronto was cousin Billie, who arrived from Rochester in the late summer, every visit memorable. More than three years older than Hanora, she could have been her twin; everyone said so. They had the red hair and green eyes, and Mamo Agnes declared them to be "two peas in a pod." Billie's mother never stayed long; she accompanied Billie on the steamship across Lake Ontario, returned home, and came back after a few weeks to collect her in time for school. Billie hated to return home and told Hanora that she and her brother, Ned, lived in an unhappy household; her parents fought and her father shouted. Sometimes he stormed out, then came back to the house late after a bout of drinking. She preferred Hanora's family to her own. Hanora had parents who knew enough to stay calm. They behaved like adults. They could be counted on.

Hanora thought her cousin exotic, arriving from another country, brazen enough to complain loudly about her family life, ready to dive into adventure. The bond between them held throughout childhood. They exchanged secretive letters during winter months and invented a coded alphabet. Billie usually signed her letters *Love you everly, your cousin Billie.*

One August morning while Billie was visiting, the two went for a walk beyond the town limits and ventured into dense woods. It wasn't long before they were lost, thirsty and hungry. Billie swung gamely from thin branches that drooped down from larger branches above. She dropped to her feet and declared that they would search for food. She promised that a path would turn up, kicked at some rocks and fantasized about what they would eat when they found food. Ten minutes later, chuffed with bravado, she climbed to the top of a wild apple tree to shake down its unripe fruit. "Apples will cure starvation," she declared. She leaned heavily into a branch. Hanora peered up as the branch cracked. Billie ripped open the back of her thigh on the way down, a long horizontal tear below the buttock. She lay on the ground with a wound that refused to bleed.

To Hanora's eyes, the upper part of Billie's thigh was a slab of marbled meat that had turned itself inside out. Tearless, stoic Billie was unable to move, so Hanora had no choice but to abandon her cousin while she sought help. Where? Not only was she lost in the woods, but she was also trespassing.

She ran in any direction, no direction, and arrived at a split-rail fence, which she followed, at a steady, breathless run, to a farmhouse. The owners of the apple tree were inside. She broke into tears when a robust woman opened the door, wiped her hands on a towel and said, "What are you doing so far from town? Aren't you Hanora Oak? I'd recognize that hair anywhere. Do your parents know where you are?"

After hearing the blurted-out story, the woman's husband followed (or rather, led) Hanora to the apple tree, knowing exactly where it was. He plucked Billie up into his arms and carried her back to the farmhouse. The woman dressed the wound, and the girls were returned to Deseronto in an open wagon drawn by two horses. Billie referred to the wagon ride as "our triumphant re-entry into town." The local doctor stitched Billie together, and from that day forward she had a thick horizontal scar running along the back of her thigh.

𝄢

HANORA pauses in her walk and stands before a memorial plaque on a stone bench at the top of the hill. She looks about in all directions. The three women who preceded her up the trail are leaning into the back of a second bench, nearby. Their faces are turned to the sun; their walking poles rest against a tree trunk. They speak quietly, eyes closed, familiarity with one another apparent—and enviable. Enviable because they seem to have no cares in the world except to absorb the quiet and feel the heat of the sun on their skin.

Here we are, like world explorers, Hanora thinks. One would think we'd journeyed to the tip of Everest. And isn't there always a journey? Long or short, on horseback or camel, by train or ferry or ocean liner, or in sturdy boots up snow-covered trails. She looks down and stomps her own boots to clear ice pellets and traces of wet leaves that have stuck to the soles. She thinks of Tobe climbing the tree with no sighting of Fielding's bum. How the two of them giggled themselves into a state of hilarity when they were children. She smiles to herself.

Remembering Tobe makes her think again of the words of Zel, dead many years now. Zel was a widow in her fifties when she moved to Deseronto to start up her rooming house. She exuded spirit, strength, humour, tipping her head back and laughing with abandon. She'd sent a letter of advice when Hanora was living in wartime England. *Some advice has been followed, some not.*

If you find someone, hang on tightly. You might not realize the importance of the occasion. You might not recognize the significance of a particular hour or day or week in your life, but you can try. Pause when you watch light rippling over moving water, or when you inhale the exquisite scent of a bloom or hear a child's laughter. Pause when you are singing, or listening to beautiful music, or dancing in the arms of a loved one, or holding someone close. Every time you offer love and are loved in return, store those moments. There will be a time in your life when you will remember and you will want to remember, and you will be glad and you will be grateful, because your hoard of memories will be raided over and over again.

It was as if Zel believed that Hanora could make conscious decisions about what to remember and what to forget. As if Hanora was somehow in charge of what her brain would store and recall.

What Hanora remembers—she waves farewell to the other hikers and begins to descend the trail—is that during her earliest years, she had no awareness of belonging because belonging was implicit. She was surrounded by family. Only later, after learning that she was not a true part of the family, only then did she begin to feel uncertain, even unworthy. That is probably the word, she thinks: unworthy. The beginning of the feeling. As if, from that day, she no longer had the right to belong. The feeling had come from inside, not from anyone around her. She had lost confidence. Tress and Kenan would have been devastated if they'd known how she felt.

But all of that is in the past. She is not unhappy with the life she has made for herself. She has real friends; she has travelled the world; she has had the companionship of men, one of whom she truly loved. She has never married. When anyone did try to move in close, she found herself edging away. She knows how fortunate she is to be able to do the work she loves; her writing keeps her engaged and provides her with steady income. Her close friends are in the same business—some in towns, some in cities or other countries; they manage to stay in touch. Each knows the others are out there writing. They are conducting research, interviewing, meeting deadlines. She has lost friends, yes, but she tells herself not to dwell on loss.

And now Mariah Bindle's papers await investigation.

Writing brings joy. Tillie Olsen was in her seventies when Hanora first met her at a summer arts colony where they were on faculty. Tillie had published *Silences* a decade earlier, and she described writing to Hanora during their first conversation. She had learned that Hanora was working on a book about the overseas trade in orphanage children, and said, with a sigh, "Ah, you are writing, Hanora. Then you are in that bless'ed state."

Tillie hiked every morning up the side of a mountain and back, before the other members of the colony were up. A role model, not only for Hanora but for every one of the younger writers there. Hanora and Tillie had several conversations about war correspondent Martha Gellhorn, especially the memorable reporting she had done for *Collier's* in 1945, after her visit to Dachau. Both agreed that this was one of the outstanding pieces of reporting of the century. Martha was born four years earlier than Tillie. She and Hanora had never crossed paths.

Hanora sometimes thinks of her encounter with Tillie Olsen. She promises herself that she will get back to her own "bless'ed state."

𝄢

SHE drives to Billie's in the afternoon and lets herself in. She carries two empty boxes and kicks them down the basement stairs as she enters. She is surprised to find Billie sitting on her red-cushioned chair at the kitchen table. Her cousin seldom leaves the TV chair for more than a few minutes. A partly eaten sandwich has been abandoned on the counter. A cup of tea has gone cold. Crumbs are strewn over the counter as if they've been thrown. An unwiped bowl and dirty spoons are in the sink. Soft cheese is stuck to the tabletop. Amazing how much chaos can erupt during a single meal. Or maybe two.

Billie is staring through and beyond her. She has never acknowledged the truth that Hanora runs the house and the care program that has been set in motion over the past year and a half. If Billie acknowledges this, she will also have to acknowledge her inability to care for herself.

She focuses. "Hanora. Are you out on errands? What are you doing here?"

"I'm here to see you. I thought I'd come before the next caregiver arrives."

"One stranger was here. She prepared breakfast and left my lunch on the counter. I don't want any more."

Hanora begins to wipe up the mess.

"I went for a long hike this morning, Billie. In the park, up and around the hill. You used to walk there with Whit. And with me after I moved to Ottawa."

"The bark," says Billie. "We walked all the way up the bark."

Hanora tries to make the connection, tries to envisage the kinds of bark on the trees at the top.

"The bark?"

"The bark. You know, the bark. Mark. The one on the bench, at the top. The marker."

Hanora is thrown by the confusion of words, but relieved that Billie has resolved the issue after groping through the tangle of language stored by her brain.

"We did. It's a great hike. Not too strenuous."

"I don't think I'd tackle it," Billie says. "Not now."

"I guess not." No, she wouldn't. Not with a cane, or without. Not at all.

"I'm going down to the basement today, to do some organizing."

"Oh," says Billie, immediately uninterested.

It is only when Hanora turns away from Billie at the kitchen table that she sees the words. They jump at her from walls, cupboard doors, shelves. Yellow Post-it Notes all over the room.

Chair
Drawer
Lace (this, attached to a curtain at the window)
Kettle
Toaster
Spatula
Pepper
Fridge
Sink

Microwave
Dish soap
Tea towel
Duke (attached to an edge of frame)
Purse (purse is on the counter, note attached to the strap)
Knife

The final note is stuck to the broad blade of a chef's knife suspended from a magnetic rack on the wall.

Each label has been printed with care. Each is attached to the object the word represents. Hanora imagines Billie guiding herself, searching for familiarity in her own surroundings. Doing her best to hang on tightly. How frightened she must be when she stands in the middle of the room without the memory of a familiar landmark to direct how she will place one foot before the other, how she will move in a particular direction for a particular purpose.

Billie acts as if nothing has changed. She doesn't register Hanora's surprise.

At least she still knows which object is which. Or did she have guidance from her morning stranger? This is Billie's handwriting. Hanora inspects each word that leads her cousin in and out of her shrinking world.

Billie leaves the kitchen and walks to her TV chair. Hanora follows to see if sticky notes are attached to furniture in this room, too: *TV, bed, pillow, remote, CD, cassettes, radio.*

Not yet.

She makes a fresh cup of tea for Billie, finishes cleaning the few dishes in the sink and goes downstairs to the basement. She turns on the lights, draws a long breath and promises herself she won't be discouraged. She has to start somewhere.

She looks around. Extra furniture, unused for years. Lamps, end tables, card table, side chairs, large chairs, a metal cot, piano stool but no piano, bookshelves, Whit's easel. These will be donated to charities. She'll attempt a discussion with Billie later. For now, she begins her own method of labelling, marking furniture that is damaged or in poor condition, sorting in her mind what to keep, what to throw out.

Plastic containers filled with rags, labelled "Dusters." Stained cushions, pieces of fabric, more dusting cloths, brittle shower curtains, cobwebs, a cardboard box filled with yellowed paper towels. A mink collar, which, if worn today, would be sprayed with paint. What on earth does one do with a mink collar? Stacked flowerpots made of clay. Stacked flowerpots made of plastic. Artificial flowers glued to the bottom of glass containers; these have hardened and cannot be separated. More cobwebs. Canvas sack filled with a jumble of stinking seeds. Cans of paint, half-used, the paint thick, dried, stuck to itself. Shelves of art books and books for teaching English. These can be donated. True to character, Billie had no use for any item once it was out of sight.

Hanora finds Whit's art supplies in a metal carrying case. Why have these been kept? Tubes of oils stuck together and dried out. Brushes might be salvaged. Watercolours, disintegrated. Palette knife. Pieces of charcoal. Messy palette. Remembers Whit greeting her with a grin as he held the palette in one hand when she dropped into the studio, momentarily, to say hello.

He and Billie were suited, she thinks. They were good for each other and for people around them. They were good for me. Inclusive. Their presence was one of the reasons I moved here after roaming the world so many years.

She hears Billie's footsteps overhead. Down the hall, into the bathroom, a flush through the pipes; steps again, slowly, slowly, back to the living room. Silence. Then the blare of TV at high volume.

One box has been pushed under a built-in shelf in the furnace room. Hanora hauls it forward and opens the flaps to find a huge, soft mass resembling degenerate candy floss, dirty grey in colour. There is a note on top of the contents: *For birds, to build nests in spring.*

She reaches in, withdraws her hand quickly. Sees what it is. Dryer lint. A box filled to the top. Billie must have been collecting this since Whit died.

Surely not that long. Maybe during the past year. No,

Billie hasn't been down here for a year. Earlier, then. How can an accumulation of dryer lint be measured over time? It is saturated with dust and dirt and probably insects and other debris. Did Billie set out dryer lint for the birds? The thought makes Hanora gag, though maybe, she allows, maybe the birds appreciated the help. She thinks of herself and Tobe, sitting on the branch in the maple, creating stillness in hopes that birds would settle around them.

She begins to sneeze, closes the flaps tightly, carries the box up the stairs and puts it outside with the garbage.

She gives up. Another day, then.

September 23, 1938

JITNEY DANCE

LOW, ROLLING HILLS. A BARELY DISCERNIBLE impression of gaining altitude. Stand of tall pines on the left, another on the right. Brick farmhouse, red barn. Split-rail fence. A barrier of stacked boulders. Inimitable landscape of the Canadian Shield. The silver hood ornament on Tobe's car: the flying lady, naked goddess, sleek and elegant. The auto, dark wine in colour, also sleek, with large headlamps and long hood.

Hanora turned to look through the rear window. Breeda was in the rumble seat with her friend Sawyer, known to them all as Saw. He had come along for the dancing and would be company for Tobe on the late drive home. Breeda was gesturing with her hands, talking nonstop. From inside the car, their conversation could not be heard. The topic would not be Hanora's adoption; she was sure of that. She had asked Breeda to keep the news to herself.

Tobe was trusted. Hanora knew he'd be sympathetic no matter what she spilled out, and everything did spill out, for the second time that day. Tobe patted her hand, her arm, while he drove. He was taller than she was, still lean, still the mop of brown hair. A habit of becoming perfectly still and nodding almost imperceptibly while listening. They had loved each other since they were children. He was athletic, too, and joined every team in town that would have him: baseball, hockey, track. He had finished school one year before Hanora, and wanted to marry, right away if she'd have him. His birthday gift to her was beside her on the seat: Gellhorn's book *The Trouble I've Seen.* He'd known exactly what to buy.

But she hadn't been able to enter a conversation about marriage. Not yet. And Tobe did not push. Her life was beginning; she wanted to get out into the bigger world. Tobe was following the path set for him by his father. The town's industry had shrunk, especially during the Depression. The town's population was only fourteen hundred. Tobe's father needed someone he could count on to help keep the family business going.

"Don't you see how complicated everything has become?" she said.

Tobe glanced over and put his hand over hers. "You're

the same person I've always known, Hanora. You resemble your parents and always have. Nothing has changed about the way you were raised. The way we grew up together."

But she was not the same person. She had, that day, divided into two. Tobe, sensitive to her moods, was trying to understand.

"It's possible that I might have a different name," she said, though she was finding that difficult to believe. The idea of a second name was too new. She was trying to work out ideas as she spoke.

"I have no history. Think of it, Tobe. You know, with a good deal of exactness, who you are. A history of the Staunford family exists. Therefore, you have a history as well. I never had to think about this before, because I knew my place in the world. Or thought I did. I somehow feel . . . I feel that I don't have the same position I had up until now. The position within my family. Even though I'm Tress and Kenan's only child. People who know who they are don't have to examine this. Their identity is in place. They know who they are. You know who you are." She realized she was repeating herself.

They were silent for a while. Hanora couldn't shake the sense of gloom.

After a long bend in the road, the Pavilion came into view. The tips of maples along the lakeshore and beside the road shone brilliant yellow in the late glow of sun. Music could be heard ahead; the Aces were playing. Breeda shouted excitedly from the rumble seat and pointed out her aunt's house across the road.

They were dropped at the front door, with Tobe and Saw standing long enough to be introduced. ("Aunt Marlo, I'd like you to meet Tobias Staunford. And my friend Sawyer.")

From the lower veranda Hanora watched Tobe park the Buick outside the Pavilion. Immediately, the coupe was surrounded. A man hopped onto the running board on the right and peered in at the mohair-covered seats. Another hoisted a foot to the metal heelprint above the rear wheel and looked down into the depth of the rumble seat. Others ran their hands over the flying lady, whose presence never failed to raise comments and smiles. Tobe quietly enjoyed fielding questions about the coupe, which attracted attention no matter where they were.

When Breeda and Hanora went upstairs to stash their overnight clothes, Aunt Marlo tagged along. As Breeda had predicted, they were assigned the bedroom closest to the upstairs veranda, the one with the overview of the Pavilion and Stoco Lake. Hanora could hear sax and piano; she could hear trumpet. Cars were edging down the slope along one side of the Pavilion like floats in a slow-moving parade. Young men had collected at the corners of the building. Some were tipping paper bags. Alcohol was never served inside the dance halls.

As she watched, electric lights burst into colour around the pillars by the entrance gate into the grounds. Couples strolled across the grass. A cluster of dancers gathered on the outside steps. She and Breeda went downstairs and ran across the road. The air was balmy, still humid. Their legs were bare; they were wearing sandals and light dresses. They had promised Aunt Marlo that they'd have a good long visit over breakfast the next day.

Tobe and Saw had bought strips of tickets—four for a quarter—and were waiting. Extra tickets were tucked into their pockets. The big room was cleared after each dance, the jitney box near the entrance ready for the crowd that would pass through the gates and swell back onto the floor.

Hanora was not prepared for the size of the dance hall or the height of its vaulted ceilings. Hinged shutters that swung inward and upward were latched to support beams that were part of the ceiling structure, the entire length of the Pavilion on both sides. Lights had been dimmed. On the far side and through the open windows, the lake could be seen shimmering in the near dark. There were no screens; girls waiting to be asked to dance were sitting on benches and batting at flying insects, probably mosquitoes.

The four joined the moving crowd while dancers jostled to get into place before the band started up again. Beyond the wooden railings that enclosed the dance floor, people were in constant motion along the indoor promenade, a width of about five feet. Men were seeking partners; some were hurrying to the canteen to buy a burger and pop, some strolling to be seen while they waited for the music to start up again. The musicians had set up their instruments on an elevated stage at the far left. Tobe dropped a ticket into the jitney box and Hanora found herself part of a crowd surging onto the dance floor. The music began, and someone tapped her arm. A woman in her fifties, perhaps sixties. "Oops!" she said. "Wrong person. You look exactly like someone I used to know, but I'm mistaken. Lord, there must be more than a hundred and fifty people on this floor. Hey, what a good-looker, your partner," she shouted over the noise. She raised a hand as she backed away, and was swept off by her own partner before Hanora could respond. Hanora did not see the woman again the rest of the evening.

The band was playing "Back Bay Shuffle." The three dances that followed were fast, and Tobe and Hanora hardly paused to take a breath between. "You're possessed," he shouted, laughing.

And that was the way she felt. She didn't care how fast they danced, whether onlookers liked the jitterbug or thought it indecent. She didn't care if their dancing was admired or ignored. She and Tobe danced well together, she was aware of this. But she was also in her own space, surrounded by high-stepping, strutting, twirling dancers, the sounds of hundreds of feet pounding out the beat on hardwood. Tobe was right there to grasp her hand, her arm, her waist; he was right there to catch her.

At the end of eight dances, out of breath, they squeezed through the crowd and exited before the floor was entirely cleared in preparation for the next dance. She couldn't see Breeda or Saw, though she'd glimpsed them across the room during the fifth dance. She and Tobe went outside to cool off.

They wandered around the far side of the building and stood by the shore, the lake expanding out and out before them. A shadow glided past in the dark, taking Hanora by surprise. A canoe slipped into the boathouse beneath the dance floor and disappeared—two figures in silhouette. She barely heard the paddles, the lap of water as the canoe entered the boat stall.

The night was surprisingly still, considering the commotion inside the building with the music starting up again. The band rolled into "Sing, Sing, Sing," and dancers were back on the floor. Benny Goodman had played that piece at Carnegie Hall in January. She'd have given anything to be there. Billie attended, and sent a letter from New York that contained a breathless account of the historic evening. *A landmark concert*, she wrote. *Jazz and swing at Carnegie Hall. Who would have thought? The audience was not made up entirely of young people. There was plenty* *of white hair scattered throughout the hall. When the band started up, everyone wondered what the reaction would be. A worrying silence, at first. But then, things got going. Feet started to tap, old feet and young feet. Fingers snapped, knees swished and swayed. How I wish you'd been there, Hanora. And Krupa on the drums. Spectacular. This was a revolution! I paid $2.20 for my ticket. I mean Hallman did. He bought the tickets. Don't give me hell. I'm still with him. He took me to the Goodman concert, didn't he? My parents think I ended the relationship, but I can't give him up. You know all the reasons (& we do take precautions). Destroy this letter. Love you everly, B.*

Unknown to her parents, Billie had been having an intimate affair with Hallman—she referred to him only by his last name—ever since she'd taken an apartment in New York City. Her parents remained in Rochester, where they'd always lived. They had met Hallman once, when he'd accompanied Billie to Rochester, and they had instantly disapproved. *He's too old for you. He'll bring nothing but trouble.* Not that they didn't have trouble enough in their own marriage. According to Billie, they had stayed together so long, they no longer knew how to live apart.

Yellow leaves crunched underfoot. Tobe had his arm over her shoulder and pulled her close. They walked along shore until they reached a canopy of trees, then turned to walk back so they could dance some more. Tobe nodded to people approaching from the opposite direction. Hanora leaned her body into his. As they walked, he kissed her temple, the side of her cheek. With Tobe, she was safe.

She was also on the lookout for faces. Faces that belonged to men and women the age of her parents, faces of people her own age. Perhaps—she held her breath, this was a new thought—perhaps sisters or brothers. And why not? She would like to question the older woman who had mistaken her for someone else. She dismissed the thought, and reminded herself that this could happen to anyone. In any case, the woman had vanished.

But Hanora remained vigilant. She was watching for hair colour. Gesture. Voice, a laugh, a likeness of any sort. She'd always been a listener, but now she had become a watcher, too. Thoughts darted through her mind. Escape routes, reasons to go off by herself to pursue . . . something. My life, she told herself. I am going to pursue my life. I can be anyone I want to become.

She made up her mind that evening, while walking with Tobe, that she would get away. She would leave. Not forever—she didn't want to leave Tobe forever. She would save her money until she had enough to travel, even for a short time. She was going to create an adventure of her own. She was someone different from the person she had believed herself to be, which meant that she could become someone different in fact. She had no idea how she would accomplish this.

She would ask Billie to join her for an adventure. Tress and Kenan could hardly object. They might even think of Billie as some sort of chaperone. She was, after all, older than Hanora, and they knew nothing of Billie's affairs. If they knew they would probably disapprove.

Hanora would write to her cousin, knowing that Billie's response would have everything to do with the state of her current infatuation with Hallman. She, too, might be ready for change.

As for Hanora, she was in a state that fluctuated between disbelief and a strange sort of relief, as if she had known about her adoption all along. She would remain alert. Especially over the next months, while she was saving money. She would tell no one that her private search for her birth parents had begun. Because her search had to be exactly that. Private. Except from Tobe. Tobe was smart enough to guess, anyway. He had known her as long as she had known herself.

FACTS ABOUT CHEESE

FROM THE NOTEBOOK OF HANORA OAK

National Cheese Week will take place Nov. 7–12, 1938.
Cheese is a Vital Food. Serve it daily!

WE are informed that one pound of cheese equals nearly two pounds of meat in food value. All hotel dining rooms and restaurants should be honouring National Cheese Week by serving local cheese on every menu.

FIFTY or more salesmen representing cheese factories arrive in the city of Belleville, Ontario, every Saturday throughout the year. This is our biggest home industry, a million-dollar industry. Think of the numbers of visitors who will be here during National Cheese Week! *(Guess the exact number of visitors and win a block of Old Cheddar.)*

CHEESE helps to prevent BRAIN FAG. Many people who feel "all in" at night have tried eating more cheese, and they tell us they experience a new vitality.

NOTES from interview with Annie May, cheese factory worker:

"We have a counter at the entrance to the factory . . . where we sell cheese by the chunk or by the slice to the locals. People from away will drive a good many miles to get here, our cheese is that special. Well, during the past summer, one elderly couple drove here every Saturday noon in their '37 REO truck, on their way to picnic by the bay. The boys in the factory tore outside every week to look at the truck — where would you see one of those again? The owner told me only seven have been manufactured! Seven! The old couple carried in pieces of homemade bread and asked me to slice their cheese right here, while they made sandwiches. Now, you should know that we are not permitted to have onion inside the factory because of the odour, but the old couple — don't write this down, or you'll get us all in trouble — well, every week they brought in three slices of onion, layered between folds of waxed paper. Two were for their own sandwiches and one was for me. They

got to know me and like me. So I added my slice of onion to my sandwich when I took my break. Nice change from plain cheese, bread and butter. Did one slice of onion hurt anything? Not on your life. I ate it; it wasn't as if I left it lying around. Even so, you'd better not mention that in your article, and for cripes' sake don't tell my boss or I'll be fired."

JANUARY 1939

ATTEMPTS

S HE WROTE TO THE ADOPTION AGENCY. SHE SENT
letters to hospitals in the Toronto area requesting
information about the birth of a baby girl with the
given name Hanora, birthdate September 23, 1920.

Information confidential.

She contacted Children's Aid Societies, child wel-
fare departments, family services. She inquired about the
Adoption Act.

She had travelled to Toronto, alone, in December,
hopeful of gathering information, of being given access to
a birth registry.

Documents sealed. Officials trained to deny.

One afternoon, she visited her grandmother, Mamo
Agnes, at the hotel. She took the risk of speaking alone
with her, telling her that she wanted to find out information

about her birth parents without hurting her mother. Telling her that she had to understand her background. She asked her grandmother, who was seventy-one, to keep their conversation confidential.

Mamo Agnes had no information Hanora didn't already have. She had not been told about the locket. She asked to see it, but did not recognize either locket or chain. Hanora watched her grandmother's face and believed she was telling the truth. Mamo Agnes said that she had abided by Tress's request to say nothing to Hanora about adoption until her parents were ready to tell her themselves.

Hanora asked Breeda to go ahead and question her father to find out what he knew. "Be subtle," Hanora cautioned.

Breeda could get nothing from Calhoun. If he knew anything, he wasn't saying. But what would he know? He rarely went to Toronto, except at the end of summer to take in the Exhibition. Hanora would have been adopted in November. Breeda asked him to think back to 1920, the year of her own birth, to try to remember what was going on at the time.

Nothing but dead ends. Nothing Hanora did not already know.

"I asked him if there had been any teenage girls around who became pregnant and discreetly disappeared to visit an aunt for several months," said Breeda. "He was shocked by the question, probably because it came from his daughter," she added. "Anyway, news like that would hardly have been published in the *Post*."

This was what Hanora wanted published in Calhoun's paper, and in every newspaper in the province:

Woman born September 23, 1920, Toronto, Ontario, seeks birth parents for the following reasons:

She needs to know why she was given away.

She would like to understand why society feels she should not ask questions about her birth, and why this secrecy must be honoured.

She wants to find out if she was wanted or unwanted.

If wanted, why can she not be acquainted with the circumstances of her adoption? Was her mother forced to give her up? Was this a selfless act? She has a profound feeling of empathy for her unknown birth mother.

She wants to let her birth mother and birth father know that a part of her is missing. She believes it's possible that a part of them is missing, too.

She wants to fill in the gaps, close the circle.

She wants to know if she resembles anyone. She wants to know how others perceive her.

And whose personality traits she has inherited.

She wants her birth parents to know that she carries with her a permanent feeling of loneliness.

She wants to meet any brothers or sisters she may have.

She wants to reassure her birth parents that she is an important member of the family that adopted her, but she needs to know where she belongs in the larger circle, the greater world.

Was she conceived in violence? She would rather know than not know.

She wants to feel complete.

She wants the questions to cease.

She wants to move on.

She wants to be at peace.

She wants to know if her mother did not love her enough to keep her.

MARCH 22, 1939

ON THE TRAIN

HANORA CHOSE SECOND SITTING. CLAM BOUIL-
lon, chicken supreme with fresh mushrooms,
mashed potatoes, carrots, her own pot of tea. For
dessert, fig pudding with hard sauce, a piece of Canadian
cheese. She felt the urge to write on the order pad: *What
kind of cheese is "Canadian cheese"? Our finest Ontario
Cheddar? Ask me.*

She ate everything set before her.

She wanted to linger among her fellow travellers, all
of them unknown. She missed her parents, thought of the
tearful farewells that morning. She called up her strengths,
reminded herself that adventure lay ahead. She squirmed;
her girdle was tight, uncomfortable. She was not ready to
retire to her compartment. She tried not to yield to the
sway of the train, tried to ignore the looks of the steward,
who hovered, ready to clear her place.

She glanced at the couple across the aisle; they were behaving as if embarrassed to be together. The man was in his thirties, grinning nervously, his eye teeth pointing like nibs. In contrast, the woman was all softness. Dove-grey hat pushed back over curls—the only woman in the dining car to wear a hat to dinner. She was fussing with her table napkin. She folded, unfolded, scrunched it inside her fist, dabbed at her lips.

The two were speaking rapidly but in low voices. *No, no. Leave it be. Leave it, I said.* Dishes rattled in the galley.

Hanora sipped at her tea. Watched tiny waterspouts erupt around the inside of the cup. Rested an elbow on the linen tablecloth, lifted the silver-plated teapot to feel the measure of its weight. Lifted milk jug and sugar bowl in slow motion. Poured a second cup of tea just as the steward ushered two women to her table. One beside, the other across. "I hope we aren't disturbing. These seem to be the only seats available." The one beside introduced herself as Marie. The other was her sister Annette. The steward seated them without a glance in Hanora's direction.

She was happy to meet anyone at all, and shifted in her seat as if she were the one joining the table. The women picked up their pencils and ordering pads, apparently entirely comfortable in dining cars on iron wheels. They ordered fish, put down their pencils and began to talk about themselves. They were returning to New York after visiting a third sister in Montreal. "Our fiancés died in the Great War," said Annette, as if she must explain from the outset. "We've never married. So many men didn't come home, you know." They looked at each other glumly and Hanora thought of her father, who had come home, but wounded, damaged. She'd never understood for certain just how extensive the inner damage really was. Her mother, who had known him since childhood, had provided few details. Hanora had pieced together what she could, but the topic was seldom discussed.

Marie perked up and began to talk about their sister, Mona, who worked as a seamstress for Holt Renfrew. Mona's talent, she said, was astonishing. Any grand store would be lucky to hire her, and she'd had offers. Everyone wanted her. But she was loyal to Holt.

"Mind," said Annette, "she can't afford Holt's clothing for herself, even though she sits in a room, surrounded by mirrors, and stitches their clothing all day. You'll never guess what she does. She takes an envelope of Holt's tags home and sews them into the outfits she buys at other stores—stores that aren't so dear."

"She has a sense of style," said Marie. "Dresses, a tailored jacket I'd love to own. A dress for dancing, another for dining. Her closet is filled to bursting with clothing tagged from Holt's."

Annette picked up the story. "We love visiting Montreal.

Mona lives with her husband—he's a bookkeeper—in an apartment right downtown. Their place is too small for visitors, and that is our lovely excuse to stay at the Windsor. The corridors are wide enough to allow for a horse and carriage, if ever one could get into the hotel. Every time we come to Canada, we treat ourselves to a special dinner in the hotel dining room. Our little luxury. Our gift to ourselves."

Hanora laughed along with the sisters, while continuing to glance at the man and woman across the aisle. Maybe they'd met recently and were headed for a passionate tryst. Not in a compartment as small as hers. Not likely. They had probably booked into a bedroom for two. When she returned to the sleeping car—Pullman, she told herself; call it a Pullman—she would pull out her notebook and record details and observations of her first-ever experience on an overnight train.

On her way back to her compartment, she passed a door that was partly ajar and heard a man singing softly while strumming an instrument, perhaps a mandolin. Low, deep voice, almost gravelly. She could see outstretched legs, shiny caramel-coloured shoes, royal-blue socks, but not his face; he must have been sitting sideways on the edge of his bed. He was singing "Goodnight, Irene" and she joined in silently, the lyrics repeating in her head as if a sleepy country band had taken over her mind.

While she'd been eating fig pudding in the dining car, the attendant had been busy in her compartment. He'd flattened the armchair, stowed the cushions on the floor and pulled down the bed from the recess behind the seat. Her tiny room was now converted to a pallet for sleep. She was sorry she hadn't been there to watch.

She locked the door, then removed her pumps and shoved them into the square metal locker overhead. Peeled off skirt, blouse, stockings and tight girdle—all of this while seated on the mattress. With the girdle off, she could breathe again. "Damn, damn," she said aloud. "I should be writing about constrictive undergarments, about designers who create clothes that bind and torture. But who would publish such an article? Damn again."

She stretched her legs until her bare feet pressed against the wall. Her father had told her before she left, "You'll be feet toward engine if you're travelling Pullman." He had not once left Deseronto since coming home from the Great War, but there wasn't much he didn't know about trains. She flung her stockings over a hook above the bed. The pouched-out heels swayed overhead and she laughed, thinking of the ads about SA—stocking appeal.

Do you have runs? Snaky seams? Puckery heels?

She was guilty of having puckery heels. She should be guarding her stocking appeal by using a special soap that would "save elasticity." She knew very well that ads kept newspapers running, but she wondered why Calhoun did not discriminate when he ran them in the *Post*.

Men of 30, 40, 50 who want vim and vigour for their rundown bodies! Try tablets of raw oyster stimulants.

There wasn't a man in her town who would take raw oyster stimulants—at least she couldn't think of one. Maybe men with rundown bodies had secret lives she didn't know about. Maybe they sent away for products that were delivered furtively, by mail. If Tobe were with her, she would ask and he would tell what he knew. "Vim and vigour" and "raw oyster stimulants" were definitely about sex. Who else would discuss such things with her but Tobe? She and Tobe had done their own experimenting, in private, and this did not involve raw oyster stimulants.

The train lurched and she glanced at her reflection in the compartment window. The person she saw was Hanora Oak, half-undressed, gold locket around the neck. A locket once owned by a mother she did not know. She had little information beyond what she'd been given the previous September. She made a point of wearing the locket hidden beneath her dress or blouse or sweater. To spare Tress and Kenan? She couldn't have said exactly why. They must have seen part of the chain; they must have known she had it on every day.

During her December Toronto trip, she had made an attempt to ask innocent-sounding questions of a great-aunt in that city. But lips had narrowed and closed. The aunt knew nothing. The answer remained the same. Adoption records are sealed. Your mother adopted you here in the city, that's all I know. Hanora believed her. What would this aunt know of a stranger giving up her baby for adoption?

She had also hoped to find the office of the adoption agency the way it had been in 1920. She pored through old city directories and came up with a street name but learned that the agency had moved years before. Still, she located and walked to the old address and stood on a city street looking up at a row of third-storey windows. She might have changed families in one of those rooms. Unless she'd been adopted from an orphanage. From the vague information Tress had imparted, Hanora understood that her birth mother had given her up directly. The day she was told, on her birthday, she had not visualized an orphanage. There had to have been a middle person. She wanted answers, but found it difficult to question her parents because she did not want to upset them. They had provided as much information as they felt obliged to do, and that was the end of the discussion.

From the street, Hanora had stared up and willed the building to release the memories it held. She entered, pretending to have a destination, and took an elevator to the third floor. From inside the cage of the ascending elevator, she passed Ladies' Wholesale Linens, where women worked at long tables in an open room that took up the entire second floor. Maybe her birth mother had been a seamstress. She stepped off the elevator and found herself facing two offices: a partnership of accountants, an import business. Nothing else.

𝄢

THE train raced south. She looked beyond her reflection to watch shadows leaping through darkness, silhouettes of branches, trees felled by winter. Ice lined the edge of the track. She pulled down the blind, and hung her skirt and blouse over a hook beside the window. The train was slowing, coming to a stop, perhaps to dump ashes, take on coal. The whistle wheezed, a thin, reedy noise, as if the sound had become stuck while trying to escape.

She had brought a copy of *Collier's* with her, and she slid the magazine across the top sheet. She stifled a shriek when three grey fingers emerged from beneath the cover. Her own glove. She tucked the glove away, picked up the magazine and checked the list of contributors. She had sent one article to *Collier's*, but it was returned in short order. She was disappointed until she'd seen that the response was from no other than William Chenery. He had scrawled a note in pen across the top of the first page: *This is promising. Please try us again.*

The wheels of the train began to clack and rumble beneath the bed again. So loudly, she felt that she could reach through the floor and touch the tracks. She had been travelling on trains since childhood, mostly day trips to Belleville with her mother or Aunt Grania, sometimes with Breeda, or overnight trips to Toronto to visit relatives. The past summer, while she was staying with an aunt and uncle in Toronto, Tobe arrived and took her to the CNE Tent to dance to Tommy Dorsey's swing music. The year before that, they had danced to Guy Lombardo. They'd have danced all night if her aunt and uncle hadn't been waiting up for her.

She felt a rush of panic, of regret. Earlier in the day, Tobe had accompanied her as far as Montreal to see her off on the New York train. Before she climbed aboard, he made a solemn announcement that if war was declared, he was joining up. She refused to take this seriously, found it impossible to imagine him in uniform, his thick hair shorn. And why would he wait until she was about to board before imparting news like that? Crazily, hopefully, she told herself that war would be prevented. The world was not going to allow it to happen. She wondered, given Tobe's propensity to solve problems peaceably, how he would fare in the midst of violence. She could not think of anyone less warlike.

On her knees now, she wriggled out of the last of her

underwear and jammed it into her locker. Naked except for the locket, she propped pillows behind her, pulled on a nightgown and slid between the sheets. The compartment was warm; she had no need of a blanket. She reached for the locket—a habit now—and smoothed her fingers over its surface. During the December trip to Toronto, the trip she thought of as the true beginnings of her search, she'd consulted a jeweller. He'd checked the locket thoroughly and assured her it was made of gold. Because of the design, he identified its origin, with some certainty, as European. It was impossible to be more accurate without other markings on the locket itself. The style of the letter *H*—its loops and curls—indicated central or eastern Europe; perhaps the Austro-Hungarian Empire, but that was a guess. He could not be certain of age. All exciting clues, none of which led to answers.

Hanora dug into her shoulder bag and checked her passport and money to ensure that she had both. She dug deeper and pulled out two small black-and-white photos. She placed them on the ledge of her compartment.

AUNT ZEL'S PHOTO

T HE FIRST HAD BEEN PUT INTO HER HAND THE previous day. She had walked to the rooming house to say goodbye, and stayed for a cup of tea. Just before she left, Zel handed her a small envelope containing a five-dollar bill, to "buy yourself a treat." Tucked into the envelope along with the bill was a black-and-white photo of two women, one of whom was Zel. She had removed it from her own album, she said, because she didn't want to be forgotten while Hanora was out gallivanting around the big wide world.

"There isn't a photo of me alone in existence," she said. She was speaking more rapidly than usual, perhaps embarrassed at presenting a photo of herself. "In fact, there aren't many photos of me at all. I can't remember who took this, but it was before you were born. Someone from town, for sure. You'll recognize the bay. I'm on skates and in costume, and I'm with a friend who moved to the States a long time ago. I haven't skated since arthritis took hold of my joints. You and I skated together when you were a child, do you remember? You've always been good on ice because your parents started you early. It didn't hurt that the rink was an extension of your backyard."

"I remember someone's mittened hand holding mine tightly. I remember how my ankles ached from collapsing inside my skates while I was learning. Not to mention cold fingers inside mittens."

"That's the Canadian winter story," said Zel. "Cold fingers inside mittens. Your mother—or maybe your father—would have been holding your hand." She pointed to the photo. "I hope this will help to keep you connected to town while you're away. If you look at it now and then . . . well, you won't forget me. It's taken from a bit of a distance, but it's the best I can offer."

Hanora hugged her, assured her that she was not going to be forgotten. If Zel wanted her to keep the photo with her, she would honour that request. She loved this honorary aunt who was more than a generation older than her parents, and who had been a part of her life since she was a baby. Zel, with her wonderfully dusky voice, her ability to listen, was someone she'd been able to confide in through the years. She had not, however, told her about being adopted. Even though she trusted Zel, she didn't want speculation going on in the background while she was figuring things out on her own. Any time she made inquiries, she ensured that news of her search would not get back to her parents.

But every lead had been blocked by a dead end.

She settled back against the pillows and examined the photo more closely. Zel had been in her fifties when it was taken. Every winter, people in town dreamed up an assortment of costumes for the outdoor masquerade on ice. Tress had created her share during Hanora's childhood: quite contrary Mary, Canadian autumn, the hurdy-gurdy man. One year, Hanora and Tobe went as Betty Boop and Popeye. Another year, Hanora and Breeda dressed as Jack and Jill. When they were seventeen, they were Little Lulu sisters, complete with careful ringlets they created from black yarn. The winter before that, they'd dressed as hula dancers and wore heavy leggings under grass skirts. It was one of the coldest days of the year, but freezing temperatures did not dampen their spirits.

On the back of the photo, Zel had written "Maggie and me." Her friend Maggie was the younger of the two. Poised, slender, she was dressed in an angel costume. She was laughing, the occasion one of happiness. The word "Peace" was printed across a sign that hung from a double ribbon around Maggie's neck. There was no mistaking the message.

The photo was undated, and Hanora assumed it had been taken immediately after the Great War. Or perhaps after the Treaty of Versailles, when people believed that another war could not possibly be on the horizon. Civilization was given those few years of hope. But that was before the invasion of Manchuria. Before the bombing of Guernica. Before *Anschluss*. Before the madman named Hitler occupied Prague—and that, only a week ago. The warmongers were restless. Three weeks earlier, France and Great Britain had recognized the fascist dictatorship of Francisco Franco as the legitimate government of Spain. She thought of Julian again, his mother sobbing as she held the article from the *Star*. Hanora wanted to write more articles, and more.

She returned to the photo. Maggie's partially visible wings were oversized, long and delicate, constructed from soft cloth, probably wired to keep their shape. Zel, the taller of the two, was dressed as a jester, or joker. She was wearing pantaloons with a multi-patterned tunic overtop. She was thick at the waist, but the costume was flattering to her figure. An elaborate feathered ruff was twined about her neck. Her cloth hat had three extensions, a bell hanging from the tip of each and dangling over the ruff. Arm in arm, the two friends posed in the sun, challenging the viewer. Was "peace" anything beyond a jest?

The town judges must have liked the costumes, because the women held between them a banner that proclaimed them to be winners of first prize. A first prize that would have been announced in the weekly *Post*. Every year, Calhoun ran a double layout of masquerade photos at the beginning of February. She wondered if he would miss her reporting. She'd promised to send articles from time to time.

She switched off the overhead light and turned on the night light, which cast a soft glow. This leg of the journey would last until morning. She was headed for New York. The next day, she and Billie would board the SS *Champlain*. In twenty-four hours, they'd be sleeping in a cabin at sea.

"The sea," she said aloud. "The cold March sea." She wanted to try out the words; she wanted to create a picture of herself boarding. She had never seen an ocean liner except in photographs. Famous people might be on board, maybe even movie stars. Spencer Tracy? Bette Davis? They'd won Oscars a few weeks earlier, for *Boys Town* and *Jezebel*. No matter who was aboard, she and Billie would be there, heading for a continent across the width of an ocean. Her cousin would be at Grand Central to meet her in the morning; she would know what to do and how to act. Billie was used to living in the big city. She was now working as a receptionist at the offices of Tangee, which was becoming known for rouge as well as lipstick in the cosmetic industry.

Of course, I'll come to Europe with you, she wrote, after Hanora had suggested the trip the previous fall. *Save every penny, and so will I. Tell your parents I'll arrange tickets from New York to Le Havre. (The best cabin we can afford!) I want to go to England, which means you and I will have to part ways after the first week—let's spend that first week in Paris. We could meet later in London, if at all possible. I want to sail on the French Line because I've heard wonderful stories about the SS Champlain. I probably won't stay more than a few weeks in all—I might be able to beg a full month, but I'll have to return to my job. I'm lucky to have this position and don't want to give it up yet. I'll bring samples with me. A whole range of colours in those tiny sample tubes I get free.*

Eventually, who knows, I might go back to school and move away. I've been thinking of escaping my ties here. I know you said you wanted to travel to the South of France after we land in Europe; I know you want to get closer to the Spanish refugee situation for your work, but I plan to stay away from trouble as long as I can. Maybe, when I'm in England, I'll get to see the king and queen!

Think of the fun we'll have aboard an ocean liner. I hope Hallman will be sorry I'm crossing the ocean. It will be good for him to know that I'm capable of saying good-bye. I've always, always wanted to sail the Atlantic. Love you everly, Billie.

𝄢

HANORA was grateful to Billie for referring to her work. She was glad they would be together during the first week in Paris. After that, Hanora would be on her own, a thought that frightened and exhilarated.

"Goodnight, Irene" started up in her head again. The refrain had lodged in her brain when she walked past the caramel shoes and royal-blue socks, and she willed the tune to fade into the noises of the train. She wondered if she'd ever sleep. Not with clattering wheels beneath her bed. Relax, she told herself. You are out in the big world Aunt Zel talked about, and the world is going to get bigger. Don't be afraid, but don't fool yourself, either. Focus on the journey. Anything can happen. Keep your notebook ready. Write about everything. Ominous events are happening in the world, but this is a beginning for you. Facts are facts and cannot be meddled with. Write what you see. Send back the news. If you write well enough, people will buy your work. Now try to get some sleep.

But she wasn't ready for sleep. She picked up the second photo and held it near the night light. She turned it over in her palm.

KENAN'S PHOTO

K ENAN HAD DEVELOPED THE PHOTO, ONE
Hanora knew well. She'd given him a camera on
Christmas Day 1937, and it soon became clear that
he valued it as he did no other possession. She had worked
hard to save the dollar it cost, and Billie's older brother,
Ned, in Rochester, sent it directly from his workplace at
Eastman Kodak. That same Christmas, Tress had given
Kenan rolls of 127 film. He had been taking photos ever
since. He taught himself to develop film at home, in the
unused and dark cold cellar. Kenan was entirely comfortable in the dark.

He was putting together an album of photos, his own
private discoveries. The photo Hanora carried in her purse
was taken the day she was told of her adoption. She'd carried it with her from the moment it emerged from the
darkroom.

Unlike Zel's photo, Kenan's was dated. From earliest childhood, Hanora knew that her father was methodical and organized. She and her mother had adjusted to the order he needed around him. For a long time, she had believed that all fathers were precise in the way Kenan was. As she grew older, alert to slips of conversation between her mother and Aunt Grania, she learned that Kenan had also been carefree, a charmer, intensely loyal, a dancer, a man who could make others laugh. The war had changed him in some ways, but not all. He was a loving man to his wife and daughter, a good friend to Aunt Grania and Uncle Jim.

Her father kept himself behind the camera, never in front. There were no photos of him in his new album or in anyone else's, as far as Hanora knew. Except the one she'd seen of him as a young man, taken long before the war. The one in Aunt Grania's album.

The photo in her hand contained a caption on the back, as did all of Kenan's photos. His captions meant something personal to him. Hanora had given the photo her own title, not the one written by her father. For her, it was *Invisible 1938*. Because, at first glance, there was nothing to be seen.

She tried to recreate her last birthday from Kenan's point of view.

She had rowed out into the bay with Breeda. She heard the buzz in the sky before turning the boat and heading for shore. Kenan, who reacted to all sound as if trained to listen, heard the same buzz from inside the house. He leapt from his chair, grabbed his cap from the nail beside the door and took long strides out to the street. The peak of his cap was tilted over his left eye, which was permanently sealed. His dead hand was tucked deep into the dead-hand pocket, to keep the arm from swinging wildly. Hanora knew that people in town referred to his wounds as "Flanders disease." He was received by men on the street with a respectful nod of the head. After he passed by, there was an occasional muttering of "the Somme." In the town's eyes, no distinction was made between Belgium and France or any other place he might have served. There was no real information to be had because Kenan said nothing about that time. If a question had been posed—but a question was never posed—two words would have sufficed as the answer: the war.

The last war. The world seemed to be heading pell-mell into another.

She went back to the buzz in the sky, Kenan in the street. He flipped up the viewfinder with his thumb, the Brownie a perfect fit inside his right hand. The camera's movements were controlled by the five fingers of his good hand.

He pointed the lens to the sky. Did he aim blindly? Did the Brownie lens take the place of his sealed eye? He pushed the shutter at the bottom edge and heard it click back. Snapped the viewfinder into place, returned to the house, tossed his cap over the nail. Checked the circular window at the back of the camera, went directly to his notebook and wrote, *Moving aeroplane, Sep. 23, 1938, H's birthday.*

Only after he developed the film, looked through history books and checked atlases, only then did he complete his notes, his version of what September 23 presented to his mind.

Beneath the words "Moving aeroplane," he had written in minuscule letters and enclosed in brackets: *(Sep. 23, 1835, HMS* Beagle *sails to Charles Island, Galapagos, Darwin aboard).*

Recent past did not interest Kenan. For him, recent past meant war. Perhaps, when he wrote the caption on the back, he'd been acknowledging Hanora's desire for adventure. Or maybe he was creating a memory for himself. He would have experienced loss that day. And Tress. All three had lost something vital and important on September 23, 1938. Months had passed before Hanora allowed herself to realize how difficult the day had been for her parents.

She turned back to the photo, searching for what Kenan might have seen. The edges were worn from repeated inspections, the surface glossy but dim, more grey than white. At the upper edge, she spotted the tiniest cross imaginable. The cross might have been planted at the top of an invisible hill, the destination of pilgrims who made impossible treks and wore themselves out trying to reach the summit to kneel before it. But this was not a cross. It was an aeroplane, exciting to see in the nothingness of its surrounds. She knew that people still came out of their houses and barns, stopped work in the fields or errands in the streets, to look up to the sky when they heard the telltale buzz overhead. In town that day, Kenan had taken the trouble to capture the image on film.

Hanora understood nothing of her father's intent. He chronicled his way through life, inventing ciphers, connecting present with distant past. A speck of aeroplane in the sky was linked to an event that had taken place more than a hundred years earlier. Perhaps he wondered what Darwin would have thought of flying machines. Kenan predicted that aeroplanes would eventually be bigger, faster, more useful. He was emphatic about the importance of inventions of the future. No one, he emphasized, knew what these inventions would be. Otherwise, wouldn't the idea of future be meaningless?

Hanora pushed the photo back down into her bag. She was not certain what the image meant. What mattered was that her father had given the photo to her. She pulled up the blanket and lay on her side, facing the compartment window. And fell into instant sleep.

SWITCHED IDENTITY

H ER OWN NEW CAMERA, FOR WHICH SHE HAD
paid $1.25, was tucked inside the purse slung over
her shoulder. Tobe's hickory-brown suitcase had
been sent ahead to her cabin. At the time she borrowed it,
she'd told him, "You see? I'm not going away forever. I'll
have to come back just to return your suitcase."

She was three steps ahead of Billie on the gangplank.
The two were ready for anything. Hallman had not visited
Billie to say goodbye. Miffed at her willingness to leave
him, even for a short time, he had ended their affair a week
earlier. At Grand Central, Billie told Hanora she was glad
to be getting out of the country. She did not want to be
reminded of the controlling Hallman every time she passed
doorways of city restaurants and clubs. Hanora understood this to mean that Billie was devastated and looking
for new adventure.

They were led to their cabin, and there discovered the wash basin full of flowers from Tobe. The card with them said, simply, "Hurry back, I'll be here." Propped on the bureau were "Bon Voyage" telegrams from Tress and Kenan, and from Aunt Zel. A quick look around was enough for Billie to realize that Hallman had sent neither flowers nor message. Billie's parents, too, had been silent about her departure, though she'd phoned to say good-bye the day before. All three had withheld affection as if affection were a weapon to be strategically concealed. Billie turned and went straight back up to the main deck to watch the activities below. Hanora followed.

People had been gathering along the pier while passengers continued to board. Friends and relatives below were shouting up to their loved ones, who crowded along the railing. While Hanora and Billie watched, a large group began to board, and cheers erupted from the crowd. A bottle of whisky crashed and glass scattered. More cheers. "Bon Voyage" signs were held aloft; music started up from somewhere below. Hanora and Billie could hardly believe their eyes when they saw a man who appeared to be Duke Ellington boarding with his entourage. The musicians waved to their fans as they hustled on board, laughing and joking.

"I must be the only New Yorker who didn't know Duke Ellington would be sailing on the *Champlain*," Billie said. "Shows how wrapped up I've been in my own sorrows." Certainly, it seemed as if every fan in the city had turned out to see Duke off on his voyage to Europe.

$$\text{\textbf{〇:}}$$

WHEN the *Champlain* finally pulled away almost noiselessly from the dock, or so it seemed to Hanora, the cousins leaned into the railing in a kind of reverie. Others around them were silent, too, as if everyone had drifted inside a soundless interval the moment land was left behind. The Statue of Liberty could be seen through the mist. The magnificent superliner beneath their feet headed in the direction of open sea.

But Billie was brooding. Hurt and ignored by her family and by Hallman. So Hanora was not entirely surprised when she whispered in her ear as they stood by the ship's railing.

"Why don't we change identities while we're on board, Hanora? I need to be free of myself, just for a while. We're almost the same height, same colour hair, same colour eyes. Who would know? We can be anonymous. We could do it for a lark. For one week while we're at sea. That will cure me of Hallman, I know it will. We can swap passports if we have to. And I can pretend I have a new life."

Hanora jumped in after only a moment's delay. "Yes!" she said. "Let's do it." And to herself she thought, *My new life is also about to begin.* The idea—the fact—of her adoption was still raw after six months, and she would wonder ever after if that was the reason she so quickly agreed to Billie's mad idea. Her cousin, as usual, was charging into adventure, and would not be looking back.

The two laughed quietly. In that moment and for the next week, Hanora became Billie Read and her cousin became Hanora Oak. Until they disembarked in Le Havre, they told each other. Only until then. They knew no one on the ship and no one knew them. How could they possibly be tripped up—except by themselves?

1998

THE MOVE

ETAILS HAVE BEEN LOOKED AFTER. HANORA
expects complications but cannot predict what these
will be.

The previous day, Billie phoned the apartment twenty-
eight times and threatened to bar the door if strangers
attempted to enter her house. She ranted into the answering
machine. She ranted when Hanora picked up the phone.
Hanora stopped answering when the evening caregiver
arrived at Billie's home to help her prepare for bed. Billie
did not bar the door for that stranger, who agreed to stay
until the client—as she referred to Billie—was sleeping
soundly and Hanora arrived to relieve her.

Hanora spent the night in a spare room upstairs.
Because Billie lived so close, it was the first time Hanora
had actually stayed overnight. She didn't like being away

from her own bed. She wriggled under the covers, turned side to side, slept only a few minutes at a time. She kept waking, having two-sided conversations in her head. "Why?" Billie pleaded through chaotic dreams. "Why must I leave my house?" The monotones of reason rang hollow all night long. In the morning, Hanora had no idea how many hours she'd slept or if she'd been awake the entire night. Perhaps the pleas and replies had been part of the dreams. Her brain refused to rest; the voices would not shut down.

$$\mathcal{I}\colon$$

Now it is the dreaded day of the move. For a fleeting moment, Hanora wonders if she should call everything off. Create some other solution with doctor, caregivers, nurses, coordinators, strangers. She briefly considers her own health. Has she had one peaceful night of sleep the past six months?

Billie might live a very long life. She cannot stay in her house alone.

The argument in Hanora's head goes on and on.

The residence into which Billie is moving is called Respiro. For the first few weeks, until Hanora is able to organize furniture and hire a moving van, Billie will use furnishings temporarily provided in her suite, which is on the ground floor of the two-storey building. She has two attractive and comfortable rooms, and a private bathroom. After a trial period, her own furniture will be moved in. This affords time to decide what to take and what to donate or put up for sale. Hanora is hopeful that Billie will become involved in those decisions. She hopes she will choose specific furniture, paintings and decor after seeing the suite. There are books to move, too, but Billie stopped reading a long time ago. She can no longer focus, or follow the written word. She cannot concentrate long enough to get through a page of a novel or even a short article in a magazine. She stares blankly at the covers of books and magazines as if these are mildly interesting objects that have nothing whatever to do with her.

As for clothing, Billie filled the upstairs closets with seasonal coats, dresses, jackets, blouses, slacks, sweaters and footwear after Whit died. When she had her bed moved down to the living room, she stopped going upstairs and soon forgot what she'd placed in the bedroom closets. But with the upcoming move to Respiro, decisions had to be made. Hanora spent several days of the previous week parading clothes past her cousin for approval. Billie sat upright in her bed, pointed, exclaimed, made decisions. About some items, she declared, "I have never seen that before in my entire life." The clothing to be kept was packed into two large suitcases and taken to Respiro in advance of her arrival. This, Billie accepted as a natural unfolding of events.

At the appointed time, the doctor arrives at the house and Hanora braces herself for conflict. Braces herself for anger. But Billie suddenly withers, capitulates. The doctor reminds her of the reasons she requires more care. Billie listens attentively. She looks to Hanora and asks, as if an entirely new topic has been introduced: "Do *you* think there's anything wrong, Hanora? Do you think I need more care?"

Hanora wants to weep, but does not. She explains that Billie will be moving to a place where she will have help round the clock.

They carry on.

Passively, heartbreakingly, her beloved cousin walks out of the house, supported by the doctor's arm. She climbs into his car. He hands the cane in after her, and drives her away. He carries the bag containing her medications and the medication sheets, which he will turn over to the medical staff at Respiro.

Hanora follows in her own car. Heaped onto the back seat are toiletries, pillows, Billie's blankets, writing paper and pens, jewellery, two purses, coats for various seasons, her CD player, a box of CDs and videocassettes—"I want to bring all of the movies. I want all of my music with me." Hanora also has the framed Duke Ellington photo and two of Whit's paintings in her car. One painting is a watercolour of Billie's childhood home in Rochester, New York, where she spent the first two decades of her life. The other is a likeness of the red-and-white house Billie and Whit shared from 1953 to 1990, and in which she has remained until this day.

The actual red-and-white house fades from Hanora's rear-view mirror as she turns the corner.

𝄢:

HANORA stays with Billie at Respiro all afternoon and into the evening. The first thing Billie does in her new place is turn on the television, which is hooked up and ready to go. While she stares blankly at the screen, Hanora arranges her cousin's belongings in the bedroom, checks dresser drawers, sets up the CD player, puts discs within reach and waits while Billie has dinner. This first evening, a tray is brought to her room. Starting the next day, she will be taken to a large dining room at the end of the hall. Staff members come to her unit to meet her. Everyone is kind. She asks a nurse if the year is 1964 and looks around in genuine surprise when told it is 1998.

At the end of a long day, close to ten o'clock, Hanora takes her leave. Nurses have been in and out. A worker helps Billie into nightgown and bathrobe. Billie again asks if the year is 1964.

Hanora hugs her cousin and promises to be back the next day. Billie looks her over and shrugs. "There are strangers in this hotel," she says. "But don't worry about me. I probably won't stay more than a few days. You should look after yourself more," she adds. "And wear your clothes right side out."

Hanora looks down and sees that her red pullover is inside out. The inner seams display a thick red ridge across both shoulders. In the morning, in Billie's house, she'd grabbed up the clothes she removed the night before, and put them on before going downstairs to make coffee and to start getting Billie ready.

She is so beyond weariness, she doesn't care and has nothing to reply. She hardly knows her own name. She drives home and parks the car in the underground lot. Filament is getting out of his car at the same time. He tips his imaginary hat and says, "Evening, Hanora." She is surprised, because she is certain he has never spoken her name before. They've often greeted each other on the elevator or in front of the mailboxes, but that's been the extent of their interactions. Filament has a cherry-red spot in each cheek; perhaps he's had wine with his dinner.

His heavy wool overcoat is open. He is formally dressed and wears medals across his chest; he must have been at an official function. Hanora didn't know about the medals; they're probably from the Second World War. Or perhaps the Korean War. She realizes how little she knows about Mr. Filmore. She almost asks where he's been. Almost invites him to join her to share a bottle of wine. She wants to spill out everything that's been going on these past weeks and months. The past year. To anyone. A stranger would be best. If Filament would rather talk, she would listen. To stories about his life or anyone else's. Anyone's life but Billie's. She'd say, "Look, I've been so upset, I wore my clothes inside out today."

Filament ushers her into the elevator and they stand in silence, side by side, facing forward.

He looks over sympathetically before he gets off on nineteen, and asks if she is all right.

She is so moved by this gesture of kindness she can scarcely respond. Her fatigue must be visible. The most she can muster is a nod, a quick thanks.

She lets herself into her apartment and pours a neat Scotch. She wonders how Kenan and Tress would have behaved if either had suffered from dementia. Thankfully, both had long lives and were spared the indignity. She wonders how one would have coped if responsible for the other. In ways that Hanora is now responsible for Billie. How can anyone, for that matter, understand how a primary caregiver copes? Well, no one. Except those who have done the work. And they know how high the cost: the emotional cost of watching a loved one slowly robbed of intellect.

Hanora is grateful that she never had to become parent to either of her parents. That must be the most difficult situation of all. She tried to visit her parents as often as she could during their final years. She still grieves their deaths. She is glad that Kenan kept up his photography until the year he died. She hasn't looked at his albums since they came into her possession following Tress's death in 1987. Until recently, the albums were stowed in the basement storage room of her apartment. But the shelves in the storage room are being replaced by the owners of the building, so she has carried the albums upstairs while the work is being done.

By the time Kenan died, he had filled three albums with Deseronto photos, all of which he developed himself. She remembers leafing through the pages during a visit to her parents' home, and realizing that Kenan had not lost his obsession with the lives of adventurers and explorers.

The albums are now arranged on a prominent shelf in Hanora's living room. Some evening, she promises herself, I'll take them down and examine them carefully. See if I can understand how he worked at unravelling the complications of his own life.

God knows, he dealt with enough complications after his experience in the Great War. Until she left home in 1939 to sail on the SS *Champlain*, she had been a daily witness to the way he worked at erecting secure boundaries around himself. He functioned within circumscribed but manageable routines. The routines were of his own invention and offered safety, protection and, presumably, comfort.

But isn't it strange, she thinks, how traces of ourselves, the ones we leave behind, are so often by way of the written word. It was never enough for Kenan to allow his photos to stand alone. He felt the need to assign words. Not that anyone would ever comprehend what those words meant. Nor would this have mattered to Kenan. What was important was that the words had meaning for him. Maybe, she thinks, maybe he never felt whole after returning home wounded in 1918. Perhaps he could have taught me a thing or two about feeling complete. Or perhaps that should be *incomplete.* For wasn't it incompleteness that reverberated like an echo, again and again, throughout one's life?

She allows herself the memory of staring up at those third-storey adoption agency windows in Toronto, searching long ago for her own sense of wholeness.

Everything long ago.

And now she follows her impulse to examine Kenan's albums, and goes to the shelf and pulls them down. She places them on the living-room table and opens the cover of the one on top. The black pages are laced together, the laces threaded through punched holes at the edge of each page.

She is too fatigued. She cannot enter Kenan's world right now. All she can manage at the end of this day is to stare out her twentieth-floor window into distant city lights.

WHAT SHE FINDS

━━━━━━

$\int$ HE ENTERS THE RED-AND-WHITE HOUSE AND realizes it's one of the rare times she's been here alone. The house has always welcomed her: Billie and Whit, or Billie alone over the past eight years. There has been no reason for Hanora to be here by herself except when Billie and Whit vacationed and asked her to stop in to check the mail and water plants.

The space feels empty despite the furniture still in place. The bed has been stripped of linens; the living room is bleak without Billie in her TV-watching chair. Two of Whit's watercolours hang on the walls. The air is stale, though it's been only a week since Billie moved. The thermostat has been turned down. Hanora opens windows in the kitchen, bathroom and dining room. She opens front and back inside doors to let in natural light. The temperature is warm today, the sun shining. A blessing, she tells herself, and thinks of Zel. Hold close the blessings. Value each and every one.

She plans to do a cursory inventory of the contents of the house. Prepare and sort for the movers. Make a plan. Make several plans. Set aside the items mentioned for Ned and his daughter in Billie's will and take them to Billie's storage locker at Respiro, which is in the basement of the residence.

The space under the stairs in Billie's house also has to be cleared. Hanora will set aside the seaman's chest Billie purchased in Portobello Road and deal with it later. Billie asked her to take it away after her kitchen was painted.

"I don't want the thing," Billie told her. "It's yours. I don't know what's in it anymore. Old things I haven't looked at in a thousand years. Papers, old greeting cards Whit and I saved, though I don't know why. Photos you probably took with your camera when we sailed to Europe in the Dark Ages. I'm not sure exactly what's there, and I don't care. If it's out of sight, it doesn't exist. But I knew the frame with Duke's photo was at the top, and I have that now. That's the only thing I want. The chest has always been meant for you, and I want you to have it now." All of this said with lucidity. Genuine affection. Warmth.

Hanora will move the chest to her apartment after she has made decisions about the rest of Billie's belongings. For now she plans to fill garbage bags and boxes. Grapple with the task at hand, shelf by shelf, cupboard by cupboard, closet by closet. If necessary, she will bring in a helper to assist. Once the house is completely cleared, she'll hire a cleaning crew to go through the entire place.

She enters the kitchen and starts by opening the top drawer of the kitchen cabinet. A shock of memory. Billie shutting the drawer hurriedly on the day of the MoCA test. The mass, the mess of pages she tried to hide. Here they are, scrunched and battered, folded and refolded. Writing pads crammed with scrawled entries, loose pages, notebooks, lists on the backs of empty envelopes. Paper three inches deep.

Hanora digs to the bottom of the drawer. More of the same. Every sheet covered with dates and times. The earliest go back two years. The writing is sometimes slanted from the upper corner, sometimes from the lower. Most writing is horizontal but with cramped additions around the edges. There is no order to any of this. There are hundreds upon hundreds of entries.

JAN. 1/97
4 a.m. can't sleep, warm milk, hot coffee, bed, up again, stared out window into dark, lie down, can't sleep, hear pulse in ear, loud and fast, rapid heartbeat, something wrong, should I call ambulance?

8 a.m. toast—half piece, jam, tea, oatmeal, spoon peanut butter

*9 a.m. stranger scrambled egg, ate because she nagged.
She wished me Happy New Year.*

 *12:30 p.m. drank cup of chicken soup, tasteless, crackers
(2), tea, apple*

 *5 p.m. frozen dinner, heated in m-wave, pasta, veal,
some leftovers*

 9 p.m. prune juice

MAR. 17/97
*3 a.m. shot of whisky, stared out window at snow, fell
into bed*

 5 a.m. warm milk, sleep, no sleep

 *9 a.m. milky tea, whole pot, made porridge, hate por-
ridge, supposed to be good for me*

 *10 a.m. coffee, left tap on in bathroom just for a minute?
flooded floor, sopped up with towels*

 11 a.m. coffee

 *12:45 p.m. bread and butter, can't be bothered with
lunch, slice of cheese*

 *5 p.m. coffee with baked potato, chicken breast, ate half,
carrots and peas mixed*

 9 p.m. coffee, bed, up at 11, warm milk, can't sleep

MAY 22/97
*H brought homemade butter tarts last night while visiting.
I ate 6 for breakfast.*

10 a.m. tea, strong, no milk

12:25 p.m. opened tin Campbell's soup

4 p.m. Meals on Wheels arrives—white sauce popular with someone, not me. Chicken. Brussels sprouts.

9 p.m. ice cream, cherry-vanilla, glass wine, throat lozenge, more wine

11 p.m. warm milk, tried to pay bill, messed up chequebook, cheques missing, accounts mixed up, maybe tell H?

In the midst of the lists of food, she has interrupted herself, as if she suddenly thought of this.

Baby turkeys: Don't let their feet touch wet ground. Make sure there's wire underfoot. Or bring them inside. My father made a mistake thinking he could raise a few in a small pen behind shed. Neighbours on street weren't happy. He brought them into the house in cardboard box on a rainy night. The rest of us asleep. Baby turkeys ran around kitchen all night because they got out of box. Shit everywhere in the morning. Good thing door to next room was shut. Huge fight between my parents after everyone got up. The usual yelling and shouting, recriminations and outcries. Ned left for school early, good for him, he escaped.

JUNE 17/97

Phone rang. Let it ring. Cried. Can't stop crying.

Phone rang again. Again. Again. Picked up, couldn't understand what woman was saying.

Phoned H—don't know who the woman was. Maybe call was important.

Can't stop crying. H says she'll come over. Put Meals on Wheels dinner in fridge

Two glasses wine

JULY 23/97

7 p.m. Man came to door, looked at me through window, didn't let him in, didn't answer bell, hid purse in oven. He did not look like good provider.

Called H. Help!

AUG. 7/97

Skipped breakfast—drank tea

1 p.m. stood at window after stranger left, opened tuna, ate out of can

1:50 p.m. stood beside freezer, ate entire package frozen cookies

5 p.m. no hunger after cookies, thought I'd be sick, sucked lozenge

11 p.m. cream of wheat, hankering for, still constipated

Sep. 11/97

6 a.m. Coffee. Tea. Coffee again.

2 p.m. Lettuce-tomato sandwich

5 p.m. Meals on W, don't like dinner, white sauce on fish, stranger said eat it anyway

Dec. 31/97

Breakfast—leftover Chr. turkey white meat

Lunch—leftover turkey dark meat, heated gravy, cranberries resemble blood pellets

Supper—leftover dressing, 2 cherry tomatoes, green beans. H arrived with dinner but I'd eaten. Forgot she was bringing dinner tonight.

Bed—warm milk after H left, no sleep, never sleep, do I sleep? Mixed up pills. Might have taken twice, maybe three times, better not mention to strangers. Definitely not to H. If I do, she'll return, take pills away.

Feb. 14/98

Stranger brought candy hearts for treat, cinnamon taste. Ate red hearts for breakfast.

11 a.m. egg—tried soft-boiled, mess on plate, too runny, hate runny eggs

12 noon—tea, sugar, did I ever take sugar in tea? Don't tell H. She'll think I'm batty.

1:30 p.m. phone rang, man on phone told me my credit card cancelled. How will I pay for anything? Called H.

Hanora remembers Billie's upset over the cancellation of her credit card, which she had used in the past for phone orders. Payment of her bills became erratic, and was finally forgotten completely. When Hanora arrived to help solve the problem, Billie was angry. She shouted as if she believed Hanora was responsible for the cancellation. In fact, Hanora had no idea that Billie still owned a credit card. Hanora rooted through desk files and found old statements, unpaid. Billie calmed down when shown the unpaid balances and ever-increasing interest charges. She declared that she would cut up her card. Which made no difference, as it had already been cancelled.

Billie yanked the card from her wallet, pulled scissors from a drawer and sat at the end of the kitchen table. Slowly, deliberately, she snipped away until the card was an array of tiny chips. She glared at Hanora, forgot the fragmented plastic strewn over the end of the table and rested her bare arm on top.

When Hanora got up to leave, promising to settle the bill from Billie's bank account, Billie was in no way grateful. She raised an arm to rest her chin in her hand so she could stare at the door while Hanora exited. The lower part of Billie's arm was imprinted with a kaleidoscope of coloured plastic pieces, all pressed to her skin. These did not fall off when she raised her arm. If she noticed she didn't let on, and Hanora was beyond telling her.

Billie stayed like that, glaring, the plastic chips attached to her skin while she watched Hanora put on her coat.

"Goodbye," she said coldly. A single chip dropped off her arm and fell back onto the table. She looked down and brushed it to the floor as Hanora left.

𝄢

HANORA leafs through more pages. On and on goes Billie's recorded history. Every item of food she chewed, every drink that passed through her lips—all have been listed on rough scraps of paper, scrunched-up pages torn from scribblers, intact notebooks. Some pages have a half-sucked lozenge stuck to them, as if Billie hurriedly removed the lozenge from her mouth and dropped it into the drawer.

Her penmanship is sometimes frantic, sometimes heavily scored or traced over and over for emphasis. Many pages have Hanora's phone number scribbled along the top or bottom, underlined, as if Billie was desperate to remember how to make contact.

How long has Billie's memory been slipping away?

She has written a history of eating. Of sustenance.

A history of insomnia.

A history of tears.

And fears.

On paper, as if to make herself real, Billie has been doing whatever she could, in futile attempts to preserve her sense of self.

1939

THE LADY CHAMPLAIN

RUNNING. THAT'S THE WAY IT FELT. RUNNING up and down stairs, in and out of corridors, exploring the outer deck, running into people they'd just met. Trying to see everything at once: every room, lounge, café, in the daylight and in the dark. Becoming accustomed to the roll of the ship. Seeing the occasional puddle of emesis at the bottom of stairwells, quickly cleaned up by staff. Knowing that passengers with *mal de mer* were begging to have weak tea or broth brought to their cabins.

Hanora and Billie tried to remember names, including their own.

There they were, on the *Liste des Passagers*:

Miss Hanora Oak
Miss Billie Read

For their first dinner, they were led to a table for six, their seating for the duration of the voyage. The dining room was two decks high in the centre, adorned with iron-work along the upper walls. Marble stairs led down and into the room from two directions. Grand, everything grand.

An American woman named Ruth was seated at their table. She greeted them as if she had recently suffered a grievous circumstance. Hanora was fascinated by the way her face saddened, the way her mouth exhaled a soft breath, the way she tilted her head and mourned her way into conversation. In fact, once past the mournful greeting, she was surprisingly cheerful. She was not much older than Billie, and said she planned to disembark in Plymouth, where her husband, a British pilot in the RAF, would travel to meet her. She'd been in Boston visiting family and was now returning to her marital home in the north of England. She was slim and wore a black dress, black stockings, black shoes. The only adornment was an emerald-and-diamond ring on her left hand. When Hanora admired the ring, Ruth said it had been put there by her husband and she had not removed it since. He wore a wedding band, she said. But she wore the emerald and diamond.

Ruth was certain they were heading into war and missed her husband "an awful lot," but she declared her intention to enjoy every minute at sea, especially with so many musicians aboard. "I do love to dance," she added. "I hope the ship's musicians are up to scratch. Do you think Duke will be persuaded to play?"

No one knew the answer to that. But everyone was watching for the man. He appeared at that moment, descending the staircase, and was shown to his table.

"What are *your* names?" Ruth looked as if she might burst into tears. "You're awfully alike. Are you twins?"

A quick glance, and Hanora and Billie reminded themselves of the switch.

"I'm Hanora Oak," said Billie. "This is my cousin Billie Read." The two tried to be serious, turned away from each other so they wouldn't collapse in laughter. They were saved by the arrival of the waiter, who identified himself as Hugo — white shirt, black trousers, slicked hair. He would be looking after their table the entire week. He placed menus before them, gave a slight bow and told them he'd be back. The menus were in French. Printed at the front of the menu along the bottom were the words "*En mer, le 23 Mars, 1939.*"

Immediate chatter ensued. There were so many choices. Who would interpret the chef's creations, the ones that weren't obvious — *Mousseline de Marrons, Filets de Rouget au Gratin, Coupe Rêve de Bébé*? Hanora, for one. She had taught herself some French, but could not help except to say that she was certain *marrons* meant chestnuts.

Hanora looked around at the other tables. The instrumentalists were in different parts of the room, most at tables for four. Hanora saw Tizol, Hodges, Cootie Williams, Tricky Sam. Ivie came in, and took her place with Duke and Rex Stewart and a woman Hanora didn't recognize. Loud laughter was coming from the table next to Hanora's and she turned to see Billy Taylor, the bassist, holding up pictures of steak and potatoes and pie. He was trying to show these to the waiter, even while the others at his table roared with laughter. "He can't speak the language," said one of his tablemates. "He cut these out of magazines because he's afraid he'll go hungry." The waiter was laughing, as well. Far across the room, six nuns sat together, smiling at the eruption of noise from the musicians.

Another person was led to their table, and Hanora again reminded herself of her new name. What she saw first was one caramel shoe, then another, and a shock of royal-blue socks. This time, the wearer of the shoes had a face. The man wore an open-necked blue shirt, sports jacket, tan trousers, no tie. He was in his thirties, six feet tall with a slouch. He folded himself into the chair next to Billie and grinned. The voice—he introduced himself as Angus—was the gravelly voice Hanora had heard on the train the night before. Billie shook hands, gave her name as Hanora and said she was happy to meet him. She leaned in closer. Hallman was forgotten.

"Goodnight, Irene" had not faded into the noise of the train after all.

The final companions at their table for the week were a couple in their thirties who introduced themselves as Frank and Frankie. They shrugged, saying people were usually surprised that they had the same name. Frankie was pale, the curls around her face almost white. She wore round, rimless glasses and a washed-out print dress, as if she were making every effort to impersonate an old woman. Frank had a wild look and was always laughing, always cheerful. He had genuine affection for his young-old wife, and as it turned out, the two knew every dance step invented in the past dozen years. On the dance floor later that evening, other dancers moved to the edges and left the centre clear, just to watch them do the Charleston and the Lindy Hop.

Foxy, who considered himself a ladies' man, was another matter. He wasn't at their table in the dining room, but later in the evening showed an interest in all women who were unaccompanied by men. After dinner, he moved from table to table in the lounge, asking women to dance, staring at them with small black eyes. Like Frank and Frankie, Foxy knew all the steps.

While the music played, while intrigues and encounters began to take shape, Hanora was watching faces. Every face was new. There was no chance that any relative of hers, apart from Billie, would be aboard a ship leaving New York and heading across the ocean, but she couldn't stop looking. Searching for family had become her habit, her practice. She paid attention to expression, imagined likeness, no matter how small. She watched the many ways people relaxed into, and took for granted, the state of belonging. Not long ago, she had been one of those people. Before her last birthday, she had never given her identity a thought.

Undoubtedly, there were others aboard who had been adopted. What was she to do? Ask the captain to send out a bulletin? Request adoptees to report to the editor of the ship's paper? Would she meet, interview, find out what they knew of themselves? Ask if they had concerns, deeply personal concerns? The daily paper was printed in both English and French and reported world news and news of the stock market, but why couldn't it turn to something more intimate?

She did not approach the editor of the ship's paper. Her search was her own obsession, and though at times she was tempted to tell Billie, she held back.

She wanted no one else's input. She'd promised herself that she would tell only Breeda and Tobe. Billie was impetuous, sometimes unpredictable. At the moment, she was having the time of her life pretending to be Hanora. Billie had left her own identity on the pier in New York. Now she was meeting people, practising new dance steps, engaging the musicians in chatter and laughter. And dancing late every night.

At the end of the entertainment in the evenings, Hanora returned to her cabin, looked in the mirror, stretched the skin at the edges of her eyes, pulled at her cheeks and mouth, created a variety of facial expressions.

She tried to imagine what it would be like to resemble a father more than a mother, a mother more than a father. What could that be like? To have someone to resemble? There had to be other restless souls out there. Like her own.

She crawled under the covers and did what she did every night: forced herself to try to conjure a remembered detail about her birth mother. She told herself she would never stop trying. And she *had* been able to create an image in her mind. A shape, the outline of a woman's face. The face had not a single feature. She had conjured a woman without a face.

1998

MARIAH BINDLE'S EARLY DIARY

ANORA LEANS OVER THE BOX SHE HAS labelled "A," and reaches in. Pulls out a diary with a pressboard cover, brittle, one hundred years old. Ninety-eight years, to be exact. The cover sheds tiny yellowed chips along its edges, and she's careful as she turns the first page. If Mariah were alive today, she'd be almost 112.

Billie is settling in at Respiro. She has care. The staff is attentive. Her chosen items of furniture won't be moved for another week or more, which means that Hanora can begin to get back to work. Or pretend to. Maybe, just maybe it will be possible to focus. To fully concentrate on the book she plans to write.

𝄢

THIS is the overview of what Hanora has learned so far: Mariah, born in 1886, youngest of five children, grew up on the homestead on the Canadian Shield. Throughout her childhood, she demonstrated a gift for drawing. She drew portraits of family, classmates and friends, and sketched rural scenes. She filled diaries and notebooks with sketches, along with a running commentary about various aspects of her life and the lives of others around her. When she was fifteen, a teacher named Mrs. Banco arranged Mariah's first solo exhibit in the local one-room school. As the years passed and Mariah showed no interest in marrying—she worked steadily to help her parents on the farm as older siblings married and moved away—her mother urged her to find a way to support herself. In 1908, in her twenty-second year, she moved to Toronto, supposedly to study at a secretarial school in a private business college for young women. Instead, and contrary to the wishes of her parents (both believed she could not earn a living by painting), she found an art teacher and supported herself by helping in the kitchen in the downtown boarding house where she lived. She worked out a schedule for study and one for work. She joined an art class and began to experiment with oils. Eventually, she sailed to Europe and spent time in southern France, learning what she could, painting and meeting other artists. From there, she travelled to southwest England. In Cornwall, she delighted in the exuberance of colour. She was comfortable in St. Ives, and painted landscapes of hill, sea and sky. Her work there—her drawings of fishermen, their boats and their families—was particularly detailed.

She returned to Canada at the end of the Great War, gratified at the serious recognition her paintings were receiving in her home country. She moved back and forth between Toronto and her parents' farm, always painting, and returned to southwest England again during the thirties. Once more, she lived and painted in Cornwall, where she became friendly with a British artist named Lizzie. From there, she moved to Coventry, perhaps to follow Lizzie. They were residents of that city at the outset of the Second World War. During one of the bombing raids of Coventry, in April 1941, Mariah was struck by falling debris. She suffered a serious concussion and was unconscious for a time—whether hours or days, Hanora has yet to find out. Mariah remained in England for the duration of the war, and returned to Canada in early 1946, bringing her wartime diaries with her. Her papers ended up in several locations in Ontario as a consequence of moving about so much. In June 1946, on her sixtieth birthday, she died in the Eastern Hospital for the Insane in Brockville, where she'd been taken because of what was reported to be unmanageable depression and "senility." The present-day relatives are the ones who reported these latter facts.

𝄢

HANORA had taken a cursory look at Mariah's early diary before, but did not have a chance to read all the way through. Now she wants to organize the materials chronologically. As far as she can tell, this diary, dated 1900, contains the first of the artist's writings. Eventually, every copybook, sketchpad, diary, writing tablet and loose page will be spread out over the living-room floor. For now, she wants to get through the reading and create a plan for the book. There will be surprises; there are surprises in every quest. The thought of the unknown makes her eager to immerse herself in work.

Starting back at the beginning is a safe choice. In 1900, Mariah was fourteen years old. Handwriting indicates a mature fourteen. Her cursive style is careful. Neat, but not ornate. Slanted to the right. Sometimes in pen and ink; more often, especially later, in pencil. Sketches are scattered through the pages, each sketch a window into Mariah's life.

9:

JUNE 28, 1900
Thursday. My birthday. Father announced that I am fourteen years high and asked if I'd grown overnight. He had me laughing as I twirled for inspection.

Here is my sketch of family around the table—from memory, as I'm this moment propped in bed. Mother made a three-layer cake. She had saved walnuts, as a surprise, for the icing. My older brothers and sisters—my eldest brother returned with his wife for the party—are leaning in while I blow out the candle. One thick candle is meant to represent all my years so far. The candle in my drawing is too thick, but I won't erase. The likeness of family is to my satisfaction. Quick lines. That's what I want to do. Quick lines that reveal something distinct about each of my brothers and sisters and my sister-in-law.

Wild strawberries have been spotted here and there along the edges of the ditches and roads, and farmed berries will soon be ripe. I've been offered a job picking on the Freeman farm—one cent a quart. After the strawberries are done, the raspberries will ripen. I'll be earning money for art supplies, and the extra cost to me will be an aching back and purple stains under my fingernails. Mrs. Banco, my teacher, says she will order items for me from Toronto. Half the money I earn will go to Mother, the other half to my work. Not that Mother takes my art seriously. As far as she's concerned, picking berries and preserving them for winter are tasks more important than anything I might draw.

Mrs. Banco told me to stay in touch over the summer months, now that school is out. She reminded me to ask Uncle Oryn to keep an eye out for second-hand art books while he's travelling the countryside. Uncle Oryn is an auctioneer, and often stumbles across unusual items. He says that if the automobile ever comes to a town or city nearby, he'll be the first to purchase. Mostly, he deals in property sales and the auctioning of farm equipment. Aunt Clarice travels with him occasionally, if he takes the democrat and she's not busy on their farm. She likes to poke around the estates when house contents are sold along with outdoor equipment. Aunt Clarice gives me more encouragement than I deserve, and I love her for that. She and Mrs. Banco assure me that I can "do something" with my art. Beyond that, I don't really know what "doing something" means. It is up to me and how steadfastly I persevere. Aunt Clarice suggested that I accompany her to one of the auctions on a summer day when I can be spared from home. "Bring your sketchpad," she added. "You never know what you might see of interest along the way—or what you will witness at our destination. You'll be wanting to draw other parts of the countryside."

Mother calls out from her room, asking me to shut off the lamp. She worries about fire in the bedrooms. Before I do, I'll sketch this fluted dome, my favourite of all the lamps in the house. I wish for colour, but blacks and greys must do. After I pick berries, I will have a little money to buy colour, glory be.

DIGGING UP OLD THINGS

BILLIE TELEPHONES IN THE EARLY EVENING. Weeping. Almost wailing. "Please come, Hanora. I'm having so much trouble. I'm afraid. Please come and help me." She will not or cannot say what the trouble is.

Hanora dumps her just-made tea down the sink, throws on a jacket, races in the car to Respiro, parks, signs in. She proceeds down the hall at a half run, and when she walks through the door and into the suite, Billie looks over and says, "Hanora! I wasn't expecting you. Are you out doing errands at this time of night? It's almost dark."

"I came because you phoned. You asked me to come right away because you needed help."

"I certainly did not. I haven't been near the phone all day." Billie is truly indignant.

She continues to deny, so there is nothing more to be said.

Hanora decides to stay with her awhile. She makes tea and pours a cup for each of them, and sits across from her cousin. She pulls her notebook from her purse.

"Let's try to remember some things from the past, Billie. I want to write things down."

"Why do you want to dig up old things?" says Billie. "What's the use of that?"

"Because you'll remember things I don't. I can write down our memories. Why don't you tell me about the *Champlain*? We could start there."

She looks around the room. Billie's furniture has been moved in, and is exactly the way she wants it arranged. She appears to be comfortable with her belongings around her. The braided rug is on the floor in front of the chesterfield. The framed photo of Duke is on the far wall above a white end table. Whit's paintings of Billie's childhood home and their red-and-white house have been hung on a bedroom wall. As for Billie, there isn't a trace of the fear and anxiety Hanora heard over the phone only minutes earlier.

Hanora points to the photo. "We had a grand time on that ship. Before the war. It was the first trip overseas for both of us."

"I suppose we did. The man in the royal-blue socks. He was travelling alone. I slept with him in his cabin."

"I know you did. You made it perfectly clear that I wasn't to go looking for you."

Billie laughs until she is out of breath. Hanora hasn't seen her laugh like this for a long time. For a moment, she looks twenty years younger. Hanora can scarcely reconcile this Billie with the panicked Billie on the phone.

"It wasn't a big bed—quite narrow. But he knew what to do. You needn't write that down."

"You went into considerable detail at the time, as I recall." Hanora is thinking of Tobe during the war, how he'd appeared at her rooming house in London. How they went to a shop on the Queensway to buy tinned food, and later walked to a dimly lit underground dance hall she knew about, and danced and danced and then sat at an overcrowded table. How he reached for her chair and dragged it close to his own. She remembers the scraping of wood over floorboards, the intimacy, the privacy of the moment. How they walked along the edge of the park on Bayswater Road, and how she took him back to her rooming house and sneaked him up to her second-floor room, where she was not permitted to have overnight guests. Her landlady, a woman in her sixties who had tightly curled henna hair and was called the Fury by residents, owned a Pekingese that yipped loudly every time someone came to the front door. The landlady's rooms were just to the right of the main entrance, at the bottom of the stairs. But the Fury's dog knew Hanora well, and allowed Tobe to pass without setting off a shrill alarm.

Tobe wrote from Canada in September of '39 that he had joined the Hasty Ps and was training in Prince Edward County. No proper uniforms at first. Not for weeks and weeks. He and the boys were soon to receive the badge of the Regiment—a highlight, from what Hanora understood.

There was a rush to join after war was declared. Not enough equipment yet, not even enough uniforms. That will all come, and we'll soon be nine hundred strong. Boys have enlisted from every corner of Hastings and P E Counties. We've had to take over the canning factory in Picton for barracks. I don't mind the drill, the discipline, the route marches. And we will be paid regularly. After the lean years everyone has been through, a regular salary is a wonder to most. Especially the boys from the farms. I was home to Deseronto recently—had all of a day and a half off—and dropped in to see your folks. They worry about you being there, with war declared. I reassured them, told them to remember how sensible you are (?!) and said I'd visit you at first opportunity when I'm overseas.

His ship had docked in Scotland on New Year's Day 1940, but it wasn't until the Hasty Ps moved south to Aldershot, and then later in the summer to Surrey, near Redhill and Reigate, that he was able to travel to London to find her. When he arrived, he had four days' precious leave. She learned that he'd sailed from Halifax and arrived in convoy at Greenock, Scotland, on the *Ormonde*. Travel information was aggressively protected, restricted. She used her own channels, her contacts in London, to dig up information when she was interviewing and writing, but she could not compromise security. She would not have been published otherwise.

She had been sending articles to Canada, but had found part-time work assisting a dietician with a staff of three to provide meals in a school canteen. Every recipe was calculated to feed one hundred children. She wasn't used to cooking in such large quantities, and quickly learned how important it was to follow directions carefully. The salary she earned paid the rent. She wrote during her days off, and in the evenings, and at night when she couldn't sleep. She wrote as often as she could. The *Star* bought two of her pieces, one of which was about the distribution of gas masks, or respirators. How civilians had to keep them with them at all times; how they practised using them during sudden mock attacks. She wrote about the wooden rattles used as alerts, and the drills that took place in factories and schools. What she found most poignant was the sight of small children involved in games and play while wearing masks and resembling tiny aliens with enormous window eyes and long rubber snouts.

Tobe was able to visit again, and then again. The men

in the Regiment moved about—training, exercising, learning to work together, learning to be soldiers—but Tobe was never far away. He told her about the bungled foray into France in June, with the Hasty Ps being withdrawn almost as soon as they'd "invaded"—this occurred at the same time the Germans were marching into Paris. After a quick recall to England, having been forced to abandon their new equipment in France, the Hasty Ps resumed their training, moving from one area of southern England to another.

𝄢

SHE thinks of Tobe's visits to London, the narrow bed in her bedsit in Queensborough Terrace, how they could not stop laughing when they tried to stifle sound. She remembers the coin-slot gas heater, the thin walls, the cold. Often there was no gas, no water. God, how she froze when she lived in wartime England! Dampness in her room. Worse in the frigid bathroom on the landing below—a bathroom shared with three other roomers. Water was heated by a coke-fuelled boiler. If and when there was hot water, it was rationed. She shivered violently in front of the small sink and mirror, wondering if she would survive the removal of her clothes long enough to get clean. Wondering if she could manage two inches of warm water in the tub. Tobe bathed with her in that warmth. He washed her back, her shoulders, her face. "You still have a few freckles," he said. They had added a kettle of boiling water to what was already in the tub, a sanguine attempt to make it warmer.

She watched Tobe to see what had changed. Hair shorter, but the infantry hadn't been able to thin out the thick mop on top. The kindness on his face: that had not been taken from him while he was being turned into a soldier. His shoulders were wider, more muscular after months of training and physical exercise. Hardening training. He was self-assured, more decisive than ever. She sensed his strength when she saw him, felt it when she was with him. She ran her hands down over his bare shoulders. The way he looked at her. She closes the memory.

𝄢

"THE Grand Salon," says Billie suddenly. "The enormous painting of Champlain took up most of the end wall. I faced it often enough. Blue Socks wanted to sit at the same table every day. He ordered Champagne cocktails. Sometimes Chartreuse, because he liked the name. He was free with his money, so he must have had plenty. He sang country songs and I fell for his low, scratchy voice. Didn't he play an instrument of some kind? He didn't know a thing about jazz. He liked slow dances and country. But I liked the fast dances, and I liked him. I tried to show him the Lindy and he was game to try. What was his real name? I've forgotten. I was on the rebound, as the language goes. What was the other one's name? The one from New York who dumped me?"

"Hallman. He took you to jazz clubs, he took you dancing."

"His ears were too high," she said. "I shouldn't have gone out with him. Never trust a man who has oddly placed ears."

"That's the first I've heard of the ears."

"Well, it's true. And what about Blue Socks? What was *his* name?" She is sparked by memories. Wants to follow them to their end.

"His first name was Angus," says Hanora. "His full name would have been on the *Liste des Passagers*. One of us might still have that *Liste*, stored somewhere. Tell me more about the Grand Salon."

Hanora, too, is trying to recall detail, though she didn't spend much time in the Grand Salon. Angus and Billie played cards there during the daytime. Along with the musicians and Ivie, who had their cards out every day. There was a large smoking room, too, and card playing was continuous, night and day. The pillars in the room were decorated with impressive—almost life-size—carvings of kings, queens and knaves, along with the suits: spades, hearts, diamonds, clubs. Blue Socks kept a queen of spades in his pocket, for luck.

In the evenings, Hanora danced, as everyone did. The music, the atmosphere, the dancing were charged, as if passengers believed this would be their final voyage. For many, it *was* their last peacetime voyage. But not for Duke and his orchestra. They toured with huge success in Paris, Belgium, the Netherlands, Denmark. In Sweden, they did a fifteen-city tour and were wonderfully received. But it was more and more apparent that war was closing in from all sides, and Duke had become uneasy. The news of his tour was widely reported when he and his musicians, travelling through a portion of Germany en route to Denmark, were forced by Nazi soldiers to leave the train. They were held up in Hamburg for hours before being permitted to move on.

After playing in Copenhagen and then Sweden, the musicians sailed to England. Hanora learned later that they were not permitted to play there because of a union dispute. Duke and his entourage cut their tour short and returned to New York on the *Île de France* in May, several months before war was declared, and before U-boats regularly patrolled and threatened ships in the Atlantic. By then, Billie had finished sightseeing in London and was back at her office job in New York. Hanora, who'd travelled to London from the Continent by herself in late

April, was disappointed that there would be no perform-
ances in England prior to Duke and his orchestra returning
home.

𝄢

IN the middle of the week at sea, almost every passenger
aboard—except the few who continued to suffer from *mal
de mer*—turned out to attend the Bal Masqué. Billie dressed
as a cigarette girl, with Blue Socks as her bodyguard. The
two worked in the cabin all afternoon at their costumes,
making the tray Billie wore from a strap around her neck.
They filled it with empty or partially empty cigarette packages donated by other passengers. Billie wore Tangee rouge
and two shades of lipstick, one overtop of the other.

Frank and Frankie dressed as Adam and Eve, using cab-
bage leaves begged from the ship's kitchen to cover their
skimpy outfits. Frankie looked young—her own age—for
the first time since boarding. Ruth dressed in black, as she
did every day, but added a black mask and a wig of raven-
black hair.

Hanora dressed as George Sand, in men's trousers,
vest and tie, all borrowed from one of the many costume
trunks kept by the ship for the Bal Masqué. She wore her
hair long—elaborate flowers drooping from one side—
and wished she had paid more attention when her mother

used to put her hair in ringlets. She selected *Le Dernier Amour* by Sand from the ship's library, and carried that with her. She borrowed a cigar from Foxy and tucked it into her vest pocket.

Foxy, aware of his reputation as a ladies' man, amused everyone by dressing as Reynard the Fox. He wore a hat with pointed ears that jutted through slits, and a long, bushy tail that he, too, had borrowed from a costume trunk. He moved around from table to table, asking women to dance.

The musicians danced, Ivie danced, most passengers turned out for the festivities. Hanora stood near the doorway looking on and wondering if she was really halfway across the Atlantic, while revellers paid no attention to the dark, to the endless ocean outside. The dance floor, the costumes, the partying could be anywhere. But she was aboard the SS *Champlain*, a place unlike any she had known before. A world of luxury and gaiety, her familiar world cast aside as if it did not exist. Time had come to a halt while she was at sea.

Duke approached from the corridor, a sudden presence beside her. His deep, warm voice. He was wearing a plush wine-coloured bathrobe over an open-neck shirt and casual trousers. He looked entirely at ease. He had on old slippers, the backs worn down.

He bowed, slightly. "Billie, isn't it?" he said. "Serious young lady at this moment. In a seriously inventive costume."

Hanora was caught off guard, being addressed as Billie. She recovered. "Billie Read," she said. "Well, George Sand, for the evening."

"Ah. Then Chopin is in your life."

"He is, or was."

"I played Chopin when I was a child. Both of my parents played piano. Sometimes I listen to Chopin when my life becomes too hectic. Tell me, what will the serious George Sand do when the *Lady Champlain* reaches the other side?" He rubbed his fingers across his forehead, the vertical lines between his brows. He was relaxed, in no hurry to move on.

"I'll stay for a while," said Hanora. "I want to travel in France, find out what's going on in the south. Thousands of Spaniards are coming across the border. One of my schoolmates was killed in Spain, in the Civil War." She added, too quickly, "I'm a writer," and was immediately embarrassed at having blurted this out. She was terrified that Duke would ask what she had published, but he didn't. He was interested. She had his full attention.

"That's wonderful," he said. "A fine profession to pursue. You keep following your dreams, Billie. That's what I do . . . what I've always done."

Partygoers were calling for Duke from the other side of the room, but he ignored their shouts.

"I hope writing is something you're passionate about,"

he said. "Music never seems like work to me. Writing and creating and performing—those are my passions." He reached for her hand, kissed it. "Remember to listen," he said. "And keep on doing what you love to do. I'll keep an eye out for your work."

Musicians had appeared on either side of him and were tugging him across the room.

"I have to join this party," he called back, laughing. "As you can see, I've dressed down. This is what I look like most of the time."

Only after he'd been pulled away did Hanora realize that if he was ever inclined to find anything she had written, he would look her up under her cousin's name.

The party went on and on; no one objected to the late hours. Reynard the Fox continued to put forth his best efforts to persuade women to accompany him to the promenade deck for a stroll in the dark. The ship's musicians took advantage of Duke's presence and honoured his music. Just before the party ended for the night, Barney Bigard went below and brought up his clarinet. Sonny Greer slipped in behind the drums after being beckoned by the French drummer. The rhythm changed entirely as they began to play "Mood Indigo," which pulled almost everyone onto the dance floor, swaying, humming to the easy, relaxed sound. What an ovation Greer and Bigard received. So much enthusiasm from the crowd, they went through it all again, but this time Duke quietly joined them. Hanora was on the dance floor. Frankie was sitting this one out, and Frank had asked Hanora to be his partner.

Duke's back was curved slightly over the keyboard, his bathrobe reaching the floor, hands coming down firmly—sometimes both hands, sometimes only the right while the left rested on his thigh—no music sheet in sight, no glance at the keys. He repeated "Mood Indigo," his wonderful creation, alongside the French musicians and Greer and Bigard, while the dancers moved, almost softly, about the floor. Much later, and often, Hanora would ask herself if she'd really been a part of those timeless moments of magic and music while drifting over an ocean that had not yet begun to threaten from below, in a world that was about to turn to unprecedented destruction.

𝄢

IN the daytime, Hanora read in the library or in the big lounge. She read the conclusion of Agatha Christie's 1920 novel, *The Mysterious Affair at Styles*, serialized in *National Home Monthly*. Poirot was about to gather the usual suspects so that he could announce his deductions and solve the murder of an unfortunate woman. Hanora was watching how Christie maintained suspense from one instalment to the next through her storytelling techniques.

When Hanora wasn't reading, she was on deck, walking, meeting passengers and crew, asking questions. If the weather was reasonable, she walked on the lower sun deck. Otherwise, she used the protected promenade to exercise, to meet people. Inside, she listened for music—which could erupt at any time and did, almost anywhere on the ship. When she returned to her cabin, she sat at the writing desk between the two berths and recorded her observations in detail. She disciplined herself to describe only what she had seen. She considered herself to be in training. She committed herself to her work.

𝄢

"WHAT day is it?" Billie asks suddenly. Billie worries about the days, as if they are retreating from her.

"Thursday."

"Where did the week go?"

Hanora has no idea which week she is referring to.

"Were you out shopping at night? Is that why you stopped in to visit?"

"I don't shop, Billie. Only for food when I have to. I hate shopping. Always have."

"Champlain wore a cloak," she says. "Shiny boots. Taller than the boots you and I bought to counter damp weather. Something like what you'd see in children's books."

"Perrault imagined great boots for Puss in Boots."

"Finery," says Billie. "Yes, like Puss in Boots. One of my students read the story aloud when she was learning English. What was her name? She had been in the camp, the horrific one. Well, they were all horrific. She came to this country as a refugee. She was born in France but sent to Auschwitz-Birkenau—that's the one. She was sent with those brave women of the Resistance. Most of them were captured in occupied France."

There is a long silence while Billie stares out into the dusk.

"I wish I had done more, Hanora. I used to ask myself later—after the world learned, or stopped ignoring, the details of what transpired—I asked myself what I could have done. Not many women survived. The one who learned to read *Puss in Boots* in English did. She was damaged, but while she was in the camp she refused to accept defeat."

She suddenly says, "Plume," pleased that she's found the word, and Hanora realizes she's back to Champlain again.

"A wide feather swooped around the brim of his hat. Was he holding a sword? The sails of his ship were in the background. Natives in the foreground. With fish, a teepee. The edges of the painting were crowded with trees, probably to show an untamed New France. Duke sat in that room during the daytime. Not every day. He had papers in front of him. He was always composing. People left him alone. He was given respect. He liked you, Hanora. The other man, the older one, was a musician, too. Something to do with choirs. He liked me, and we talked in the lounge sometimes, during the day. He joined Duke at his table in the dining room after the second night. Duke played piano once, at the end of one of the parties. He played 'Mood Indigo.' Put on some music, Hanora. Play Duke if you like, but with Ella singing."

Hanora searches for Ella's recording of the *Duke Ellington Songbook* and puts on the first CD. She does remember the other man, now that Billie has talked about him moving to Duke's table. Grey hair, kind face, soft-spoken. He was moving to England to take up a position as music or perhaps choir director somewhere, he had told someone. News and gossip were always buzzing around the ship. Much of the time, the man—she can't recall his name and would have to look at the passenger list—seemed to want to talk to Billie. As dinner companions, he and Duke would have had much in common. The man's face was lined, his voice low. She should have interviewed him, but she was uncertain about asking, could not decide if she should approach him. He seemed to be so self-contained, so private. She did see him walking on deck and they exchanged greetings when they passed each other. She never saw him dance in the evenings, though it was obvious that he was interested in the music being played. She remembers those things.

She and Billie listen to Duke and Ella for a while. As soon as Ella begins to sing "It Don't Mean a Thing," Billie asks Hanora to stop the CD.

"What day is it?" she asks. She looks fearful, expectant, as she waits for an answer.

"It's Thursday."

"Where did the week go?" she says. "I'm hungry and I want something, just a snack. You know, Ella might have been the boss lady, but that was Ivie's song through and through. No one could sing 'It Don't Mean a Thing' like Ivie. I don't know why Ella bothered to record it. She was so good herself, she'd have known Ivie's version was superior."

What Hanora will consider later is that many of Billie's old memories appear to be intact, that language sometimes flows unbroken. What is unknown, unpredictable, is which of the memories are real and which are not. Or how they will be expressed. Some of the patterns are not so different from the way Hanora's own thoughts meander. Billie, however, expresses hers aloud.

What is entirely different is that Billie is sometimes filled with fear as she begins to speak. She gropes for clarity, terrified that reason has abandoned her.

THE O'NEILL AUCTION

HANORA HAS READ EVERY DIARY ENTRY COVering the first two years. She is enjoying the spirit of the young Mariah, not to mention her skill in drawing and painting. In 1902 she'd have been sixteen years old, more serious than ever about her ambition to be an artist.

AUGUST 2, 1902

Aunt Clarice took me along to the Saturday auction at the O'Neill farm. I've accompanied her to three auctions during the past year, and this was the fourth. From our farm we had to travel to Tyendinaga's Ninth Concession. Aunt Clarice is accustomed to getting rhubarb every spring and apples every fall from the farm of Maggie and Am O'Neill, so she knows the way. She is friendly with the owners and we were warmly greeted by Maggie when we arrived in the democrat wagon in the late morning. Maggie has beautiful red hair and a touch of the Irish accent, and maybe I will try to draw her in days to come.

Uncle Oryn had gone ahead in the larger wagon, as he expected to be at the farm the entire day and would be bringing items back. I'm happy to say that the weather was fair. I have sketched a few scenes, all views from the democrat as we rode: an abandoned log cabin with one wall down, leaving its single room exposed; the sagging roof of a barn; a grey rock face with evergreens atop, some stretching higher than others to hog the sun. With wax-based crayons, which I ration, I created this likeness of the blue-black surface of a low-level creek we passed. I'm working at contrast between the water and the green of the bushes and grass beyond. Blues and greens. These are wonderful together.

Aunt Clarice and I so enjoyed our day. She encouraged me to talk about school and say what I have learned from the books I was given last Christmas. At a fall auction, my uncle came upon a box containing several books about the Old Masters, and these were a gift to me from the two of them. A treasured gift.

Today on the Ninth, every item of farm machinery had to be auctioned; the horses, too. The woman, Maggie, cried when the horses were sold, and she leaned her head into the neck of one and stayed by it as if she could not let go. That is the scene I'll be able to draw from memory.

There was a glum feeling about the whole affair, and I began to feel badly for the couple, though Aunt Clarice assured me that Maggie is not sorry to leave the farm. A large crowd turned out for the auction—entire families, in some cases. In part, I believe it was to say goodbye, as the couple is to move south, to town.

Uncle Oryn started the auction with the sale of machinery and barn equipment. Because household items—those that the couple were not keeping—were to be auctioned last, Aunt Clarice and I took the opportunity to bring out our modest picnic lunch and seek a spot sheltered from sun, not far from the farmhouse.

We walked to a nearby copse and spread a blanket on the ground. The two of us were alone in that beautiful spot, and it was there that I was told the saddest of stories. Aunt Clarice was moved by being there, and wanted to share the story she knew.

Maggie and Am's two young children, their only children, had died of the diphtheria four years ago, during the unforgiving winter of '98—a winter every one of us in these parts remembers. One of the children was a baby girl, the other a two-year-old boy. The babes could not be buried until spring, when the ground thawed, and because of this their bodies had to be bundled and kept in a wall of snow outside the farmhouse throughout the remaining cold months. They are now laid near the spot where we had our picnic, beneath the same trees that shaded us as we sat. The graves are unmarked but the location splendid. I was awed to be in that place and have done a sketch on the adjoining page. I suspect that the graves—Aunt Clarice told me the babes are laid side by side—are completely sheltered by the spreading maple; there was a slight depression in the earth beyond the place where we laid our blanket. I hope I've been able to create the feeling of sanctity. It is a challenge to create a mood of terrible beauty.

𝄢

HANORA sets down the diary and tries to take in what she has just read. The grief of the parents would have been unspeakable. She knows the name O'Neill because it is a family name, but she has never heard this heart-rending story of the O'Neill babies, which would have taken place a generation before she was born. Tress was an O'Neill before marrying Kenan. Her grandparents and uncle, who ran the hotel, were O'Neills. She knew there were Irish relatives scattered about the northern farms, but had never been taken to the area as a child. She could be distantly related to this family.

She realizes that of the entire extended family in Deseronto, she is the one who has moved about the most. Especially during and after the war. Overseas travel is something she takes for granted, and has since she first left home in 1939. Perhaps this would be the time for someone to draw up a family tree. She can't do this herself— not in the immediate future, while she's working on the Bindle book—but she'll investigate and find out if anyone has researched the genealogy of the O'Neills. No point in doing the work if the research has been done. It takes time to track down births, marriages and deaths, and to fit patterns together.

The sketch that accompanies the diary entry of that August day in 1902 includes a tree trunk drawn with wide swaths of charcoal, opposed by thinner branches and broad leaves, all of which overshadow a soft, grassy place. Small and uneven rocks are heaped purposefully at the widest edges of the copse. There is a feeling of generosity about this drawing, a feeling of reverent quiet, with sunlight splashing through openings in the branches above. Mariah was skilled enough, even at sixteen, to capture with immediacy the mood of that sad and beautiful place.

Someday, Hanora tells herself, I'll drive through the area, road by road, and find the place myself. It can't be far, probably a few hours by car.

One more thing on her list of things to do. There is no one left to ask about location anymore. Well, remote cousins would be living around there somewhere. Descendants of descendants of pioneer families. She could also return to

Deseronto to see who is still around town. Breeda, for one. Breeda never left. She and Saw raised their family there. They stay in touch once a year, exchanging messages at Christmas. Calhoun is still alive and lives with Breeda and Saw. Calhoun is now 103.

Hanora could also look through county atlases in the Ottawa libraries, to search out the names of previous owners of farms along the Ninth. That information is readily at hand.

When she does, eventually, drive to the area, she'll start with the essential drive to the Madoc area and visit Mariah's birthplace, the farm that belonged to her parents. She will find out who the present owners are and ask if they'll permit her to walk around the property. This will all be material for her book. On the way home, she'll stop in Deseronto to see Breeda and Saw and Calhoun. It's been a long time since she visited her hometown; she hasn't been back since Tress died.

1942

TOBE

—————

N THE SUMMER OF 1942, THE HASTY Ps WERE
still in the south of England. Most recently, they'd
moved inland to the Horam area in Sussex. Tobe wrote:

*You will like the area, as I do. Rolling hills, woods,
fields. Endless pathways and trails. An elderly man
in the town told me that this was the site of an
ancient forest. We help out on nearby farms when
we can. Which doesn't feel much like soldiering,
but the boys like to spend their time this way. So
many in the Regiment grew up on farms. We all feel
that we can contribute if help is needed. We've been
called "plough jockeys" by some of the other units,
but we laugh that off and don't accept the name as
insult. We also help when there is rescue work to*

be done after bombs have been dropped on houses or farm buildings in the area. This is a sad business and has been happening more and more frequently, though the targets are usually farther north, mainly factories and industries. Overall, the bombing here has been nothing like what you have experienced in London. But any death is tragic when it comes from an attack in the sky, and when those on the ground have no opportunity to find protective cover or defend themselves and fight back.

A number of our boys have married local girls around the area. We've been in England so long, some have young children now. Perhaps those with new families will find it difficult to leave when the time comes to fight our share of the war. We know our turn is coming. We can't be in training forever, despite this being our third year in the country. A fact almost impossible to believe. I scarcely believe it as I write. But true. We are in our third year. As a Regiment, we are ready, and no one can pretend otherwise. For a while, we were at the coast, ready to help fight off invasion. But invasion did not come.

When you visit, I'll meet you at the train. I sent details earlier, and will hope that the schedule doesn't alter between now and then. I've found us a place to stay. One of my buddies, Jack, who grew up in Bloomfield in Prince Edward County, has married an English girl. He and his wife, Evelyn, share a home with another couple in the village, and live in the back part of the house. A private entrance opens out from the kitchen to a small garden with a low stone wall. Jack stays with Evelyn as often as he can. While you are here, they'll be away a few days to visit Evelyn's parents in her hometown in Surrey. The place will be empty and we'll have it to ourselves. What luxury, to have you to myself for three entire days. Hurry up. Hurry up and get here. I need you with me.

There was a dance in the evening at the local hall, and Tobe's friends would be there. He wanted to introduce her around. After meeting her at the train, Tobe took her to Jack and Evelyn's house, but momentarily, to drop off the hickory-brown suitcase, the same she'd borrowed from him when she sailed on the *Champlain*. They walked hand in hand, the air warm on her bare arms. She had thrown an open cardigan over her shoulders, thinking she'd need it later. She wore her hair long, partly rolled across her forehead, the ends curling up from her shoulders because of the tight pincurls she'd worn under her turban at work earlier in the day. As they neared the hall, she saw that the place was overcrowded and dancing was under way. Men and women were trying to squeeze through the main entrance. Tobe told her that the band was local, made up of older men, along with a female singer. They knew how to play what everyone wanted to hear: Glenn Miller, Artie Shaw, Benny Goodman. Music from America had arrived. The dancers knew every piece and shouted out the titles.

Tobe led her by the hand to a corner where two small square tables had been pushed together by a group too large to fit around them. His buddies had been expecting them and let out a cheer. "Red! Over here, Red." Everyone knew who she was, and she allowed herself to be called Red—though she'd never put up with the nickname before. The room was heavy with noise, the dance floor crowded, swirling with bodies. The throb of music, foot tapping from the sides, the quick beat, the warmth in the room from body heat. Eyes toward the musicians. Almost every man was in uniform, except the older men from the village. The intimacy between her and Tobe, the intensity. She began to understand, intuitively and with certainty, that nothing would be like this again. Every second she and Tobe spent together was fraught with happiness and foreboding intertwined. When she'd first seen him from the window of the train, when he'd reached for her hand as she stepped off, even then she had known that they would not be able to protect or defend what they shared or who they were together, as one. She pushed back her darkest thoughts. She did not discuss them with Tobe because he would already know. But during the moments they had in the present, the hours, they permitted nothing to come between them. Others greeted her heartily, shook her hand, hugged her, pulled her up and onto the dance floor, but she always knew where he was. She also understood, from that evening forward, that Tobe now had two loves: his love for her, and his love for the Regiment, his commitment to the boys he worked and trained alongside. Different kinds of love, but there all the same. All evening, she fought off sadness, even when she was so entirely happy.

The music was coming at her from all sides. The band struck up "In the Mood." Another cheer. She danced with Tobe. Heard his voice expressing concern about her staying on in London, but that was nothing new. He'd been telling her that for the past two years. During the Blitz, the bombing had been relentless; so far, she had survived. When bombs rained down upon the city, she did not believe she would escape death; rather, she believed that because others stayed, she, too, could stay. She helped when help was needed. She carried on with her work at the canteen during the day. Fixed her long hair into pin-curls. Wore the turban and took the pins out at night and watched her red hair curl up at the edges. Wore a smock overtop her jumper. Many children in the city had been relocated to the countryside, but many stayed because they had nowhere else to go. The children needed to be fed. At the canteen they were sure to receive a nourishing hot meal. Some families who had been bombed out of their houses went to the British Restaurants instead of the canteens. These were set up by the Ministry of Food and were known as Community Feeding Centres—until Churchill changed the name.

Hanora could have worked at any of those locations, but she decided to stay with the canteen because she considered herself part of a team. By now, she was accustomed to following recipes meant to satisfy one hundred ravenous appetites at a time. She stirred five pounds of macaroni into huge pots of boiling water, added mustard, added cheese, tried to make cheese sauce from what was in the kitchen that day or from what was rationed. She'd been shown how to stretch the ingredients with a bit more flour, a bit more water instead of milk. Some days, hunger was sated with repeated helpings of potatoes and gravy. Meat was often available, but never in huge quantities, and never minced. The kitchen crew made stews and pies; occasionally there were roasts. Sausage was a mainstay— sausage and mash—but only a tenth of any sausage was meat; fillers had to be added, often bread or flour or oats. They did have a supply of carrots, parsnips, cauliflower. Every menu depended upon what could be obtained, what could be stored, supplies on hand, seasonal foods from allotments. Eggs, butter, sugar, tea, jams, marmalades, cheeses were all rationed. To make bread, it was her job to rub in the fat, cream the yeast with tiny amounts of rationed sugar, add warm water. She learned to test loaves fresh from the oven by ensuring that they gave off a hollow sound when knocked. She thought she would gag if she had to look at another hundred portions of bread pudding. And then another hundred, and another.

But she knew how to make the children laugh when they arrived for their meal. The children could make her laugh, in return. Many, like her, were high-spirited. They soothed one another's fears. She looked out for the children who had lost their parents to bombs. Orphans who were living with relatives or had been taken in by neighbours.

At night there were other things she could do. She assisted families in the Underground shelters. Bodies curled against one another between track and curve of wall. Cups were held out for water she poured from watering cans. There were children to be settled, to be cheered, to be made less afraid. She carried a notebook in her bag, and a pencil, and she made notes and reminders to herself. Some mornings when she emerged from the Underground, the damage was so extensive, she was astonished that any structure in the city remained standing. A double-decker bus nose-down in a giant hole in the road; houses collapsed at the end of her street, across the park, at the corner. Tumbled stone and brick, fractured beams, fires, glass crunching underfoot, pillows and tangled mattresses pierced by metal and wood. The dead.

Children combed through rubble and came up with a dartboard, a mangled chair. Girls and boys picked up pieces of metal for trade, hoping to find a scrap with German markings, which would ensure value for the purposes of barter at school. When Hanora was in her own room, she wrote. She wrote everything. Described scenes, individuals, families, children she encountered daily. She did not want to self-censor, but was aware of the tight controls over wartime press. She worked at ensuring that her writing was muscular, stronger, concrete. Now that the Americans had declared war, the demand was greater from US publications. The articles she wrote were published as fast as she could file them, even though anything sent by cable was also censored. Her name was becoming known to readers of at least a few magazines. The editors wanted human-interest stories, stories that would help families at home learn of the hardships, the tragedies and the joys experienced by a population much closer to enemy action.

From time to time, readers' letters were forwarded by editors. The letters asked if she could find out about a particular person, asked about the fate of some loved one who hadn't been heard from in a long while.

The bombings in her own area had become less frequent. And Tobe would be leaving soon.

He was speaking about the Regiment, the men desperate to involve themselves outside of England. The Hasty Ps were tired of waiting and preparing, the methods of training changing constantly as war progressed elsewhere. The longer the men remained in England, the more dissatisfied they became. Current rumour was that they would finally be sent somewhere, perhaps North Africa or the Middle East. There was no end to the confusion of tangled information. He declared that he and Hanora should marry before he left. He added that with an emphasis unusual for him. And was silent for a moment, while she considered.

"It makes sense," he went on. "Everything about us makes absolute and perfectly good intelligent, logical and crazy sense. Who could love anyone more than we love each other? No one." While she was in his arms on the dance floor, she had to agree. But quietly, to herself.

They were on their way back to the borrowed house. Trying to make their way through the blackest of nights. Tobe had a small electric torch and switched it on for a second, shining the tiniest cone of light ahead of Hanora's feet. She tripped, and tripped again, which started them both laughing. She felt as if she'd been drinking wine, but she had not. She'd had nothing but some sort of sticky-sweet punch at the hall.

The leather strap on one of her sandals had partly torn while she was dancing, and now, on the way to the house, it separated completely and flapped at her ankle. She removed the sandal and carried it, tightening her grip on Tobe's arm to steady herself. She was glad she had packed a second pair of shoes into the hickory-brown suitcase. Sensible shoes to wear home on the train. The road was uneven, and Tobe offered to carry her. Which made them laugh uproariously again. She wondered if he had had something to drink. Several men she'd met that evening had flasks tucked into pockets. Many of them had disappeared outside for a while and returned.

"Not far now," he said, but his usually sure voice sounded doubtful, as if they might wander the village the remainder of the night. He did, finally, recognize the house by the overhang of its oddly shaped roof, and they went round the back and entered from the garden path, both stumbling now, into unlit rooms. The people who lived at the front of the house must have been in bed; everything was quiet, still.

Tobe went from window to window and pulled the curtains tight, having forgotten to do this before they left. The electricity had been working when Hanora first arrived, but was out now. This must have happened frequently, because Jack and Evelyn had left candles beside a deep stone sink. Tobe lit two, and set them into wax dripped onto saucers.

He had brought wine to the house, and now began a search for glasses. On the kitchen counter were a few bowls and a milk jug with a square of muslin stretched overtop, tiny beads hanging down to weight the muslin.

She heard him curse, reach for something on a kitchen shelf. She watched as he picked up a small glass elephant. Candle in one hand, elephant in the other. The ornament was green and had an opening at the top; perhaps it was a miniature planter, though there was nothing growing inside. Tobe opened the top drawer beneath the counter, shoved the elephant out of sight, shut the drawer.

"Why did you do that?"

"An elephant with trunk down is bad luck. Trunk up is fine, but I don't see any of those around."

"Your mother's, on the sill," she said. "Those trunks were up. But I don't remember you being superstitious. You're like my aunt Grania."

"Maybe I've become that way since becoming a soldier. Anyway, I heard enough superstition from the Irish in town when I was growing up. And so did you." He turned his back to the closed drawer, found two pewter goblets, poured the wine with care, deep purple pooling beneath the rims.

Their portion of the house had no bath, but there was a shallow sink in an alcove beyond the bedroom, with a curtain pulled round a semicircular track to afford privacy. Jack and Evelyn must have negotiated an arrangement to use the bath in the other section of the house, perhaps at weekends.

The bedroom was immediately off the kitchen. The fireplace in the bedroom was unlit, coal scuttle at the ready. But the fireplace wasn't needed this August night.

Tobe had taken a candle and moved on to the sitting room to check out the gramophone. He put his finger under the thorn needle, which he declared to be unfit. He quickly removed the thorn and took a few moments to sharpen it against a sandpaper strip kept handy. Hanora watched his long, thin fingers, the way his skin glowed in the small circle of light offered up by the candle. His profile was distinct inside the circle, his body in darkness. He moved and an enormous shadow flickered, like a threat, across the ceiling and the blackout curtains. A momentary shadow, momentary threat. He moved the candle again and peered into the arm of the gramophone to ensure that the thorn was secure. "We have choice," he said. "There are half a dozen recordings here. How about Shaw's 'Dancing in the Dark'? That would be appropriate. Or Duke and 'Jitterbug's Lullaby'—how about that? I don't think I know it."

"Let's start with Duke. That was recorded the year before I met him on the ship."

He wound the gramophone and placed the thorn at the outer edge of the record. She took the second candle through to the bedroom and went to the alcove to change into her robe. From the bedroom, the kitchen was an open doorway leading to blackness. The outside door was locked. The music was playing softly when she returned, barefoot. He restarted the recording from the beginning. Volume low, the room dark except for the flickering of two flames. She blew out her own candle, leaving one.

"Johnny Hodges, listen," she said. "He's brilliant." The sax had put out its solo call and was circling the room. Drum soft in the background, mood slow and lazy, sax echoing from the dark corners of the room. A shiver of vibration followed, muted trumpet, trombone, Duke subtle on keyboard, drums always present, never intrusive but pushing forward with a low, slow, steady beat. Tobe held her and they danced, Hanora naked under her robe, arms around his neck, listening as each musician faded to the next, and then Hodges circled back for the final solo. Music from afar. From another world now.

She stopped. A long, full moment of stillness, pressed against Tobe. He stayed with the pause, did not attempt to move until she spoke.

"Aunt Zel," she said. "Advice she sent in a letter. About storing. About pausing to store important moments."

He returned to the gramophone and set the thorn again.

"I need you with me," he said. "I meant that when I wrote to you, Hanora. And I mean it now."

"I am with you. I'm here. I'm always with you. You know that. But I need time, just a little—to find out more. Someone knows something, I'm sure of that. I just haven't figured out who the person is. And I cannot—absolutely cannot—go back to my parents to ask. If I haven't found out who I am by the end of the war, I'll marry you then. Anyway, we're together more now than if I were at home waiting for you to return. And I'm not going back without you." She realized, as she spoke, that she meant those words; she had no intention of going back without him. "Who else do you think I'd marry? There's no one in my life but you. What difference does it make if we're married or not married?"

"We'll talk this through again," he said. "We'll talk about what you've found so far—which isn't much, I grant you. But sometimes the answer you seek is right under your nose. And if a new clue turns up, you'll be off on another search. I'll help you. But you will marry me. As soon as we can arrange it."

"When the war is over, of course we'll marry. I'll be here. I'm just thankful that you understand. I only want to know who I am. Only." She wasn't able to make light of this. "And I'm not feeling sorry for myself. It's because . . . it's because I feel as if part of me is missing. If you suddenly found yourself in this situation, you'd want to know, too."

He had stilled again.

"I keep sending out letters. Now I'm trying to get more information about the locket. A jeweller in London told me he's almost certain it's from 1850s Vienna." She felt for it around her neck. It had aged gently, beautifully. For almost a century it had been worn and loved and cared for, and now it was hers to own and wear. It pleased her to think that Vienna was in her background. But how? She thought of writing to Aunt Zel about the locket. Aunt Zel had tentacles out in the community and had always been honest with her. And Aunt Zel travelled to Toronto from time to time. But how could anyone track a locket that had travelled from Vienna to Toronto in an unknown period? Given the influx of immigrants to the country during the nineteenth century, it could have belonged to anyone. A treasured family heirloom.

Inside the locket, Tobe's picture faced her own. The photo of the two of them had been taken by Kenan in the backyard, the day she left home. One day before she sailed on the *Champlain*. Tress had watched from the step; Tobe's parents walked over from their yard to say goodbye. This was months before Tobe joined up. Before war. Kenan mailed the photo as soon as Hanora was able to send the address of her bedsit in London. When she came in from work at the canteen one afternoon, she found the envelope in her mail slot inside the front entrance. She had cut around the faces and inserted them into the locket. The expressions on the faces told a story of believing anything was possible. Anything and everything. Tobe had smiled when she'd opened the locket to show him.

She wondered what Kenan would have written as a caption. Or if he had made a copy for his own album. The photo he sent to London was unmarked, and she assumed that this was deliberate, leaving space for her to write her own note on the back. But she had not. She'd cut the images into oval shapes to fit the sides of the locket.

Tobe led her to the bedroom, set his candle on the bedside table, went back for the wine. He rewound the gramophone, reset the thorn on the same recording. Pulled off his clothes and crawled in beside Hanora and they clinked glasses and drank. They lowered themselves down under the covers of the narrow bed. Tobe's feet were partly over the end of the mattress. They laughed and curled round each other. His body heat.

"I can tell you who you are," he said. "I know in the finest detail who you are."

She ignored this, smoothed her hand down his side.

"Is the music too mournful?"

"Not mournful," she said. "Duke called this a lullaby. Languorous, maybe. Perfect for dancing in a dark room in a stranger's house in a village that may or may not be bombed. Perfect for lying in bed by the light of a single candle with a man named Tobias."

"And a woman named Red. Who has freckles sprinkled across her nose as if someone shook them over her, like cayenne pepper."

"Careful."

He blew out the candle. Slipped his arm under her shoulder, pulled her closer. The trumpet shivered. The music soft. Insistent.

Hodges' solo was circling back one more time. They'd finished their wine. Tobe shifted until they were face to face. "Perfect fit," he said, and he shifted again, as she did. "And will you store this moment, too?"

"I will," she said. "And so will you. We'll make it last."

The record continued to its end. And then there was a single jarring noise, and a crackling. The needle stuck in the final groove, the whirr and whirr unheard, while the gramophone finally wound down to silence.

MARIAH'S 1903 DIARY

————————

MAY 14, 1903

Thursday. One and a half months left until I am free for the summer. Free of my tormentor. And then?

Since Mrs. Banco moved away, I have felt desperation at the lack of good teaching. Mr. Comfort, and he is far from comforting, looks upon me as some sort of rebel, someone who refuses to align to his standards and never will.

"So, Bindle"—he never calls me by my first name—"it is the art world to which you aspire. And for my own edification and for the edification of the class, will you name any five great women painters in the world? For that matter, even two?"

My classmates put down their pens to listen. Not even the dabbing at edges of inkwells can be heard. My friends are sympathetic and give support later, when we are out of sight of Comfort. No one wants to cross him because he is capable of making lives miserable. He is the person of power in the room.

I do not reply.

I never let him see how I truly feel.

He addresses the class.

"Have you learned the Dobson poem assigned?"

"Yes, Mr. Comfort."

"Stand, then—you, too, Bindle—and recite together."

Fame is a food that dead men eat,—
I have no stomach for such meat.
In little light and narrow room,
They eat it in the silent tomb,
With no kind voice of comrade near
To bid the feaster be of cheer.

Today, he had us sit in our seats just as we were about to launch into the second verse. He wasn't interested in the friendship half of the poem. His aim was to ensure that I would feast sourly on my own ambition.

But Comfort will not hold me back. Though I say nothing to his face in class, and complete my assignments so that I may sit the end-of-year exams, I resolve that he will not stand in my way. Not that I wish for fame. Far from it. I wish only to pursue what I believe I can do, become what

I am capable of becoming. That is to paint and draw the world as I see it. And I plan to see the world. As much as I am able. The important people to convince are not teachers like Comfort, but my parents. Who have already begun to wonder how I will accomplish what I am setting out to do. They are in no position to help financially, and I will have to make my own way.

Here is my sketch of Comfort. I admit that I exaggerate the mean-spirited expression on his wretched face. He takes cool pleasure in baiting me. But I remind myself: the more he goads, the stronger I become.

As for his body, his stomach is so large it protrudes in front of him. As if a pendulous overripe plum has swelled out of proportion and leaped under his shirt and stayed there, creating a mass that hangs precipitously over the belt that holds up his trousers. It is this mass that leads the way when he stomps around the classroom in his self-important manner.

1998

INVITATION

===

HANORA IS SORTING IN EARNEST NOW. ITEMS are set on the living-room rug in rows so she can get down on her knees between them. She separates drawings that are dated from those that are not. The latter are put into an archival-safe folder for protection. She'll place them in context later. This might not be complicated because Mariah, accustomed to keeping a diary, often provided a written commentary around the edges of drawings, or on the surfaces themselves.

One journal is entirely unlike the others, though there are different styles of notebooks and sketchpads within the body of work. Some have ragged edges and show wear; others are in reasonable condition. Presumably, Mariah had to rely on what she could find in the shops of the country she lived in at any particular time.

The one journal that stands apart from the others is also the thickest. Filled with cream-coloured paper, it contains her entries and drawings from the years in Coventry. Odd, Hanora thinks, because there was a severe shortage of paper during the war, and I had difficulties getting my hands on any for the writing I was doing in London.

Hanora's first book was written during the Blitz, about the Blitz, the brutal bombardment that went on for fifty-seven consecutive nights. The day-to-day story of citizens who remained in the streets of London, inside houses, in the Underground at night or in shelters they'd built themselves, or who crawled under stairs or beneath tables or other large pieces of furniture—not that those kept bombing victims alive when their once-protective houses tumbled down around them. She focused on individuals, stories about how women and men and children managed and how they helped one another, and what kept them going and enabled them to endure the horror of death and destruction on their streets throughout the nightly and even daily bombings. She wrote about spirit and courage and determination. She wrote about the myriad ways Londoners dealt with fear and anguish and how they kept on with their lives. These were first-hand accounts. The book was published in North America one year after Pearl Harbor was bombed. Mortality figures were not included in her book, no information that could feed the Nazis. The

figures were not given out, in any case. The book caught
the interest of the public, and went into several reprints,
which was enormously satisfying. The knowledge of the
book being "out there" kept Hanora going during a long
stretch between that and her second book.

꠰꠰

MARIAH must have purchased her thick Coventry journal
before the war and saved it for the last. For it does appear
to be the last of the artist's diaries. There are earlier periods
of her life not accounted for in the papers laid out over
Hanora's rug. Some years spent in Europe have no docu-
mentation, which means that diaries were lost or discarded.
A single diary from southern France does exist. And two
thin sketchpads from Cornwall, mainly St. Ives. Hanora
hopes that loose paintings and drawings will make up for
any missing diary years.

She now has a good idea of what remains to be read and
how long this will take. She does not want to be so methodical that she kills her own creativity, but she has begun
to look inward, beyond the rows of paper laid out over
the rug. She begins to imagine the contents in another sort
of order, one that will become the structure of her book.
She does not want to impose structure early, because she
knows from experience that the book's pattern will emerge

in its own time. Still, she needs a place to start; she wants to write the first chapters, even as she continues to read the material at hand.

✿

FILMORE is retrieving his mail when Hanora takes the elevator down to the main floor. He tips the imaginary hat, after which they stand and talk while she clears the mail from her box. She checks through the envelopes. Several bills: electric, water and sewage, heating—all forwarded from Billie's house. So far, the upstairs of the red-and-white house is empty. Another week or two, and the main floor and basement will be cleared of the last furniture, much of which will go to resettlement programs for incoming refugees from Bosnia-Herzegovina and Sri Lanka. New residents to the city are in need of furniture, having left everything behind. What remains in Billie's house will partially furnish two small apartments.

In a week or two, Hanora will hire a team of cleaners, including window cleaners. After that, the house will be listed and hopefully sold. The phone has been disconnected, the furnace turned off, the water temperature turned down. June will soon be here, and with it, summer.

Filmore is full of surprises. On the way up in the elevator, he stands tall and holds out a monthly photography magazine for cursory inspection of its cover. He confides that he's been interested in photography since childhood, and writes a monthly column for the magazine he holds in his hands.

Hanora hears herself inviting him to look at Kenan's photos.

"My late father—adoptive father, the only father I knew—put together a few albums, which I now own. His first camera cost a dollar. A 1937 Brownie I gave to him for Christmas. A cousin who lives in the States worked for Eastman Kodak and sent it directly."

"I have a 1937 Brownie in my collection," says Filmore. "I would be pleased to see your father's albums. Delighted." Ah, the old-school manners.

"I have no idea what to expect," she says. "I leafed through one of them years ago while visiting my parents. My father was private about his discoveries. Or what I think of as his discoveries. Every photo was taken in Deseronto—do you know the place?"

"I've seen the sign from the main highway, but never pulled into the town," he says.

"My father was a veteran of the Great War, and had his own way of doing things. He never left town after coming home wounded in 1918. That I'm certain of. I found out, late in my childhood—I was in my teens—that he didn't leave the house for more than a year after coming home."

Filmore nods as if he understands. His facial expression shows that he does, in some way, understand.

He tears a small strip from an envelope and writes his last name, which she already knows. He adds his phone number and email address. She'll send an email and tell him when to come to her apartment.

As he leaves the elevator on the nineteenth floor, Hanora realizes that she doesn't know his first name. It must begin with *R* because that's part of the email address.

This is what happens with apartment living. She recognizes faces but doesn't know full names or personal details—except when it comes to residents who live on her own floor. She meets the same people in the elevators, exchanges greetings, listens to reports on the weather. The place is a bit of a vertical village. She can tell who is eternally cheerful, who is mournful but kind, who wards off conversation, who fills every gap with babble, who stares at the floor when others talk, who is hard of hearing, who has an antenna up for gossip, who struggles with health or mobility issues, who gets by no matter how dire the situation, who strides through daily activities with vigour, and who wags a warning finger, threatening anyone within hearing distance that problems will be reported to management. She knows which families have children and where the children go to school. She could make a greater effort to socialize, but she always seems to be working, or solving Billie's problems.

Filament is making an effort to socialize. And now, she supposes, she is, too. And realizes that she spoke of Kenan as her adoptive father. She has been silent so long, she is astonished that this fact has come out in casual conversation. *Tell a stranger what is most important to you.*

When she is back inside her apartment she turns toward her hall mirror. What she sees is the woman she has always been, for years now with short hair, still a bit of red, but deeper red, especially at the back. The rest is grey. She is paler now. She is lean and she is fit. She loves to walk. She has aged but doesn't give age a great deal of thought. Instead, she thinks of the work she is doing, the work she has done. This is how she defines herself. She has no idea what other people see when they look at her; she hardly cares what others see when they look at her.

She hasn't cooked for a week and would be grateful if someone were to cook for her. She's been making sandwiches lately, or opening tins of soup. She is desperate to get back to the rhythm of writing every day. Once Billie's house sells, she'll be able to breathe freely. Her time will be her own.

If she is to write the book, she must gather peace around her. Otherwise, she will never fully concentrate. But she is determined. And she is, gradually, earning back her peace. As if peace is a reward for some kind of penance, she thinks, wryly. These days, if she works for an hour and a half without interruption or emergency phone calls, she is filled with optimism. Some days, if she writes well for ten minutes, she is happy. A full day's work and she might tumble over in a state of ecstasy.

𝄢

SHE sends Filmore an email and asks if he would like to stop by in the evening, around seven. She'll work as much as she can today, see what she can find out about Mariah after the artist returned to Canada in 1946. How did it come to pass that she lived out her final days in the Eastern Hospital for the Insane? Hanora has to look for answers.

Later, she will go through the drawings, one by one. She may also put a note in several newspapers to see if she can track down any privately owned paintings. She'll soon be told what her publisher's budget will permit in terms of reproductions—colour and/or black and white. In her book, she will describe some of the sketches she has in her possession. Not that she owns those. She owns only the one she was given by the family, the one on her office wall: the child holding the shell, the mother looking on with love.

She has an urge to reach for her locket, rub it between her fingers. But the locket is in a drawer of her jewellery case. Someday, the province will open its adoption records; she knows this, and so does every other adopted person seeking or not seeking information. So does every birth parent who gave up a child. She thinks of the unknown adopted men and women out there as her brothers and sisters. They would know the feeling she has of having worked at her adoption her entire life. Every one of them, or almost every one, will have gone through a prolonged reluctance to upset the applecart by speaking frankly to the parents who adopted them. Every one horrified by the thought of hurting the people who gave them a home, and who loved them and brought them up as if they were their own offspring. But why, if everything was so loving and good, did the questions of identity have to be set aside?

Because the subject is so emotionally charged, it might as well be an exposed wire.

Because some issues will never, ever be resolved.

While writing her book about the trade in orphans, she interviewed twelve adults who were adopted. And listened, again and again, to identical stories, identical words. *I don't want to hurt my mother. I don't want to upset my father. I don't want my parents to think I'd have preferred a different kind of life. I had a great upbringing. I feel I should wait until they die before I investigate. I've been lucky. Yes, I've been lucky. I'm so fortunate.*

And what of the adoptees who did not feel so fortunate? What if adoptive parents were not loving? That, too, happened. *I was always on the outside. I never really felt that I belonged. I knew I was different. I felt different, looked different, wasn't at all like my brothers and sisters. I suspected I was adopted even before I was told. When I was older, I saw photos of myself as a baby and thought, Oh, that tiny, lost child.*

Well, she'd behaved as most had behaved. She did not go back to Tress and Kenan to insist on having more information. In 1938, they had made it patently clear that the discussion was closed. She'd respected their wishes, and maintained her silence. It seemed pointless to do otherwise. After decades of travelling down blind alleys, she'd long ago accepted the fact that she does not and probably will not own her history. Maybe that's why she has been so interested in everyone else's. She's never had a history of her own.

Which can also be seen as nonsense, goes the old argument with herself. She has a very complete history, comprising work she has done, decisions made, people met, travels undertaken, stories written, books published, friendships near and dear—including one with a close friend, another writer, who was also adopted. And the world is full of orphans, displaced children, street children, missing children. All they want is a home. Any home.

Understanding all this, having made a commitment to be silent, why, then, does she continue to glance into mirrors in shop windows, in stores, in public washrooms, in airplanes, on trains, anywhere, on the chance that a detail she hasn't noticed will be newly revealed?

Why, after all this time, does she stare into her bathroom mirror every night before bed?

Habit. Something she has done since she was eighteen. No one will ever know the ways she has scrutinized her features, tried out different expressions. Looking for . . . well, what she was looking for was never found. And what difference will it make now if adoption records *are* finally unsealed? Her birth parents won't be around. Not a single person involved will be alive.

Still.

FILMORE

FILMORE ARRIVES PUNCTUALLY, HOLDS OUT HIS hand and shakes hers as if they are meeting for the first time. "Robin," he says. "Robin Filmore. British parents, first-born, the name was favoured at the time. There was Robin Hood in the background, and that helped." He laughs. A confident laugh. He's lived with his name a long time.

She has not been expecting a Robin. And in he comes.

Once they have drinks in hand—he, too, drinks neat Scotch—he asks to see Kenan's albums. These are on the living-room table, where she placed them weeks ago. Each one thick and full.

"My father learned darkroom skills after he was given his first camera," Hanora says. "He used the cold cellar in our house in Deseronto. It had shelves, and he installed a sink. He was completely comfortable there. He was never afraid of the dark. When he began to develop film, everything was black and white. Especially the first few years. That remained his preference, even after colour film was commonly available. Everything about photography amazed him. He was entranced."

She is thinking of the photo she carried in her wallet for decades. *Invisible 1938*. She framed it after she moved to her present apartment. She had to look several places before she found an appropriate frame: two layers of glass that allow the caption and notes on the back to be seen without removing the tiny photo. She has come to think of this in some complex way as her birthday-adoption photo, and she keeps it near. As familiar as it is, she still has to examine the face of it before she can locate the image of the plane. She goes to her office now, retrieves it and brings it to Robin. He turns it over and reads aloud, "'Moving aeroplane, September 23, 1938, H's birthday. September 23, 1835, HMS *Beagle* sails to Charles Island, Galapagos, Darwin aboard.'"

"That was my father's way of making sense of the world. Every photo has a caption."

"Your birthday is in September?"

"The twenty-third. That particular birthday was a rather remarkable day—one I've had to consider ever since."

"Ah," he says. But he does not pry.

They have to sit at the dining-room table because the

rug in the living room is covered with Mariah's documents and there's scarcely enough space to walk across the room. Hanora makes no excuses but tells him this is how she works. Eventually, in an orderly way, the papers will be moved to her office. After she begins to write the book.

She gathers up Kenan's three albums, brings them to the dining room and watches while Robin opens the first. Turns pages. Examines closely. The earliest photos are, according to him, "Wonderful images."

"What was your father's name?"

"Kenan Oak."

Robin repeats this and nods as if the name suits the man responsible for the photographs he is scrutinizing.

"He used to write notes on the back," says Hanora, "but once he began to mount the photos in albums, he printed directly on the pages, above or below, as you can see."

This is what they see on the early pages.

An electric Redi-Heat iron, photographed from three angles, its black handle shining. *Tress's first electric iron, manufactured in Deseronto. (France 1609, Champlain recruits artisans and settlers.)*

A compact radio, also made in Deseronto, an early one owned by Kenan and Tress, but photographed from the back. *Arvin radio, 1938. (France 1624, Champlain gives an account to the king.)*

A long, sleek auto from the late thirties, the auto polished to gleam, an unidentified woman perched glumly on its running board. Perhaps a visitor staying at her grandparents' hotel? *Deseronto, June 10, 1939, Main Street. (Philip Turnor, June 10, 1790, held up on journey northward to Lake Athabasca. "My loitering my time at this place can give no satisfaction to any party.")*

Tress and Grania with Mamo Agnes. They are looking out over the bay in three different directions, as though their aims and thoughts have been scattered by a cold wind. *Deseronto 1939. (Dec. 1492, Columbus: "The wind blew hard ... and caused the anchors to drag half the length of their lines.")*

Windows of the brick pumphouse next to the waterfront, large rocks heaped below sills. *Pumphouse, July 1939. (Quebec, July 1608, Champlain begins construction of storehouse and first habitation.)*

A group of men with shovels and picks, clearing debris from the ruins of a burned house on Main Street. *Deseronto, devastating fire. (Aug. 1492, Columbus: "I passed this night near Tenerife, where the great volcano on that island erupted in a fiery display.")*

The widow of postmaster Jack Conlin grinning to the camera while rubbing clothes down a scrub board outside her back shed, immersed to her elbows in soapy water. *Deseronto resident, Oct. 21, 1942. (Bahamas, Oct. 21, 1492, Columbus searched for fresh water, people fled the village, leaving household goods.)*

A weather-beaten boat, pulled up on land, resting on low stumps. The boat has holes in its side and is partly filled with snow. Long grasses are flattened underneath, their tips jutting through an icy crust. *Deseronto, winter 1943, by the bay. (1914, U-boat sinks three British cruisers.)*

That's the first of Kenan's notes she's seen with a First World War reference—one unrelated to discovery. She wonders if there are other captions of this nature. From a period of violence he would have known intimately.

It is not possible to read these notes without wondering how Kenan's mind worked, how he made associations, how he was fascinated by discovery, how he juxtaposed old and new worlds. How he dug in, after the war, in a small town, and lived partly through the adventures of others. But he never stopped learning, never stopped trying to piece together information.

They come to photos devoted only, it seems, to September 23 in various years.

"Your father loved you," says Robin. "He never let a birthday go by without a photo and a caption."

Here she is at different ages and stages. Childhood photos had to be captioned after the fact; most would have been taken by her aunt Grania, the only one in the family who had a camera during the Depression. Perhaps after Kenan was given his camera and started an album, he asked Grania for copies of earlier photos.

She remembers a few of the adult photos that were taken during visits to her parents. If Kenan hasn't recorded the exact year, she can guess by the outfits she is wearing. After she moved away, she wouldn't have been near the town on her birthdays.

Some of the other captions he wrote:

Sep. 23, 1768, James Cook sails near Grand Canaries during 1st world voyage.
Sep. 23, 1846, existence of Neptune confirmed.
Sep. 23, 1938, Neville Chamberlain meets Hitler, second round of discussions/Hurricane ravages New England coast.

This last photo was taken near a window, afternoon sun pouring in, following the eighteenth-birthday supper the day she was "told." Slices of cake can be seen on a table in the background. Tobe and Saw and Breeda would have picked her up in the McLaughlin Buick minutes later.

Her adoption birthday. So there were two photos: the

plane overhead while she was out rowing on the bay, and this birthday cake photo. Memorable day for Kenan, as well.

"Would you permit me to go through the albums at my leisure?" says Robin. "I'd be interested in writing a piece for the magazine about the photos *and* the captions. The captions by themselves are unique. But the photos are crisp, wonderfully developed. These are unusual images. Some are studied, some entirely spontaneous. Or so they appear."

Hanora smiles to herself. And grants permission. He tells her he would like to start with the first album. Take his time. Follow up with the other two albums later.

She pours them both another drink and they talk for a while about Robin's contributions to the magazine. She is curious to hear what he has to say. He tells her that photography is a hobby he developed over many decades. His late wife, Enza, had been interested, too, and had her own camera. His children—four children—well, they send photos of the grandchildren. The family is scattered across the country. Robin's arms stretch out to the sides as he says this. "They're busy," he adds. "Working, raising children, the steady lineup of unending tasks Enza and I faced at one time."

He speaks modestly and gives the impression of having a love of life and a sense of humour. He asks about her research and she mentions Mariah Bindle and the connection between them, which is partly geographical. She tells him why she was drawn to Mariah when she first came upon her art.

"Mariah," she says, "would have known some of my parents' Ontario relatives, distant relatives. Family members who farmed, mainly Irish settlers. I plan to drive to the area north of Highway 401 and up to the Madoc area, after the weather improves. The original Bindle homestead is up that way. I'll be looking around, taking notes and certainly photos. As it turns out, Mariah lived in wartime England, as I did, though we were in different cities. Our paths never crossed. I suppose our lives were parallel in some respects: two women trying to make our way in different fields. But she was born thirty-five years before I was. I'm hopeful that some of my experiences will help to shape the book I'm writing about her."

"I'd be happy to come along for the drive," he says. "I could bring one of my cameras, or I could bring camera *and* car, which would leave you free to look about—give directions and take notes."

Not something she had considered, but she thanks him and tells him she'll let him know.

When he stands to leave, he thanks her warmly. He takes the first of Kenan's albums with him, but at the door something drops out of the back: loose papers, two items. Hanora stoops to pick them up.

One is a newspaper clipping describing the Westinghouse Time Capsule, deposited September 23, 1938, at the site of the 1939 New York World's Fair. The other she instantly recognizes as the backyard photograph of her and Tobe, taken by Kenan the day she departed for her first trip to Europe. She slips the photo into her pocket.

The capsule, according to the clipping, is meant to represent twentieth-century civilization at a moment in time, the items buried within its torpedo shape for the next five thousand years. The capsule is not to be opened until the year 6939.

"I remember reading about this," Hanora says. "There are numerous items inside: a kewpie doll, a copy of *Life* magazine. I think there's a light bulb, too. I'd have to look up the list of contents again. Lots about language and explanations of what the human body can do. I can see why this would have fascinated Kenan. He'd have enjoyed imagining future explorers, five thousand years to the day, hauling the capsule out of the earth and breaking into it to see what discoveries are inside. The meeting of past and future."

"Your birthdate, again," says Robin. "The day the capsule was deposited. Did you know that a second capsule was placed at the same site during the sixties? At least I think it was the same site."

"If I once knew, I've forgotten," says Hanora.

"I'm not sure what was in the second capsule. Many items from the thirties would have been out of date by the time the sixties rolled around. Now I'm curious and will check it out when I'm home again."

Robin shakes her hand as he departs. Tells her he has read and enjoyed several of her books. The one about the Blitz was familiar territory. Well, familiar in ways that war can be. "I was with the British Eighth Army," he said. "In North Africa. After that, we fought our way north through the boot of Italy. A lifetime ago," he adds. "But as they say, 'memories ever-present.' And I met Enza there, in a very small village. I went back for her after the war."

The door closes behind him and Hanora locks it and leans into the wall. Italy. A lifetime ago, yes. But her heart is pounding. She closes her eyes, waits until the pounding stops.

She turns and catches a glimpse of herself in the hall mirror. Be calm, she says to the image in the mirror. Be calm. The feelings are always there, just under the surface. You know that. You've always known that.

She pulls the photo from her pocket. Taken by Kenan, identical to her own copy, the one he mailed to England. She cut the faces of hers into ovals to fit the locket and has never removed them.

It is the caption she wants to see. What was in Kenan's mind that day? What was he thinking the moment of taking the photograph?

Nothing about discovery or exploration, but in retrospect, a prediction of war. The impossibility of preventing young people he loved—her and Tobe—from running headlong into it. The caption is from Dickens.

Kenan owned the entire set of Dickens' work, fifteen volumes, shelved in the enclosed veranda of their house in Deseronto, where he did most of his reading. When he looked up from the page, he wanted to look out over the bay from his wicker chair. He was safe there.

Hanora now owns and treasures those fifteen volumes. Illustrated, with gilt titles, they were a Christmas gift from Tress the year before Hanora was adopted. Tress inscribed only the first volume, "December 1919."

The caption Kenan chose for the photo was a warning, a prediction from *A Tale of Two Cities*. Although the book title is not included, Hanora recognizes the words: "It was the spring of hope, it was the winter of despair, we had everything before us, we had nothing before us . . ." The date is written in minuscule figures: *Mar. 22, 1939.*

Kenan knew that war was inevitable, even though he refused to discuss the possibility. He didn't try to stop her from leaving, but he must have worried constantly. She looks at her own face and Tobe's—how young, how determined, how open to experience they were. She remembers that Tobe's parents were standing in the yard near Kenan when the photo was taken. They had come to say goodbye before Tobe accompanied her to Montreal, where she was to catch the overnight train to New York. It was Tobe's mother who gave her the issue of *National Home Monthly* to read during her trip. The *Monthly* had been running the Agatha Christie mystery, and Mrs. Staunford and Hanora were following the instalments.

Enough for one day. Enough for one evening. She has to alter the course of the monologue that is running through her brain. She looks into the mirror again and tells herself to stop. Stop.

At least she isn't wearing her clothes inside out.

1942–43

PREPARATIONS

———

TOBE TOOK HER TO THE VILLAGE STATION IN THE afternoon, and handed his suitcase in after her when she'd boarded the train. "Nice piece of luggage you've got there, miss," he said, and she couldn't help laughing.

She stumbled as she sat down, and experienced a physical sensation that she could only describe to herself as the unknown rising up to meet her. How could anyone foresee what lay ahead? She put her hand to her throat. She thought she would not be able to breathe.

Everyone in the country knew that the fighting, the bombing, the killing and destruction would go on and on. Man against man. Weapon against weapon. Arms against arms. Nation against nation. Neither she nor Tobe had any idea where he would be sent, or when the Regiment would be shipped out of England. She stared in the direction of the village long after the train had pulled away and the station was out of sight.

𝄢

THE morning had been unsettling. Jack and Evelyn returned two hours before Hanora was to leave for the train, and the mood between her and Tobe was immediately broken. Not intentionally. Jack went out of his way to be friendly, to make her welcome. It was clear that he and Tobe were close. She listened to their banter and watched Jack draw deeply on his cigarette. One cigarette after another. He was thick through the chest and shoulders, five foot seven or eight, dark hair, a vertical scar at the edge of his left eye and extending down over his cheekbone. He rubbed at it every once in a while, probably from habit. Or maybe the scar had resulted from a recent accident and he wasn't accustomed to feeling it there.

Evelyn was as fair and slim as Jack was dark and stocky. She chattered while she prepared lunch. She was cheery, couldn't stay still. Hanora imagined her going around a crowded room from person to person, keeping spirits up. It was certain that she kept Jack's spirits up; they had met at a dance the year before, and he clearly adored her.

Tobe became quiet, content to listen while they sat around the kitchen table. There was more talk. Evelyn and Jack announced that their first child would be born the following February. They all celebrated the news. A record was put on and Glenn Miller and His Orchestra played "My Blue Heaven" in the background while Evelyn laughed and chatted on. There was little time to be alone with Tobe after that, except for the walk to the station. On the way, Hanora remembered the elephant in the drawer.

"They'll think it's gone missing," she said. "They'll think I put it in my suitcase."

"*My* suitcase," said Tobe. "I'll take responsibility." He laughed, and shrugged. "They'll find it. If they don't, I'll mention it to Jack." He wasn't concerned; he just didn't want to look at it when he was there.

𝄢

They'd planned to spend Christmas of 1942 together, but Tobe had to cancel. There was nothing to be done but wait for him to contact her again. She had no idea where he was.

Tress and Kenan sent cards and letters (her father reminding her to keep her guard up because *Life Is Treacherous*; he did not mention the word "war"). Aunt Zel wrote, Breeda and Saw wrote, as did Tobe's parents. Hanora received care packages in early November—sent well ahead of Christmas to ensure arrival: apples wrapped individually in newsprint; a Christmas cake; Belleville cheese; heavy stockings knitted by Tress to keep Hanora's feet warm at night; two copies of the *Post* from Calhoun, along with a note: *There's a job waiting when you come home.*

She sent articles to Calhoun from time to time. Always a profile of an individual. She wrote about what that person was doing in London and how he or she was managing within wartime restraints and conditions. She found Canadians to interview, and there were many in London. She met one woman her own age, Caroline, at a shop in Westbourne Grove, and after that they got together occasionally to share a pot of tea. Caroline had come from Montreal and was married to a British soldier. She had been working with the Red Cross in London since the beginning of the war. An Anderson shelter had been built in the garden behind her flat, and Hanora was invited to stay during a raid if she was in the area when warnings were sounded. "It's cold, and it's damp, and can get wet and muddy," said Caroline. "But we feel somewhat safe in there. Not totally, but somewhat."

𝄢

EARLY Christmas morning, Hanora walked through her London neighbourhood alone, hat pulled down over her ears, scarf twined about her neck, shoulders hunched against the cold. The air was heavy with mist. She looked up to grey skies. She went to work and helped with preparations for the hot Christmas meal. The menu that day included hundreds of servings of special pudding, and she was put in charge of that. She became the Christmas pudding person. She sang Christmas carols with the children and alongside women she worked with, as well as women she knew from Underground shelters and from hours spent queuing for rations. Everyone made the best of the day and the best of what they had. The children were happy with their small treats. On the way back to Queensborough Terrace a man walked toward her with a sack of coal on his back. He was covered in grime; his face looked as if he'd blackened it intentionally. "Hello, love," he shouted out cheerily as he passed. "Happy Christmas."

𝄢

WHEN Tobe was finally able to visit, she learned the reason for his earlier cancellation: two weeks before Christmas, the Regiment had been taken north to Scotland for assault-landing training. Rumours were flying about once more. Tobe told her the boys called them "latrine rumours." Wherever the Regiment was headed, the approach was going to be by water.

He arrived in London from East Sussex, where the Regiment was sent after the rainy month in Scotland. He told her how they'd worked and trained non-stop, going up and down the sides of ships; he told her about landing in barges, crossing beaches under mock fire. All the while, soaked through by bone-chilling rain.

Everything done in preparation. But for what, he didn't know and wouldn't have been permitted to tell if he did.

"Do you remember how I made whistles?" he said. They were crossing Bayswater Road at the end of her street and followed it until they could find an entrance to the park. They took a well-worn path and headed for trees along the far side. Despite the chill, a man with white hair was bundled up and seated on a folding chair, reading. Hanora had made sandwiches from slices of meat she'd been given at the canteen. She'd baked the bread herself.

"Whistles? Sure I remember. One day, your collection was lined up on your mother's sill. You made some of them from the maple in our backyard. With your pocket knife. You were so careful about selecting the small branches. You preferred ones that had already broken off so you wouldn't damage the tree. There couldn't be any little twigs coming off the sides; I remember that. And you tapped the bark with that tiny hammer you carried over from your house. You taught me."

"Could you still make one?"

"Probably. We had to twist the bark without damaging the branch—the branch that became the whistle."

"And cut the V, and the sliver of wood from the end."

"Yours was always sharp, decisive," she said.

"And yours a bit ragged."

She shrugged. "And then we slid the bark back on. I was good at that."

"Sometimes I'd like to return to that backyard, doing nothing more important than making whistles," said Tobe. "Sitting on the thick branch in the middle of the tree, waiting for the birds to settle."

"We did learn to be still," she said. "And quiet. We didn't blow whistles when we were in the tree."

"We got through all those childhood years, and after that all the way through the Depression, and now we are part of a war. Has the world moved any further ahead since your father came home from his war?"

There was no answer to that. They both knew Tobe would be facing something he had never faced before. She tucked her free arm into his and pressed herself against his side.

That was as close as they came to discussing the war. Tobe maintained his extraordinary calmness. They had three days together in London, and three nights.

The first night of the three was spent in an Underground shelter that was overcrowded when they arrived. They had planned to look up a dance hall outside her area that evening, but sirens began to wail while they were in the street, and they had to follow signs to the nearest shelter. They ended up sitting on the stairs of the Underground, deep below the streets, leaned into each other all night. They were exhausted from lack of sleep by the time morning came. Hanora had to work that day and stumbled through the damage, through smells of dust and fire and ash and cinder, sometimes the odour of gas. She returned to her room as soon as she could after the children at the canteen had been fed. Tobe had taken advantage of her absence to catch up on sleep, and was still sleeping when she returned. If the landlady knew he was there, she did not complain to Hanora. The Fury now had her own friend, never named, but referred to as "my gentleman friend." The Fury mentioned him every chance she had when greeting Hanora; she and her gentleman friend made a point of staying deep in the cellar of the house during air raids, and did not go to shelters. They had met, Hanora was told, while queuing for rations, and it was love at first sight. The Pekingese was not yet convinced, and nipped at the gentleman friend's ankles and chewed at the cuffs of his trousers. The Pekingese was jealous, she said. He'd just have to get used to sharing her.

Every moment shared by Hanora and Tobe during the three days they were together led to the lovemaking between them at night. Every look exchanged. Every touch of skin. Every moment heightened because they knew they'd be separated when his orders came through. They walked the streets arm in arm, hand in hand, sometimes in silence. They stopped at an underground club to have a drink. They danced to slow music; they talked to two other couples at their table. They found a restaurant with an entrance several steps beneath sidewalk level, but it was so full they returned to her room and lit candles and made dinner from what she had saved and from rations he had brought with him. They called it their smorgasbord, and Tobe opened the bottle of wine he'd brought and they turned it into a feast.

At night, Hanora barely slept. She watched over a sleeping Tobe—since he'd been with the Hasty Ps, he could sleep anytime, anywhere, standing up if necessary—as if watching him would also keep him alive. She'd become used to writing at nights when he wasn't there, or writing in the shelters, and sleeping as much as possible during daytime hours when she wasn't at the canteen. And now it seemed to her that she hardly slept at all. She accepted this as what she thought of as her perpetual wartime state.

On the day Tobe departed, Hanora felt she was seeing him through a haze before he had even boarded the train. She accompanied him to the platform, and when he walked away, she watched from behind, the shape of his shoulders, his tall, lean body in uniform. He grinned back at her after he found a seat next to the window. Raised a hand in farewell and stayed that way, frozen in position, watching her intently while the train pulled out and she was left alone.

1998

COVENTRY

―――――――――

THE COVENTRY DIARY IS THICK NOT ONLY
because of the quality of the paper, but also because
Mariah had inserted loose drawings on separate
sheets between some of the pages. This diary was never
completely filled, but it does include the final Canadian
entries. There are several blank pages at the end. The diary
is open now, as if Mariah had laid it out on Hanora's desk
in readiness for the next entry, the next drawing.

Hanora turns to the beginning and reads slowly and
carefully, arriving at the section where Mariah received
her necessary but abrupt training as a hospital volunteer
in 1939, after war was under way. It is not clear where the
training took place, but following the November 1940
bombing of Coventry, she was working at the Gulson
Road Hospital. She was in her mid-fifties, and had every

intention of making—and did make—a valuable contribution during the early years of the war.

There are dozens of sketches, sometimes two or three small ones on the same page. The handwriting is easy to recognize. Compared to the diaries of her teen years, this writing, as expected, is more mature and confident. Drawings were done in coloured pencil, sometimes ink. Mariah delighted in colour. Her art is vibrant, alive. Before the outbreak of war, she created country scenes outside Coventry, and drawings of radiant gardens. She was pulled to outrageous colours, the blazing, the bright. She recorded the sale of her paintings during this period, and kept a list of earnings on the inside end-cover of the diary.

Further on—Hanora lifts a chunk of pages—after the bombing of the city began, Mariah's portrayals darkened: destroyed buildings, a house in greys with its entire front blown off, rooms hanging in the air so that the whole resembles an oversized but badly tilted dollhouse. There is nothing static about this work. There is movement, energy. It's as if the viewer is compelled to become part of the scene, must breathe in the soot, the smoke, the fumes.

There are drawings of a crowded hospital ward, three rows of beds the length of a room, a nursing sister reaching for a basin high on a shelf, a friend or relative seated beside someone's cot. The patient lying in the cot is heavily bandaged, face hidden from the viewer.

It is in this set of drawings that Mariah begins to depict herself within a hospital setting, even though she had trained as a volunteer before the city was devastated during bombing raids, and before the large cathedral was destroyed.

NOVEMBER 11, 1940

Last night, my friend Lizzie and I stumbled through dark streets to the local hall to listen to a Sunday evening concert. The musicians played downstairs, not quite a cellar, but we felt as safe there as anywhere, and when the sirens began their warning, we remained where we were. Chamber music was played. I greedily indulged, and had no problem surrendering to the Haydn string quartet.

This was the second luxury of the day for me, as I'd attended church in the morning and listened to the choir at Holy Trinity. The director has been there a year or more. Every one of us standing or sitting in the church was inspired by those glorious singing voices.

In the evening, at the Haydn concert, the small hall was crowded. Afterward, I felt that I would surely float across the room. As we made our way to the exit, we met one of Lizzie's friends, a man in his sixties, a cardiologist who invited us back to his place for a bite. We followed along, and when we arrived he poured us a glass of sherry and proceeded to prepare scrambled eggs and toast. Two eggs divided among the three of us, and toast without butter. We did justice to every crumb. After that he offered biscuits to dip into molasses. I was surprised at the biscuits, but he told me he'd been cooking for himself since his wife died several years earlier. The food was excellent, despite the rationing we are quickly learning to endure.

I mentioned my volunteer work at the hospital and he (his name is John—the fourth John I've met in Coventry) told me about a former colleague, a Spanish doctor who arrived for a time as a refugee from his own brutal Civil War. The Spaniard was a pediatrician and was helping to fill the vacancies left by doctors who are currently serving in uniform. He had also become particularly fond of a young child on the ward. The boy had a sweet disposition as well as a head of thick black hair. One night, very late, this Spanish doctor returned to the hospital after hours and shaved the boy's head. He believed that shaving the head would make the child strong in life. Predictably, the staff members were upset when they arrived the next morning to see this little fellow shorn. The parents, and by that I mean the young mother—the father is a fighting man, as are most young men—well, the mother was not happy about this and had to be calmed by the Spanish doctor himself. He did not make much of an apology for his misdeed, as he felt that the shearing was of enormous benefit to the child. He saw the shearing as a gift. Because the doctor himself was so likeable, he was quickly forgiven.

Lizzie and I laughed over the story, though we wondered how the child felt about the whole affair. Here, below, is my imagining of the head-shaving scene. I've used charcoal, to make the hair truly dark.

I did not tell John and Lizzie my own recent story, though I was tempted, if only to make a contribution to the conversation. At the hospital, I have been trained on a medical ward as an aide, and must perform a number of tasks to help the short-staffed nursing sisters. Really, I'm doing the work of someone in the Voluntary Aid Detachment; there is such a shortage of help. But I am not exactly a VAD. Still, I could work with the Red Cross after all the training I've been given within the hospital itself.

One task I've been taught is to give injections, and while practising, I jabbed a poor old half-rotten grapefruit so many times it finally succumbed. Where the fruit had come from, I'll never know, for I haven't seen another since, and there are no grapefruit to be had in the entire country, as far as I can tell.

For the administration of my first-ever injection, the nursing sister who was supervising offered me the choice of two patients, one of whom would unknowingly be the guinea pig. The choice was between an elderly blind woman and a woman half her age, in her forties. I buckled under my own cowardice and chose the blind woman, believing

that if I fumbled or showed fear, she would not be aware.
And so it went. I hesitated before plunging the needle into
the scrawny buttock that had been bared, and the blind
woman asked, timorously, if something was wrong. Of
course, she sensed my fear, but I carried on.

I was surveying the muscle, trying to ensure that the
tip of the needle was not only sterile but also aimed at the
correct spot. I plunged and all went well. After we left the
room, and before I took the needle and syringe to the util-
ity room to be cleaned, the nursing sister told me that from
now on, I would find it easier to give injections. The blind
woman will never know that hers was the first I ever did.

Here I am, below, wild-eyed, holding the needle in the
air—but really, I see that this has turned out rather car-
toonishly. I will, however, vouch for the expression. My
own, that is. The expression, I would say, is valid.

Hanora turns to the entries after November 14, when
so much of the city was destroyed.

NOVEMBER 16, 1940
The bombing went on for what felt like twenty-four hours,
though I'm told it was twelve, in all. The sirens sounded
shortly after seven in the evening. Having finished my shift,
I was with Lizzie when we took shelter. We who tried to
stay alive beneath the horror of this attack felt that the

bombs would go on dropping forever. Indeed, the effects of this will stay with us forever, and no one believes otherwise. I speak of those of us fortunate to be alive. Hundreds were killed, hundreds injured. The damage to the city is unspeakable. There are no detailed numbers yet. Lizzie and I have rooms in the same house and our own dwelling is largely undamaged, though the windows have shattered. We were in the shelter most of the time, and when I tried to reach the hospital in the early morning, I was turned back. I've since been told that many of our patients were moved.

One of Mariah's Coventry drawings depicts the inside of a small bomb shelter. Half a dozen people are hunched over, sitting side by side on what could be a stone ledge. All are staring at a wailing baby who is at their feet, wrapped in blankets and arched unnaturally on a cushion, one arm and fist poking up into the air. The drawing has been executed in quick, bold strokes, as if Mariah was sketching hurriedly at the time. One of the six people staring at the baby is a very old woman who has a wizened face and wears a bonnet with ties under her chin. A flap of the bonnet is pushed back so that she can hold an ear trumpet to her left ear. She stares at the baby as if straining to hear its cries. It is clear that Mariah was trying to emphasize sound. Everything in the drawing is grey or black except the ear trumpet, which is the colour of blood.

There is another—living and breathing—sketch of a young boy, perhaps ten or eleven years old. He is wearing short trousers, a jacket and a sailor hat, and pushes a bicycle over and through heaps of smouldering ruins. It is daytime, but a haze is suggested and blurs the sides of the drawing. The expression on the boy's face is one of unconcern, his bearing almost casual as he makes his way around obstacles and toward an unseen destination.

Following that, a sketch of two civilians beside a damaged doorway, perhaps leading to a medical station. An older man rests his chin in his hands and stares bleakly at his bandaged right leg; a woman lies flat on a stretcher, her head and part of her face bandaged. Both man and woman are intentionally static beside heaps of rubble that look alive and ready to tumble.

From this point forward, most of the drawings are about war. The damaged city, the people within. Death. Shelters. Building and rebuilding, the shocked and shocking appearance of citizens, people dragging carts through streets, medical staff attending the injured.

Several drawings depict Holy Trinity, which survived the bombings even though glass shattered from many of its windows. Mariah exaggerated the spire, having it pierce the sky while people stand small below, their backs to the artist as they stare up at the peak, at the height of this amazing monument to survival. All around Holy Trinity are screes of rubble, half walls, jutting timbers, downed wires, destruction, more destruction. Already, men and women are at work, hauling away glass and brick and stone.

Hanora wants to take a break but she carries on and gets through another chunk of pages. She stops when she notices that the handwriting has changed significantly. This is in April 1941, after Mariah was injured in a bombing raid. Some pages are now undated, even though, until then, Mariah had taken care to record specific dates. The handwriting is spidery, as if her body had aged overnight.

APRIL 1941

Lizzie brought me home from the hospital where I was treated. She tells me I was unconscious for several hours after the cellar door fell through in the shelter where we'd taken refuge. An upper panel, a thick splinter of wood, struck my head as the door broke into pieces, so Lizzie says. I had been sitting on the bottom step, below. I don't remember that part, but I do remember thinking that I had to get to the hospital to work my shift as soon as the all-clear sounded. I also recall being comforted by a short woman in a long black coat, wellies and a tin hat. I had never seen her before and haven't seen her since, but I could draw her in an instant, and will.

My head hurts; my brain is partly in a fog. I can't seem to remember where I'm about to go or where I've been.

The doctor told Lizzie to reassure me that these problems will settle in time. I have bruises as large as a fist on my shoulder. My left arm suffered lacerations and is sutured. I am fortunate to have Lizzie around to check on me, and comforted by the knowledge that we live in the same house. I do not feel wonderful about adding to her daily tasks and responsibilities. Lizzie is much involved, now, in the Women's Voluntary Services. She tells me that I was in hospital two full days, though I have no recollection of this, either. At one point after I spoke to her, she looked at me strangely, as if my words had come out upside down or backwards. She did not ask me to repeat, and I couldn't have anyway, as I had no recall of what I had just said.

One new pleasure I have is a cat that has adopted me. She is sleek and black except for her astonishing white face and white paws. She wandered into our area in the night; no one nearby recognizes her or claims ownership. The cat was at first terrified. Its owners must be dead, and the startled beast has chosen me as the most likely human to provide a home. I've named her Smoke because she was covered in ash on arrival, and smelled of smoke. Now, cleaned up, she stops, tilts her head and looks me over as if giving inspection. Her eyes remind me of a blackout poster I'd almost stopped seeing because I pass it so often. I'll do drawings of both below. Smoke will be first, the poster cat second.

And now I must remember—Lizzie will be checking— that in our house we have at the ready, day and night, full water buckets, respirators, food, candles.

Hanora examines the two drawings. Smoke is as Mariah described in her diary, and is sitting on a wooden chair and staring at the artist as if posing. The poster shows the head of a coal-black cat with yellow almond-shaped eyes. The left eye contains a round black pupil, the right a vertical black slit. The print below the cat's head reads: "Until your eyes get used to the darkness, take it easy. Look out in the blackout."

She returns to the diary pages, reading further into 1941.

MAY ?? 1941
I sometimes look around and wonder where I am but don't ask for fear Lizzie or the other residents of the house will think me mad. I found myself in the kitchen this morning about eleven o'clock, and could not think why I was sitting at the table by myself. I had no recollection of moving myself there from any other place. I stood and walked about the kitchen and made my way upstairs to my room. I sat on the edge of my bed and tried to recall the sequence of events that had brought me to the kitchen table. I could not come up with any motive. I am hopeful of preventing a repeat of this kind of experience, and will have to have

my wits about me. I must remember to carry my respirator with me when I walk out. Lizzie continues to remind me.

Smoke follows me from room to room, needing to be reassured of my presence. Once accustomed to the routine of the house, she will no doubt become a more independent creature.

Evening note: Halfway through the afternoon, Smoke leaped up to the outside sill next the door and rattled the latch. She stared through the window, willing—perhaps I should say demanding—someone to admit her. Her independence asserted, she will now become intent on making us her slaves.

After this, several pages are without any date. The entries then cease, and do not resume until December of the same year. The handwriting in December is no longer spidery, but it's also not as assured and fluid as before.

DECEMBER 23, 1941

I'm glad that I have stayed on, and that I share the fate of everyone here. How can a city abandon itself? Our city—I think of it as my own now—was much destroyed, but after a night of bombing, clearing begins almost immediately. Clearing and reconstruction. So many lives were lost in the November raids last year, and again in April, that I realize how fortunate I was to emerge from my own injuries alive.

Even now, we are never certain if and when planes will threaten overhead.

After a bad spell that seemed to go on and on, my head-aches have disappeared. At Lizzie's urging I have begun to paint more. This war cannot last forever, and I believe it is important to document in art what is happening around us.

I am also able to help once more at the hospital, though I put in fewer hours and my tasks are light. There is always a need for extra hands, and I do what I can to assist the regular staff. They work long shifts and stay beyond when emergency calls. I am sorry I cannot do more.

One thing that has caused some grief and confusion is the following: A doctor who visited my ward this morning approached and spoke to me by name. He said his name was John, and repeated the name several times during the conversation. He told me we had met at a concert about a year ago. He is a cardiologist and now works at this hospi-tal, his former place of employment having been destroyed. He told me he had cooked up scrambled eggs and toast for Lizzie and me after said concert, and this I could scarcely believe. We laughed together, though I believe he was con-cerned about my memory lapse. I continued to wonder if he was joking. I have met many men named John in Coventry. Perhaps he is the one mistaken. If it is my memory that has failed, then I have cause for grief.

I have begun to long for spring and want to return

again to St. Ives, where I painted so happily. Perhaps it will be possible to travel there with Lizzie in late spring or early summer. The citizens of Coventry appear to have set in for a long war. The determination on their faces tells the story. If that is the case, St. Ives residents are no doubt doing the same.

Unable to resist, Hanora turns toward the end to have a glimpse at what lies ahead.

It appears that Mariah stayed on in England throughout the war, though there are fewer entries in the diary between 1943 and 1946. Fewer entries, but more drawings. After the end of the war, she managed to get herself onto the *Mauretania*, one of the many ships that transported close to sixty-four thousand war brides and their children to Canada so that families could be reunited. The *Mauretania* landed at Pier 21 in Halifax on February 9, 1946, carrying just under a thousand women and children.

Numerous sketches portray life on board, largely around mealtimes—images of countless toddlers scattered among the pages. There are drawings showing waves threatening the ship. Even if these are exaggerated, the faces of the new immigrants clearly show the misery of seasickness, people lying across their beds and laundry piled high. On land there are depictions of Pier 21—the walkways, the waiting trains—and an attempt to show crowds of women and small children disembarking as they arrive in their new country. Mariah notes beside one drawing: *A band played a rousing "Here Comes the Bride," but this was unappreciated by many women who have suffered during the crossing.*

Three sketches show a young girl of perhaps four or five on the train leaving Halifax. She is holding a banana, the first time she has held such a fruit in her hand. In the first sketch, she holds it with a perplexed expression on her face. In the second, she is about to bite at the peel. In the third, adult hands come in from the side to demonstrate how to pull back the peel. Extreme pleasure is now seen on the face of this child. Mariah used greys and blacks, and in contrast, created the one object of vibrant colour, the yellow banana.

Knowing how impossible it was to find a way to cross the ocean during wartime years, and even for a year after the end of the war—and having found a way herself in 1945, with more than a little difficulty—Hanora suspects that Mariah offered herself in an official capacity so that she could make this historic postwar crossing. The *Mauretania* wasn't the first ship to bring war brides; earlier ships carrying wounded soldiers had transported smaller numbers of brides and their children. But the *Mauretania* was the first "designated" ship for Canadian war brides and their offspring.

Mariah might have been paid for her work. Perhaps she offered paintings of the crossing to the government in exchange for her passage. If so, Hanora will track any of her art that might be owned by the Canadian War Museum. She wants her book, with an appendix listing Mariah's works and where they can be found, to be as complete as possible. She will be the first to set out this information. She has not yet chosen a title for her book, but that will fall out of the work itself, she hopes. She is counting on that.

No matter how the passage home was negotiated, Hanora is now certain of the dates Mariah sailed to Canada. She returned without the company of Lizzie. The plan was for her British friend to join her when civilian transatlantic crossings started up again.

Hanora will have to read the entries of the final pages before she has answers to her remaining questions. She is coming close to the end of the main body of research, which means she is coming close to writing the first chapter of her book.

LAST WORD

J UNE HAS COME AND GONE. THE CLEANING CREW scoured the basement, cleaned floors and bedroom closets, and washed shelves under sinks. Vacuumed cobwebs, replaced light bulbs where needed, wiped appliances, cleaned stove and fridge. Window washers removed every streak on every pane of glass, inside and out. The lawn care company sent a worker to mow the grass and clean up the small garden. Once the house was ready, it sold quickly. Now there are papers to sign, a meeting with the realtor and another with the lawyer, and a visit to the bank to ensure that the money has been deposited into Billie's account. Finally, she will have to let Billie know that the red-and-white house has been sold.

Filmore accompanied Hanora during her final inspection, and before she gave the realtor the okay to come and take photos. They were downstairs in the basement when Hanora opened the door of a narrow closet, a makeshift affair recessed into the wall of a side room. Although she'd walked past the closet many times, she had overlooked it earlier. And so, it seems, had the cleaning crew.

A plastic garment bag was hanging from a metal bar, suspended from two hooks that protruded through the top of the bag. Hanora unzipped the bag and discovered inside a faded yellow dress with matching jacket that Billie wore to her brother's wedding in Rochester, eons ago. Hanora saw the wedding photos after the war, and recognized the outfit immediately. The photos were taken before Billie moved to Canada, before she upgraded her education and started her new profession as a teacher of the English language.

The yellow dress was layered, with yards of a paler yellow netting overtop of the skirt. A crinkled and slightly stiff crinoline was attached underneath. When Hanora removed the dress from the garment bag, the jacket disintegrated at her touch. The dress did the same. The garment bag also fell to pieces—rotted, old, brittle plastic. Everything ended up on the closet floor, and while Hanora began to pick up the larger pieces, Filmore went upstairs to find a broom and one more garbage bag.

"That," Hanora told him, "is the closest I've come to understanding the physical surrounds of Miss Havisham."

The last item to be removed was the seaman's chest, which she had intentionally left in the house to the very end. Filmore lifted it into her car, and when they drove back to the apartment, he helped her carry it into the elevator and through the hall.

The chest is heavy, cumbersome, made of pine with dovetail joints, iron hinges and a thick circle of rope inserted into a ring at one end, for lifting. Hanora raised the lid to show Filmore the image of a whaling ship painted on the underside. The chest is filled with papers and greeting card boxes, and Hanora knows she will eventually have to sort through the contents. For now she is happy to be the new owner of this wonderful old object that has passed through known and unknown hands for almost two centuries.

𝄢

HANORA and Filmore have made a plan for a day trip in August to the homestead where Mariah spent her childhood. Hanora checked with the descendants and was given directions. They've assured her that the farmhouse is still standing, and is lived in at present. The owners have agreed to permit Hanora to walk through the house and around the property, to take notes or photos, whatever she needs for the book. "You'll find everyone up there pretty easy to get along with," she was told. "You'll be made to feel welcome. They were excited to learn that they live in a place that housed a famous artist. Especially one who will be the subject of a new book."

Hanora tells herself she'll enjoy Filmore's company. She can't bring herself to call him Robin; when she does, she thinks of Christopher Robin visiting the zoo, tramping around London streets or parks with his father or with Pooh Bear. Robin was amused when she told him this and doesn't mind what he's called, he says. He adds that he was called Filmore during the war, last name only.

$$\text{𝄢}$$

IN late July, after the money from the sale of the house is in Billie's account, Hanora drives to Respiro to visit. It is a hot day and an outdoor booth has been set up to serve glasses of lemonade and iced tea. A few staff members have come outside to be with the residents, and they carry glasses and cups to the tables. The extensive gardens at the residence are being tended along the back and sides of the building. Billie does not object when Hanora invites her to sit outside, and they make their way slowly, Billie using her cane. One of the exits is close to her suite. From there, it's a short walk to a group of chairs that have been set near the gardens.

Hanora chooses chairs that are protected from direct

sun. There are striped awnings along one side of the building, and a groomed field stretches beyond that, but is off the property. A cricket match is in progress, a game Hanora has not seen since she lived in London and watched a charity match at Lord's during the war. Billie has never seen cricket, and watches intently. Several of Respiro's other residents have begun to take an interest, and while the game is under way, a groundskeeper comes along with a ladder and sets it against the wall beyond the edge of the iced-tea booth. Some part of the roof above must need repair.

Just after the ladder is placed, a man and his visiting family members, all of them stout, sit at a table near the walkway at the opposite corner of the building and dig into the food that has been set out for snacks.

"The washing-machine family," says Billie. "They've been here before." Her voice begins to rise. "Drum barrels on legs. Washing-machine barrels with heads on top. Father, mother, daughter, son-in-law. By their fruits ye shall know them. Remember the washing machines of the forties? Their skin might have been painted white. Look at them!"

"Billie, they can hear you," Hanora tells her, in a low voice. But Billie is right—the four have the same bulge across the middle, which makes them all the same shape. Their skin could pass for painted enamel. Hanora wonders if they eat nothing but white bread and pasta and desserts.

Billie drops her voice, looking chastised. She turns her attention in the other direction, where the man on the ladder is repairing a section of the eavestrough.

"The comics," Billie says, eyeing the ladder, but she speaks more softly this time. "All those accident-prone figures walking under ladders or slipping on banana peels. Think of *Mutt and Jeff*. Or maybe the man on the ladder is climbing to heaven. Every rung goes higher, higher." She is enjoying herself. She adds, "'Seek ye the Lord while he may be found.' That man might want to rethink the length of the ladder."

Billie has been slipping into biblical references lately, and Hanora sometimes feels that they've begun to converse like ancient biblical sisters. This must be coming from some period of Billie's childhood. She was brought up to read the Bible. She mentioned one day that her father sometimes carried one around the house when he was drinking, and shouted out the Scriptures aloud. Billie was raised as a Protestant, but she set aside her religion after she moved out. Too much hypocrisy in her own home, she said.

Billie is still watching the groundskeeper. "If he wants to get to heaven, he's chosen the slow way."

Hanora is thinking of *Mutt and Jeff*, damsels tied to tracks, ballooned exclamations over cartoon figures, mischievous boys in comics, a lick of hair over one eye. Billie's childhood memories often send Hanora back to earlier times, the past unreeling in her mind.

A woman who lives on Respiro's first floor wanders by. Seeing an empty chair on the other side of Billie, she turns and comes back and sits next to her, greeting her by name.

Billie looks at Hanora, raises her eyebrows and says, loudly, "I have never seen this person before in my entire life."

The woman, a small woman wearing a cotton skirt and lightweight top with long sleeves, twists at her own arm. Continues to fidget.

Hanora is about to introduce herself, but Billie says to the woman, "Oh, do sit still," and turns back to the cricket game. The woman is already up, and wanders away.

Billie watches the woman walk toward other chairs, other residents, and this time she whispers. She says to Hanora, "The place is full of strangers."

Whatever Billie says or doesn't say, knows or doesn't know, she no longer has to pretend that she can look after the complexities of day-to-day life. She no longer has to pretend that she doesn't need assistance. She accepts help as if this is her due. She doesn't argue, and no longer shouts at the staff.

Hanora wonders if the timing is right to tell her about the sale of the house, and decides to go ahead. There may never be a right time, an exact time, a time that will fit a particular state of mind that will admit the information.

"I have something to tell you, Billie. Something important."

Billie perks up at this.

"I've finished preparing your house for sale — I've kept you posted about this over the past few months. Well, we've had an offer, a good one. I've accepted, and the house is sold. You'll be getting a good price for it."

"My home?" she says. "You've sold it? You had no right to do this, Hanora. No right at all."

"Yes, Billie. It had to be sold to pay for the care you receive here. You have excellent care, excellent meals, your own furniture around you . . ."

"You sold my home," she says again, in disbelief. "Why would you do that?"

"Because you moved out and came here. The house can't remain empty. You knew the house would be sold. We've talked about this many times."

"Well, of course," she says. "That's true. The insurance company won't cover an empty house with no one living in it."

But she eyes Hanora suspiciously.

She drinks a glass of lemonade. "Did you sell my house?" she asks.

"Yes, it's sold."

"Why would you do that?"

The same conversation is repeated several times, but Billie can never quite remember the answer or the explanation.

"Am I here, then? Is that it?" she finally says.

"You've been here four months now, Billie. This is where you live."

"That's true enough," she says. "They're good to me here. The strangers."

After they've spent an hour outside, Hanora takes Billie back to her room and helps her settle into her TV chair.

Billie thanks her. "I had a lovely afternoon," she says. "It was good to sit out in the fresh air. I don't know if that man ever reached heaven." She laughs at her own joke. She switches on the TV.

She is so easy to please, thinks Hanora. Now that she is truly being cared for. And maybe the fear is gone. And the anger. Or maybe not.

When she reaches the door, she turns to look back. Billie hasn't moved from her chair. She is staring blankly at the TV screen, but when she hears the word "goodbye," she turns her head to watch Hanora depart.

She says, with no affect whatever, "You're getting on in years yourself, Hanora. You think that because you're a writer and can put everything down on paper, you're always going to get the last word."

MARIAH'S FINAL DIARY

AFTER THE FEBRUARY VOYAGE FROM LIVER-
pool to Halifax on the *Mauretania*, after the
trip by rail from Pier 21 to Ontario, Mariah
continued to write in her diary, but erratically, between
March and June.

There are drawings and sketches, but fewer now. At
times, the images are blurred, as if the fog in Mariah's head
has returned and now extends to the world outside her
body. Hanora feels she is about to lose a friend, and is saddened by the thought of how Mariah's life came to an end.

MARCH 10, 1946, SUNDAY
I have not been able to write in these pages since being met
at the Belleville station by my eldest sister, Patricia. She and
her husband, Tom, drove me to their home and I managed
an awkward fall as I was walking up three easy steps to

their veranda. Entirely my own fault, as I was excited at the thought of my reunion with their daughter—now an adult herself—who awaited my arrival. The eccentric aunt come home, I suppose that's what they were all thinking.

The fall was a hard one. My shoe caught between steps; I went over backwards, crashed to the stone walk below and knocked my head. I'm told I was confused immediately afterward. That accounts for the troubles I've had since. Patricia insisted on having her family doctor come to the house, and he gave instructions that I am to rest. What else would he say? There is no damage to be seen. Only what I feel inside my head.

This morning, the family left for Sunday service and I told Patricia I would resume my work, writing and sketching. She was unenthusiastic, but did not discourage me completely. She asked only that I work briefly and then lie flat again so as not to tire myself.

For days, I have lain on the divan with a dark cloth over my eyes. The headaches of old have returned. I have not yet been able to walk about the streets to look for a place to live, but that is my intention. I must find a place before Lizzie arrives in the late summer. I want to be settled and ready for her to move in when she comes to Canada. She plans to stay, and the two of us will live together and work side by side as we did in England. If we manage enough funds between us, we can travel to different parts of the country, as there is much to see. I miss Lizzie and cannot wait until she sends word that she has been successful in booking a passage. We understand that the soldiers must be brought home first. And after the soldiers, the women and children who became their families. Like the passengers on the Mauretania, *a journey I won't forget. I did some of my best work on that ship, despite several days of rough seas.*

But haven't we survived the war? Every one of us who makes our way home?

For now, I want to be up and out in the winter sunshine. Soon to be spring. As I think this, I see an early robin, its brick-red breast puffed out as it perches on a branch outside. The robin—a thrush, my British friends taught me, insisting that theirs are robins, ours thrushes—well, this particular robin will be my first drawing since I fell from the steps. Finally, I set to work again.

Hanora examines the drawing opposite the diary entry. Far from being colourful, the robin is drab and slightly blurred. Hanora was expecting to see a vibrant orange-red, but this is a sad-looking creature of greys and blacks.

She continues.

MARCH 27, 1946
I've been thinking of Comfort. How he made us stand in the classroom and recite "Fame and Friendship," but only

289

the fame part. He wanted to shame me for having ambi-
tion, for having talent. I tried to believe in myself. But
Comfort would have none of that. The man is no longer
alive. And why should I think of him now, after all these
years? Perhaps because I don't forget how he goaded me in
front of everyone. "They eat it in the silent tomb." A horrid
image. Comfort may have desired a world in which every-
one would compete to see who could be most average. If
anyone stood out or differed in any way, the great plates of
the earth that some believe to exist would close soundlessly
over that person. Anyone with originality would disappear
without a murmur.

And now, having thought of Comfort, I will draw some-
thing cheerier, the robin again—though there's no robin to
be seen today. The first robin I drew turned out darker than
I'd intended. I had hoped to show off its colour.

Hanora looks for the robin but the image on the adja-
cent page is, instead, of Comfort, or a man she believes to
be Comfort. Dark thoughts of him must have taken over.
He is shown as a short, rotund man with a large protrud-
ing paunch, ruler in hand, officious expression, well drawn
by Mariah, but dark and grey. His cheeks are shaded. He
looks as if he is partly shrouded, and perhaps that is what
she intended. He faces an outline of vague shapes, meant to
be the students in the class. Their shapes resemble shades

of the underworld. There is a good deal of cross-hatching, so no individual can be made out entirely. There are only hints, again, of darkness.

APRIL 3, 1946

I sat outside on a chair for twenty-five minutes, wrapped in heavy winter garments. I felt Patricia watching me from the kitchen window. The ground is still partly frozen and the cold seeped through the soles of my boots. I did not last long, but I was happy to take the air.

Patricia hovers. Concern shows on her face. I can't stay here much longer, as I am a burden on her family. She assures me this is not the case. She is so loving and kind, I hardly know what to do next. She does not want me to leave, but I feel I should find a room, perhaps a single room until I am ready to look for something bigger. If I find something close by, Patricia will have to support my decision. I admit that I have come to depend on her. I've been feeling low.

I long for the end of spring. I long to be tipped into summer. I asked about my papers, my early diaries, the ones I left at the farm when I travelled to England the second time. The farm was sold after our parents' death. The diaries are now stored at our brother Roland's farm, I'm told. But what of the diaries from Toronto when I was in my twenties? I'm not sure where those are. I would like my papers to be in one location so I can refer to them as I wish.

And the drawings, well, there are many. The best I can do is stick them into a folder or in the back of a sketchpad. The ones that have sold? The oils? They went to their new owners with my blessings!

The last entries in Mariah's diary were written in May 1946. These run together and are largely undated. Damage to Mariah's brain from the original concussion during the bombing of Coventry must have been severe if she suffered such symptoms later. The second fall seems to have triggered a recurrence of symptoms. Including depression.

Maybe, Hanora thinks, all these factors are related — the concussion, the fall, the subsequent depression, the diagnosis of senility that became the official family story passed down to living relatives.

She won't jump to conclusions. Not until she has examined every word on every page before her. But as she reads, the entries become more and more disjointed, the drawings darker and darker. Mariah draws the same image over and over. The almost-black robin. The caricature of her teacher, Comfort. Who was never a comfort and whose actions haunted her final days.

Nothing Mariah draws during her last weeks compares with the brilliance of the work she completed between the wars, and during her time in France and St. Ives, and then in Coventry during the Second World War. And yet, every detail is a valid part of her story. When Hanora finishes writing the book, she will try to interest a gallery in sponsoring a show of Mariah's best paintings and sketches. The quality of the work is so high, there should be interest, especially if the show is held after the book is published.

She settles in to read the final pages. But not without sorrow. These are undated, the handwriting threadlike, wobbly.

I was brought here sometime in May. More than a month ago? No one tells me what day it is. This place, this large property, these many buildings are in Brockville and I have never been here before. I have my own bed.

A woman on the far side of the lounge knits constantly during the day. She is never short of wool. Who supplies the wool? She has been knitting a scarf, and I swear it is long enough to trail out the room and down the hall. She speaks to no one.

What day is it?

Someone ran by and punched another woman on the arm as she ran. I don't like that. She is dangerous. There is a bruise on the woman's arm.

The people who work here call me "dear." I want to be addressed by my name. The leaders here need a leader.

The cat outside the window has a long shadow. Too long a shadow for such a small cat. It walks unnaturally. I do not like this cat. Not like my Smoke, in Coventry. Was it Coventry? That place seems so long ago. When will Lizzie come?

They want me to eat oxtail soup at the table. I refuse. I remember the ox with the wild eye on the farm next to ours. A scary creature because of its one wild eye. Would I eat that creature or its tail? "I have no stomach for such meat."

My brother Roland and I turned the handle of the meat grinder in the back kitchen. We took turns, and fed chunks of bologna into the grinder. What came through the grid at the other end was pink and disgusting. Roland teased. He called the food "bologna worms" and tried to make me laugh. Our mother mixed pickles and mayonnaise into the worms to make them palatable, and spread them on bread. Roland had wavy hair when he was growing up. He was handsome, and married a handsome wife.

On Sundays, one of Father's uncles showed up at our farm with his wife. The two walked slowly up the lane, making certain to arrive right in time for dinner. Mother had no choice but to ask them to stay. They pretended surprise, and always accepted. But we knew they came only for the meal. It was my job to stand at the porch window and give warning. I enjoyed calling out: "Here they come. The spongers are on their way to join us for their free Sunday dinner."

I love the music from Porgy and Bess. *Sometimes, music is played here. A woman sits at the piano. Another woman plays spoons. But no one plays music from* Porgy and Bess. *The woman who plays piano has a face shaped like a plate. That wonderful choir in Coventry sang so beautifully.*

The tree with brittle copper leaves. Where was that tree? Every branch and fence post was covered in crystalline snow. Water will find its path through snow but not the other way round. Next to the house, wave formations rippled across the snowy field.

I wanted to paint the copper leaves from that winter.

Large footprints left pockmarks in melting snow. I drew those sinking caverns.

The door at the end of this room is kept locked. A nurse carries keys that rattle and clang. The window in the upper part of the door has wire mesh over it. I could draw that. Cross-hatching the mesh. We can't go to the dining room until the door is unlocked. Sometimes in the dining room, people have spills. One woman waves her tray about as if she is a lunatic. Perhaps she was once an intoxicate.

The woman who smells like lavender came and stood by my chair. I don't know what she wanted. When I asked, she replied in sounds but not words: "Hnn—hnn—hnn—huh—nn—hnn—nn—hnn."

What day is it?

The woman who runs and punches has just flitted past.

I always sit in the same place. She lurches, as if she might not come to a halt. She runs into obstacles. Sometimes she crashes into the door with the wire mesh. Sometimes into other people.

Most stay in their own space. They know what's good for them.

There was a child on the Mauretania *who was blonde with curly hair. I wanted to draw her. She was two or three years old. Young enough to be dragging around a comfort cloth, a snippet cut from a larger piece. Faded from many washes. It was the palest of blues, sky washed by rain. The cloth was stuck to the child's chin. Or rather, the child stuck it to her chin in moments of frustration and when she was tired. Her mother held her until she fell asleep. The ship moved forward through the waves, and I began to wonder if the rag was stitched to the child's chin.*

The beautiful small round face.

The delicate chin.

The washed-out blue rag.

I hope I drew those. Did I? I asked a woman here, but she said she didn't know.

Patricia came for a visit. She wept when she saw me. When I saw her weeping, I wept, too. But what is the use of crying? Patricia says I am weak. She wants me to eat more because I am too thin. I want Lizzie, but she hasn't come. Lizzie is the person who makes me feel that I belong.

An old woman comes by and speaks to me as if I am standing to the left of myself. She won't look at me face-on. She stares into a place where she and I are invisible. The old woman's discomfort has nothing to do with the hail that beats against the window. The place is full of gloom today. I can't see beyond my own centre. I could sit here all day and wonder who I am.

Cake was brought to the table at midday. The lurching woman had a birthday. A candle was lit and stuck into the icing. A candle does not shed light on itself.

We sang "Happy Birthday." The person sitting beside me told me that the people here are insane. The women reached out their hands for cake. I would like my life to be one coherent story.

The final entry has a date: Mariah's sixtieth birthday, the day of her death. The writing is not her own.

Her sister Patricia, who collected her belongings and arranged her funeral, noted:

June 28, 1946—Our beloved youngest sister, Mariah, has been taken into the arms of the Lord. She was weak and could not live a day longer. She died on her birthday.

BELLEVILLE STATION

H ANORA STOOD BACK, BEYOND THE END OF the platform. She had left Deseronto early so she would be in Belleville in time to watch the train pull in. She wore dark brown slacks and a long beige sweater, belted at the waist. She was alone. Deliberately. She wore her hair shoulder-length now, and wavy. She had become so accustomed to wearing pincurls under her turban while working at the canteen, she had come to like the way her hair curled up at the ends. She no longer used pincurls, but she had clamped wave clips into place early in the morning, and removed them before leaving home. She shoved at the waves with the side of her hand and tried to push them into place. Checked to make sure her sweater wasn't inside out.

Tobe had always liked to see her with her hair down.

She had returned in the summer to be with her parents,

and to be with Tobe's parents. She knew she would get herself back somehow; she just wasn't certain how she would accomplish this, or how soon after the end of the war. After numerous trips to the High Commission, and having made military and diplomatic friends during her six years in London, she was eventually permitted passage on a hospital ship sailing to Halifax. She avoided questions and lay low until the ship left port, and then made herself useful throughout the voyage. There were many who needed help, many who wanted to tell their stories. To anyone who inquired, she was a journalist reporting on troops being returned to their home country, returning to Halifax, to Pier 21. And she did write several of their stories.

Now, through noise that was overwhelmingly jubilant, through all the jostling while men poured off the train as others shouted from open windows of coaches, she continued to look for one soldier. Hundreds of men in uniform crammed into the space between train and station. Young boys on bicycles skirted the edges of the crowd, wheeling about in circles and half-circles, never staying still. People were milling about in a way that appeared to be purposeless. It soon became clear that the soldiers were about to regroup so they could march along Station Street, and the townspeople could see with their own eyes the men who had come home after so many years away.

𝄢

SHE knew his letters by heart. The first he sent from Italy was dated September 3, 1943.

By now you will have read about the Sicilian invasion. The Regiment has been as much a part of this as anyone, but no one would know from censored press reports. We have not given up our identity, but the reports lumped us in with "Allied forces." Our families back home would have no way of knowing where we are or which campaign we are a part of, but we don't control that. I think the releasing of information has been a fiasco, from what I'm hearing from our own headquarters. Somehow, somewhere, Canadians were mentioned, but after the fact.

Well, now you will certainly know where I am.

Our biggest challenge yet. We fought hard over the last two months, harder than we could have imagined, but our training prepared us and we move on. We lost good soldiers. Decent men, Hanora. All young, decent men.

Mail does not catch up with us often. It's what all the boys want. It's what I want. I try to write to you when I can. Most days and nights, writing letters is not possible because we are on the move.

I say your name aloud. I speak your name when I sleep.

There has been an occasional pleasure to remind us of life, not death: pomegranates, a melon, once a brief dip in the sea. Every one of us has the friendship, the backup of others. Even humour surfaces. We have good scroungers in the Regiment, the best. We manage from time to time to find bitter wine (wine nonetheless).

Keep sending letters. Doesn't matter if they arrive three or four at a time. We face a long road ahead. Every time something absurd happens—that would be daily—I think of how you and I would share the moment. War is absurd, Hanora. Utterly, devastatingly absurd.

I think of you. I pause. We sit on the big branch inside the tree, silent and still, waiting for the birds to settle. I pause again. Remember. At Jack and Evelyn's. Ah, yes.

𝄢

THE 39ers, the first to join up, had been gone since the beginning of the war. More than three hundred Hasty Ps were not returning. Tobe was one of those, a 39er now buried in a grave in Italy.

Tobe had transferred to the White Battalion.

𝄢

SHE was about to give up, believing it would be impossible to locate Jack. She'd met him only once, at the end of the three days she and Tobe had spent at his house in Horam. She remembered the colour of Jack's hair, the vertical scar at the edge of his eye, but she wasn't certain she'd be able to identify him now.

Four or five civilian men were standing on a high baggage cart, overlooking the chaotic scene. She began to head in their direction to see if they would haul her up to give her a better view of the crowd. But Jack spotted her before she could push her way through. He shouted over the turmoil, trying to get through and past dozens of men in uniform, like him.

"Red!" he shouted. "Over here, Red!"

He shoved his way forward. He looked tired, rugged, drew deeply on a cigarette in the way she remembered. His cap was pushed back at an angle over his dark hair. The scar was the same, permanently etched into his face. Older. He was older.

He pulled her into his arms and hugged her tightly. He had written to her from Italy. He and Tobe had almost made it home together. Tobe was killed in February, only weeks before the remains of the Regiment shipped north to Holland, and only months before the end of the war.

That much she knew. Now, all Jack could promise was to meet with her another day, the following week, to tell more, to fill out the story, to talk to her about Tobe's life from the landing at Pachino, in Sicily, and onward. What they had been through together from July 1943 until February 1945.

The men had begun to form up, preparing to march down Station Street. Jack's parents and his sisters had arrived; Hanora watched as he waved to them at the edge of the crowd. Evelyn and his son would be joining him from England as soon as the British, the Canadians, the High Commission and the Red Cross finalized their plans to transport the tens of thousands of war brides and their children to Canada. That was taking time, he said. A few months, in Evelyn's case. There was so much paperwork. There were documents to fill, medical exams, appointments. But his family would soon be here, and he would have weeks to get things ready for them.

"I loved him," Jack said, and he hugged her close again before he headed over to his relatives. "You did, too, Hanora. I loved him, and he was my true friend. He couldn't wait . . . he couldn't wait to get home to you."

1998

THAT'S MY BABY

AFTER WORKING MOST OF THE DAY, AFTER considering the overview of the contents of the diaries, after making a few notes on how she hopes to shape the book, Hanora drives to Respiro in the evening to visit Billie. Her cousin is glad to see her.

"Hanora. Are you out on errands?"

"No. I'm here to spend the evening with you."

"What day is it?"

"It's Friday. What have you been doing?"

"Walking up and down the halls, meeting people." Billie points to her cane as if she'd propped it against her chair only moments before.

Hanora is so relieved to hear that Billie is adjusting to life at Respiro, she goes out to the nursing station to speak to one of the caregivers she has come to know. She tells her how pleased she is to learn that Billie is walking in the halls now. But the nurse is perplexed.

"Your cousin?" she says. "Billie? She hasn't left her suite except for meals. Not once since she arrived. She goes out only when you are here to take her. She certainly doesn't walk up and down the halls."

Billie was so convincing that it is difficult to understand how she invented the information. She seemed to genuinely believe she had been out there socializing with other residents. Hanora can tell that she didn't say this intentionally, to deceive.

"Confabulation," says the nurse. "She believes what she makes up. We'd like her to move about, walk in the halls, take part in events, but she refuses. We do encourage her . . . we don't give up."

Confabulation. One more piece of jargon to consider. Not exactly the way Hanora has considered the word, if ever she did consider it in the past. She returns to Billie's suite.

Billie has been checking through her TV guide and wants to watch a rerun of a movie she and Whit saw on TV sometime in the eighties. The movie is called *Sizzle*. She remembers the music and wants to see Leslie Uggams sing and dance. A gangster film, Billie says.

Hanora thinks of her grandparents' hotel at the edge of the bay in Deseronto. She considers the rumour—perhaps fact—that Capone stayed several times under a different name, or names. Her grandparents and her uncle Bernard wouldn't have lied about that, so she assumes it is true. She never met Capone but used to watch for him. She thinks he probably wouldn't have sat around the lobby, but she kept a lookout just the same, and told herself that even a gangster had to eat. He could have been in the dining room, bolting down her grandmother's amazing meals while Hanora was sitting right there in the corner, at the family table. Many men were on the move between the two countries, criss-crossing Lake Ontario in small boats during rum-running days. She learned about that when she was older. But no one around the hotel said a word about rum-running. Not in front of her. Not when she was a child. She heard mutterings about gambling and about gangsters, but her family was careful about what was said. She and Tobe got together later to figure out the words, the meanings, the taboos that were not discussed.

Billie has trouble finding the correct channel, so Hanora makes the selection, kicks off her shoes and plugs in the kettle to make tea at the countertop. They settle down to watch *Sizzle*.

Leslie Uggams, with her smooth skin, high cheekbones and beautiful eyes, dances a fast, sexy dance to the music of "Sweet Georgia Brown" while John Forsythe looks on. Billie's left foot is tapping, tapping; she knows the music, she hums along. The mob rivalry, a story set in Chicago, progresses, and a naive—but not for long—character named Julie enters the nightclub. Loni Anderson plays the part of Julie.

"Julie doesn't know much," says Billie, clearly enjoying herself. "She doesn't know much at all. Look what's going on around her. Why can't she clue in? Everyone's crooked in this movie."

Uggams tap dances and sings "That's My Baby," and she is a wonder. The song and dance, her movements, everything about the performance sizzles with energy. Hanora would like to meet Uggams, interview her. A person that talented gives so much to the world. And her voice: so deeply powerful, it seems to echo from the back walls of the club.

Billie sings along with "That's My Baby"—a few of the lines. Her foot is tapping again.

"Uggams uses her shoulders," she says. "And why shouldn't she? They're fabulous. I used to have great shoulders. The dance," she adds. "She must have learned to use her shoulders when she learned to dance."

"She's a star," says Hanora, delighted to see Billie so engaged.

"Look at the way she can wear orange," Billie says. "I saw her on *Ed Sullivan* one time, and she wore orange then, too. You think I forget things, but I know whereof I speak.

She wore some sort of feathered outfit over one shoulder. The other was bare. She knows how to work those shoulders. Just look at her."

After Julie gets her revenge, after many twists and turns, the movie ends. Billie sits quietly for a moment, and stares at the screen while the credits roll.

"The man," she says. "The one I told you about? The one who was looking for me? He said that. He said, 'That's my baby,' when he showed me the photo."

"What photo?"

"Of him holding the baby. Our last day on board. I went up to say goodbye to Socks and the man said that, just like the song. He said he was moving to Coventry. His face was kind. He was twice my age, so much nicer than my own father. He held out the photo and told me he'd given his word that he would never speak of this, and tucked it into the letters and handed them to me. He must have been mixed up. The letters had string around them."

"What letters, Billie?"

"The ones I told you about."

"You never mentioned letters. Who wrote them?"

"I don't know. He insisted that I take them. He called me Hanora. I don't think you were around. I was saying goodbye to Socks so we could arrange to meet in London. The man might have thought I was you. I thought the letters were mine. Well, they *were* mine. He gave them to me. But I never bothered reading them. I didn't give them another thought. Socks was going directly to London, and I was right there beside him and handed them off. Socks had room in his luggage."

"But Socks left the ship in Plymouth. You and I disembarked in Le Havre."

"Plymouth was bombed eight times," she said. "I read that, after I was back at my job in New York. I told you. I went to that place where everyone assembled before getting off the ship. Socks and I wanted to say goodbye again because I was going on to Paris with you."

"Billie, you and I changed identities on the ship."

"Why would we do that?"

"It was your idea."

Why is Hanora suddenly afraid?

But Billie is afraid, too. Her memory is becoming scrambled. This happens when she is anxious.

"What did Blue Socks do with the package?"

"I don't know. It was nothing to do with me. I don't remember."

"Try. Think, Billie. Think hard. What did the man say?"

"Blue Socks? I told you. I don't remember." She stares out the window, her eyes blank. She's becoming agitated.

"The man with the letters. What did *he* say?"

"Something about not being silenced. Something about Father."

"Whose father?"

"You had a father. I had a father. The man confused me with somebody else. He was acting strangely. Socks wanted to get me over to a quiet corner. We had a shipboard romance . . . I was head over heels. I met him in London later. We had only a few minutes to say goodbye. I ran up after breakfast."

"Please. Sit quietly. Think, Billie. Where are the letters now? Where is the photo?"

"I didn't care about any of that. I handed them to Socks. I met him three times. You probably never knew that. The last time was in New York. He brought the chest back for me. That was all before Whit. I loved Whit, Hanora. He was the only one for me."

"The letters might have been mine," says Hanora. "What exactly did the man say about 'father'?"

"I had an abusive father," Billie says. "He drank. He was unkind. Your father was perfect. Uncle Kenan was so good to me when I visited every summer. I was jealous. I used to imagine that he was my father, too."

"The man on the ship. I need to know. I was adopted, Billie. Kenan and Tress were not my birth parents. The man thought you were me."

"Oh, come on, Hanora. Now you're talking nonsense." She is irritated, and clearly doesn't think much of this idea. "Why on earth would you invent such a story?

And why would you and I change identities? What would be the point of that?" Billie leans forward in her chair and rocks back and forth. "What would be the point?" she says. "What would be the point?"

She begins to cry. She's incapable of saying more. Hanora tries to calm her down. A nurse comes in to help put Billie to bed. She turns away from them both, and sobs herself to sleep.

MISTAKEN IDENTITY

H ANORA LIES IN BED. HEART POUNDING. NOT a chance of sleep. Stares at the ceiling. Goes over and over the scene in her head. More than one—a myriad of scenes. Everything so long ago. The ship. What can be recalled accurately after all this time? Everyone's memory distorted. Everyone's memory different, even when two people witness the same incident at exactly the same moment. Two onlookers or twenty-two, it makes no difference; the reports will never be the same. Remember Akutagawa, she tells herself. So many testimonies about what took place in his story "In a Grove," but no two accounts alike. Everyone with different motives in the telling.

What of her own memory? Aunt Zel warned her to guard, to preserve, the important moments so that, later, she could raid the hoard. As Aunt Zel herself must have tried to do from a past that stretched back generations before Hanora was born. How is anyone to know what to store, what will matter over time?

Maybe, Hanora thinks, maybe I managed to get some memories right. Maybe I added some of the better ones. I may have chosen others poorly. Hoarded the wrong hoard.

But she can't make light of this, even to herself.

The man travelling to Coventry was the man she had thought of earlier. She saw him when she was out walking on deck. She talked to him several times. He addressed her as Billie, knew she and Billie were cousins. He'd have known nothing of the identity switch. He wore a knitted green scarf. He seldom took it off except to dine or when dressed for the evening. Wore it during the day, wore it when out walking on deck. This memory, the forest-green scarf, has darted out from the buried hoard. And will be in her notes, she suddenly realizes. She wrote her observations when she was a passenger on the *Champlain*, sailing the ocean for the first time. Every notebook from that period is on a shelf in her closet. She hasn't looked at the notebooks for years.

She sits upright. Pulls on a robe and goes to the closet. Pulls down the one she wants, easily found. They're all in order, labelled by date. She flicks a duster over them once in a while. Has no idea what to do with them. They'll be destroyed, probably. But so far she hasn't made a move to do this. Probably because they represent her training ground. The early, rough—but detailed—recording of people and events that helped her start out in her profession.

She goes back to bed. Props pillows behind her.

Call up your feelings, she tells herself. Stay calm and call up what you saw. The day of disembarkation. First Plymouth, then Le Havre. This matters. Every detail. Memory becomes distorted along the way. Think of Billie's memory fading, replaced by some other reality.

Everything so long ago.

She begins to read.

MAR. 30, 1939—PLYMOUTH, ENGLAND!
Some passengers skipped breakfast. More than a few empty chairs. Not at our table. Excitement and buzz in the air; we're caught up in it. People reporting they haven't slept all night. Musicians in dining room. They'll disembark in France later, when Billie and I do.

Duke comes to breakfast. Ivie sits across from him. Irving Mills, too. Mills wearing spats, Ivie wearing dress with rectangular print. Wide lapel-like collar each side, reaches waist as if collar intended as vest. She smiles, gives a wave. Fabulous, self-assured smile.

Ruth in black again. Black wool dress, V-cut neckline— this time with dramatic chiffon scarf, startling cerise. Cheeks flushed, almost match scarf. She turns the emerald-and-diamond ring around and around her finger. So excited to be seeing her husband, can't keep down a cup of coffee.

Get through this part—but there's still more about her own table.

Frank and Frankie danced late last night. They ask for slices of beef with asperges *and melon. Not my kind of breakfast. Someone at table behind asks for French ice cream and waiter brings out two flavours from kitchen. Everyone roaring with laughter. Blue Socks attentive to Billie; she spent the night in his cabin. He still thinks she is Hanora. Billie says she'll correct that when they meet in April. She'll explain everything.*

The waiters move quickly to whisk away plates. Socks goes to his cabin to finish packing. Billie and I end up hurrying through meal, though no need to rush. Some people come to breakfast wearing overcoats—as if that might speed disembarkation.

Many passengers on deck as we approach land. Plymouth is spread out before us. Luggage in halls awaits pickup; people milling about in public rooms. Everyone anxious, checking passports, checking watches. Too bad, after so much relaxation all week. I mingle with crowd before going down. Have a feeling I'll miss out if I don't.

Billie and I swap our passports back. Glad to have my own again. Glad to be Hanora Oak. There's so much movement everywhere. Le Havre passengers try to stay out of the way of the mob getting off in England.

Who on earth keeps track? Plymouth, then Le Havre. After that, ship has to prepare, stock up, return to New York. Stops again in Plymouth on way back, picks up new passengers joining return voyage. Complicated trail of schedules and bookings, embarkations, disembarkations. Who keeps track?

Two assembly points. All crowded. Billie goes up first, wants to say final goodbye to Socks, wants to see him one more time before they meet in London.

I take my time, wander back upstairs. Hear the sound of a horn. Laughter from behind. A few of Duke's musicians horsing around. They're not getting off but they add to the chaos.

I catch glimpse of Fred Guy. Blue Socks edges over to speak to Guy, probably about his own mandolin, or about Fred Guy's guitar. Or maybe banjo. They played together a couple of times in lounge this week. Socks laughs and claps Guy on the shoulder.

The other musician is across the room. The older man I've seen walking on deck. He is pressed into the wall by the crowd. Wears a heavy winter coat and a knitted green scarf. I hang back because I don't belong here. But I want to see what's going on.

The room is dingy, not yet open to full light. The older man looks in my direction. He's searching for someone. He smiles at me from where he's standing, starts to make his way toward me. That's when there's a shudder and the exit gate draws back. Another surge, and bodies funnel toward the narrow opening. Billie intervenes. She's found Socks. The older man reaches her and Socks at same time. They're talking about something. Socks slings his arm around Billie's shoulder. I try not to get caught up in the surge. Have to turn away. But everything so exciting. Go back down to my cabin. Write what I can here. Soon we'll be in France. All seems like a dream. "Follow your dreams," Duke told me. "That's what I've always done."

But was it Billie the man was looking for? Was he holding something in his hand? Hanora hasn't written anything about that.

SEAMAN'S CHEST

———

S HE HAS HARDLY SLEPT. SHE CHECKS THE CLOCK—almost four in the morning—rolls over in bed, checks the time again. Drifts in and out. Wonders if the sun is up. Gets out of bed. The notebook is on the floor. She looks out at the night lights of the city, a soft orangish glow, a scene she loves, one that never repeats itself in the same detail.

She makes strong coffee. Did the older man have something in his hand? Billie remembered, said he did. The man was acting strangely, she said.

Hanora goes to the seaman's chest, drags it across the floor and into the kitchen, raises the lid. Listens to the creak and groan and thinks of the whaler who raised the same lid two hundred years ago. Wonders if the man who built the chest is the same one who painted the image of the ship on the underside.

She clears the table and begins to lift out the contents. Most are greeting card boxes of varying sizes. She opens each one and riffles through the contents before stacking the boxes on the table.

What she finds: cards sent to Billie and Whit after they met, including cards they sent to each other (or in Whit's case, several he made for Billie—she's pretty certain Billie will want to see these); birthday cards; Christmas greetings; Easter cards; Valentines; thank-you notes; and letters from Billie's former students. New Canadians she once taught. More new Canadians she helped. By donating a piece of old furniture that she and Whit had restored, or a shopping bag filled with food. By helping to write a letter to some government department or other, by organizing a picnic for her class, by making introductions to future employers, helping with applications, providing references, obtaining medical advice on someone's behalf. There are birth announcements, wedding announcements, invitations, obituaries cut from newspapers.

There are a couple of dozen photos: Billie with students, students as couples, students with babies, students with parents and grandparents who were sponsored as immigrants after the students themselves became citizens and were in a position to help.

Hanora's cards to Billie are here, postcards from abroad when she was travelling, researching, interviewing, meeting people in the Soviet Union, China, Romania, England, Ireland, France. Has Billie thrown nothing written away?

One box contains the coded childhood letters Hanora sent to Rochester during the winter months, her first correspondence with Billie. Hanora doesn't remember how the code works; she'll figure it out. And here is a photo of the horizontal scar across the back of Billie's upper thigh. A rough job of suturing, at the time. Nothing delicate here. Billie always wore long shorts in summer to cover the thick, permanent ridge of tissue. She never liked to be seen in a bathing suit, unless she wore something to cover her thigh. Hanora has no idea who took the photo of the scar. Probably one of Billie's school friends in Rochester. Or maybe her brother, Ned.

Hanora sets her childhood letters aside; she will read those later. Breaking the code won't be difficult, given the age she was at the time of writing.

She thinks about how she looked up to Billie. Her cousin: leader, creator of adventure and fun, never looking back. And yet, she stowed these markers of time past.

There are photos of Billie's early admirers. Here's one of Hallman, taken outside a jazz club in New York. Another of Hallman in front of Billie's apartment, also in New York. And then Socks, a black-and-white photo, but Hanora has no difficulty imagining the caramel shoes and royal-blue socks. This was taken *inside* Billie's apartment.

They were all in their twenties and thirties at the time. Before Billie moved to Canada after the war.

Hanora returned to Canada in 1945, but was soon off again, earning her living by bringing attention to postwar refugees, divided families. She wrote stories of individuals who survived the infamous camps. Individuals who hoped their names and photos would be recognized by family members . . . if any were living. So many people were on the move in different parts of the world, looking for a country to welcome them, to enable them to start new lives. Some people whose stories she wrote contacted her later. When this happened, she made an effort to stay in touch. Then there was the post-Stalin era to write about, the Cold War, the space race. Hanora has been most contented when travelling from one place to another.

She's nearing the bottom of the chest now. Finds two sagging Laura Secord boxes crammed with summer costume jewellery. Much of it plastic, bright, gaudy. Necklaces and chains and clip-on earrings that Billie liked to buy. The jewellery was often discarded after being worn once or twice. The founder of Laura Secord chocolates was born in Deseronto in the late nineteenth century, close to the house where Hanora grew up. That's a fact of town history Hanora has learned.

She thinks she should take a few of the boxes to Billie at Respiro. Especially the original cards Whit made for her.

Billie might also want to remember her former students and take credit for helping them create new starts in their lives. Looking at the memorabilia might give Billie a hold on the person she is. The person she was. And will give her something to do for a few days.

With the boxes removed, Hanora now finds a sturdy file folder, wider than usual. She opens it and recognizes the *Liste des Passagers* from the SS *Champlain*. There are also dinner menus—one from the night of the Bal Masqué, another from their last night aboard ship. And a few blank postcards from Paris, pub coasters imprinted with ads, brochures from the Tower of London and Westminster Abbey, jazz concert programs, a map of London, a map of the Underground, a hotel card bearing a street address— probably the hotel where Billie stayed with Socks while Hanora was travelling through pre-war France. Socks stayed on in England for a while after Billie left. When he returned, he'd have disembarked in New York on his way home to Canada.

Billie must have continued to toss things in on top of the European souvenirs. At one end of the chest Hanora finds a thin envelope containing university course information, immigration information.

And at the bottom. Beneath everything that has been lifted out. A thin bundle, tied with string. Probably never removed after being covered with souvenir papers, brochures, the folder, the ship's list, the menus. She doubts that anything was removed, by anyone, after being placed there. By Billie? By Socks? Socks stored some of Billie's belongings for her in London, and would have put them into the chest after she purchased it in the Portobello area. He had promised to deliver the chest when he returned to America, and had done that. But was Billie never curious? She threw nothing away. For her, the thin bundle was one more item, one small part of the history of the rugged old chest.

Hanora unties the string and opens the top envelope. Her hands shake as if she has tremors. She takes her time over every word, every detail.

March 30, 1939
My darling child, my darling Hanora,
I have decided to turn these over to you, random papers that survived only because of Zel and because of your late mother, my beloved Magreet. All correspondence was to have been destroyed, but sometimes when Zel sent news of you to Oswego, Magreet forwarded the letters to me in Toronto. I have a few in my possession. These I give to you.
I met your mother, Maggie, in Deseronto in 1919, when she auditioned to sing in the New Year's Eve concert. I went to your town to find work after the

war. I wanted to disappear, live in a small community I'd never heard of before, far from anywhere I had been and from anyone I had known.

Maggie was a wonderful, compassionate person. She was also a singer, an outstanding soprano. There are many things I can tell you about her, but the most important is how much she loved you. As I do. The decision to have her niece Tress and Tress's husband, Kenan, raise you was the most difficult of her life and mine. We knew, however, that they would be loving parents, and that is why you were entrusted to their care and legally adopted by them.

Maggie (she signed her letters to me as Magreet, because that is how, when I first came to Canada, I pronounced her name) was unable to leave her husband because of what they had been through in their lives, and because of earlier losses they had suffered in their marriage.

By now, you will have been told of your adoption, even though details of your birth parents were never to be revealed. That was Maggie's condition; we gave our word—the few people who were involved—collectively. Now that Maggie has died, I feel that I may speak out. I am your father. It is your right to know. Maggie died of illness, of pneumonia, only two months ago. She moved from Deseronto early in 1920, and chose Oswego, New York, because her sister, Nola, lived there. She travelled to Toronto for your birth, but returned to Oswego with you during the first six weeks of your life. She was forty-four when you were born.

Tress has by now passed on the locket. I can tell you that it belonged to my grandmother from Vienna, and later to my mother, also born in Vienna. Both women were named Hanna, and you were named after them. The locket was my gift to your mother. Maggie wanted it to be given to you. Something from both of us.

Ours (and yours) is a family scattered about Europe. The stories have not always had happy endings. My first wife, a Belgian, died in Dinant at the beginning of the First World War. She was executed, along with her parents. She had travelled there to help them shortly after war broke out. Although she and I lived in London, I had gone to Manchester to conduct a choral performance, and had not accompanied her to Belgium.

At the end of the war, I left England and the Continent, where I had lived and studied and worked all my life. There was nothing left for me there, and I moved to Canada.

Now I return to England. I have been invited

to Coventry to take over the choir at Holy Trinity Church, but temporarily, for one year, possibly two. This will probably be the last position I will formally hold.

After you read these letters, you may want to contact me. The address is enclosed. When I saw your name on the passenger list, I considered carefully how to go about this, not knowing how much you knew of the circumstances of your adoption. I leave it to you to make contact.

The photo inside this letter was taken before I moved away from Deseronto. I held you in my arms. Zel took the photo. You were two and a half months old. Your hair was as red then as it is now, the same colour as Maggie's hair, the same green eyes. Your mother was a beautiful woman. As you are now, Hanora.

From Deseronto, I moved to Toronto. Your mother travelled several times to meet me there, and I am blessed to have those memories. Each time we were together, we talked about you.

Last evening, I decided I would pass these papers on to you. I was sworn to silence by a woman who commanded my respect, and I owed it to her to stay silent. But I remain silent no longer. If only I could show you how much you have been in my thoughts *since the day you were born. It is difficult for me to believe that I have finally met you again—and by chance.*

Your loving father, Lukas Sebastian

Hanora cries and cries and cries. Her father, her birth father. She was face to face with him and hadn't known. He had loved her.

But he had been thinking of Billie when he compared the hair, the eyes. She and Billie were so much alike in their younger years, especially at the time they were aboard the *Champlain.*

Hanora had met her father. She had talked to him briefly, written him into her shipboard notebook. She has read the entry for the day of disembarkation, but now she will read what she wrote every day at sea, starting with the day she boarded in New York, March 23. There will be more detail. There has to be more.

She has names. Identities. Information. What she has sought all her life.

She tries to stop the tears. Walks in and out of rooms because she cannot be still. Returns to the kitchen. Examines the rest. The photo remembered by Billie. He placed it in Billie's hand. "That's my baby," he said. He didn't say, "This is you," because he wouldn't have known how she'd respond.

But Hanora was not given the opportunity to respond.

She stares into the faces, the small black-and-white images. Lukas is wearing what appears to be the same scarf he wore on the ship. Hanora is wrapped in blankets and he is holding her securely. Both faces are looking at the camera. They are outside Zel's rooming house in winter. Hanora recognizes the door that led into the spacious kitchen.

𝄢

WHAT else?

A New Year's Eve concert program from 1919.
Music under the direction of Lukas Sebastian
Maggie O'Neill, Soprano
Lukas Sebastian, Piano. Liszt, Gilbert and Sullivan, Claude Debussy. He accompanied Maggie when she sang lyrics from *The Mikado*. Zel accompanied another of Maggie's solos, also on piano.

Hanora's parents: Maggie and Luc. That is how he is addressed and referred to by Zel, in the letters enclosed.

AND more.

Obituary of Maggie O'Neill: who died January 23, 1939, in Oswego, New York.

Who loved Hanora's father. But remained with her husband, Am.

She reads and rereads. The letters were supposed to have been destroyed. But Maggie sent these on to Toronto. Letters that mentioned her, Hanora. Maggie shared the news with Luc.

Here is a notice cut from the *Post* in Deseronto, dated the first week of January 1920.

Found on Main Street: a woman's gold locket upon which the letter H *is inscribed. The finder has conferred a favour on the owner by leaving it under lock and key at the office of the* Post. *The owner of the locket may present herself to the editor in order to identify and claim said item.*

One of Zel's letters refers to the locket. So it was lost and then found, and Zel ended up having it in her possession. Or perhaps Maggie claimed it before she moved away and passed it to Zel, ensuring that it would eventually be received by Hanora.

Zel's letter of January 1, 1921, reveals more than Hanora has ever known, or could have guessed or suspected.

The news you await is Hanora's news, of course. I visit as often as I can, not only to send a report, but because she creates so much happiness around her. She is healthy and plump-cheeked and beautiful, just as she was when we were in Toronto in November. It goes without saying that she brings her new parents more joy than they have known since Kenan came home from the war.

I visit Tress and Kenan at their home, which is where I see Hanora. No one discusses what so few of us know. You wondered, in your letter, about the rest of the town. Not a person, I believe, has made the connection to you. Especially as it's generally known that you moved to Oswego to be close to your sister's family. Hanora has been accepted as any other child is accepted. Nothing is known except that the adoption took place "away," in the city. When I think of that day, I believe we live in the Dark Ages. Of one thing, I am certain: everyone involved is capable of closing around this secret.

I, too, am trying to understand, now that I know the entire story. I try to understand what you are going through, knowing that Am was unable to accept the child as his own. You tell me that you stay with him because of what you both had, because of what you were together in the past, because of what you both lost. Tragedy, it seems, is measured out in unequal parts among us. I know that your heart must be broken yet again.

And now Hanora understands.

The graves in the copse at the O'Neill farm, sketched by a young Mariah Bindle. Maggie and Am O'Neill. The auction of their farm, the horses sold, the babies buried, the move to town. Where Maggie eventually met Luc.

I have passed on the locket to Tress, and she under-stands that it is to be given to the baby when she is eighteen.

Someday, who knows, Hanora may own her life story.

I know you will destroy this and all my letters as they arrive, as we agreed.

In the third of Zel's letters to Maggie, written when Hanora was in her teens and forwarded to Luc:

I would like to be free to tell Hanora what I know. The stories belong to her, whether they are joyous or sad. All that I know belongs to her and to you and to Luc. If ever you give permission, I will tell her of her beginnings: her wonderful and talented mother; her humane and gentle and talented father. The great love between them. If you release us from our promise, Maggie, I will do this.

Please reconsider all of the secrecy. Will it matter,

332

after dozens of years have passed? When we are all
dead, will it matter? Hanora deserves to know.

Hanora wants to throw all the papers, the letters, the
photo, even the old chest through the wall.

No. She wants to fall to her knees.

No. She will sit in silence and give thanks, because that
is all she can do. She has no choice but to accept and understand what she has been given.

𝄢

WHO lied to her?

Everyone lied. All bound by promise. A silence insisted
upon by her birth mother.

Tress and Kenan had known the identity of Hanora's
birth parents from the beginning; they had lied by omitting
part of the truth.

Aunt Zel, who wanted so much to tell Hanora, lied
because of her friendship with Maggie. Zel, who had
known all along, and who was present when Hanora was
adopted. Who, in 1939, without breaking her word, placed
evidence directly into Hanora's hands. The photo of her
and Maggie on the skating rink. Using the excuse that she
did not want to be forgotten while Hanora was roaming
around Europe, beginning her own adult life.

Pull out the photo of Maggie and Zel. She knows where it is. She now has one photo of her mother. She will find others. She will find others of both her birth parents.

$$\text{𝄢}$$

WHO was Maggie, to demand silence, to demand this kind of loyalty and also receive it?

Her mother. Maggie O'Neill, of the O'Neill family. Who lived in Deseronto, but moved to Oswego in the States with her husband, knowing she was pregnant with another man's child. A child born of love.

Maggie, who died of pneumonia two months before the SS *Champlain* sailed on March 23, 1939. Which is why Luc Sebastian left North America for good, and returned to England.

Her father, Lukas Sebastian. The man who wore the green scarf on the ship. Who went on to Coventry from Plymouth, and who probably died there. It won't be difficult now to obtain the information.

THAT BLESS'ED STATE

―――――

HANORA SITS AT HER COMPUTER, MARIAH'S diaries by her side. She writes the first paragraphs, a symbolic start. Words will change as she goes along, as she writes and rewrites and edits. The fact that she is beginning is what is important.

Mariah Bindle was born Monday, June 28, 1886, in an upstairs bedroom of her parents' farm. The farmhouse was the original family homestead, located south of Madoc in Hastings County, in the province of Ontario. Mariah's father took horse and buggy to fetch the local midwife, having been warned not to dawdle. The midwife had explained that the birth of the fifth child would no doubt be quick, given the history of his wife's deliveries.

When the midwife was brought to the bedside, the father led his two sons and two daughters, all under the age of twelve, outside to await the news. The baby's name was decided in advance. The children had been allowed to make suggestions. If the baby was a girl, Mariah was the favoured name.

Mariah Bindle, youngest of the five Bindle children, grew up to become an outstanding artist and diarist, and left a stunning visual record of the turbulent eras that marked the first half of the twentieth century.

She stops there. Filmore is at the door, ready for their drive to Hastings County. They are expected at Mariah's homestead, but first, Hanora will visit the Ninth Concession. She has directions to the former O'Neill farm. The farm where Maggie and Am lived at the time of the death of their babies. Cause of death, diphtheria. Cause of heartbreak, death. Hanora's half-brother and half-sister. She will visit the site of their unmarked graves. She knows their names.

Donal.

Annie.

She has looked up the record of their births and deaths. Once she had a key piece of information, the rest was easy to find. She also has the date of the auction and sale of the farm before Maggie and Am moved to Deseronto. Before Maggie met Luc.

Can sorrow and joy coexist? They did for Maggie. And for Luc. They do now, for Hanora.

She will bring some of Mariah's drawings with her on the trip. She wants to be certain she's in the right place when she and Filmore walk around the farm. Filmore will take photos. She has the drawing of the copse where Mariah and her aunt Clarice ate their lunch on auction day in 1902. The drawing shows the indent in the earth beneath the shelter of the maple. The owners of the property know Hanora is coming and have assured her that they are aware of the location. They will lead her to the spot, not far from the original farmhouse. The ground has not been disturbed since the burial.

𝄢

THEY set out early. Hanora's plans are ambitious. If necessary, she and Filmore will stay at an inn in Prince Edward County overnight, and complete their journey tomorrow. Hanora doesn't want to rush or be rushed. She will take notes and she needs good, clear photos, especially of the property and the farmhouse—both outside and in—where Mariah was born more than a century ago.

This probably *will* end up being a two-day trip, because she has also promised to stop in Deseronto on her way home, to visit Breeda. Hanora feels the need to see her childhood friend, as well as the town and all its changes. If, indeed, it has changed at all since Tress died. She will have to see for herself.

She is comfortable travelling with Filmore. He is good company. He makes her laugh. They have enjoyed many evenings together, and have been out for dinner several times. He is now working on his article about Kenan's photos.

Her new friendship with Filmore is an unexpected event in Hanora's life. She was content to be alone, live alone, work alone. But now she looks forward to the time she spends with him. She has told him the story, the stories, recently uncovered. He has not told her about his time in Italy, but that will come. She wants to know what happened there; she wants to hear his stories. She met several times with Jack, and knows what the Canadians did—what Tobe did, how he lived and died—but she wants to hear Filmore's stories, too.

Both she and Filmore are old enough to know that life moves on. That people learn to live with love and regret and loss. Sometimes loss is so great, there is nothing to be done, nothing to be said. Both have learned to welcome happiness, friendship, companionship, when these present themselves. They learn anew. Count their stars. Look up or do not look up. Make choices. Continue to create the lives they want to live, to become the people they want to be.

IDENTITY?

———

T
HE WEEKEND AFTER THE TRIP, HANORA VISITS
Billie on a sunny afternoon. She carries a plastic bag
that contains two of the card boxes from the seaman's
chest.

Billie is in her TV chair and looks over when Hanora
arrives.

"Hanora. Are you out doing errands? Is that why
you're here?"

"I'm here to see you, Billie. I brought some old things
you might like to look through."

"You and your old things," says Billie, but her interest
has been sparked.

Hanora suggests that they go outside to sit in the gardens, and Billie readily agrees. She doesn't leave her room
when she's alone, but she likes to be out in the air and will
go when Hanora is there to take her.

They choose a circular table in the garden. A wide lawn umbrella inserted through a hole in the centre of the table provides shade. There is a slight breeze, pleasantly warm air. Hanora feels the breeze against her skin and sinks back in her own chair after Billie is settled. Her cousin moves more slowly these days, and is beginning to look frail. Her cane is hooked over the arm of her chair. Hanora looks at Billie and wonders if she would ever be able to understand.

She removes the lid of the first box and passes it to Billie. This contains the cards of thanks from her former students, along with photos they sent over the years—marriage clippings, obituaries, life stories, Christmas cards.

Billie becomes excited. She doesn't recall names, but some are written on the backs of the photos. Others are only dated. She laughs aloud in pleasure.

The second box contains a few coded letters from childhood. Hanora wants to see what Billie can make of these. And the photo of the scar.

Billie is confused by the letters and doesn't remember receiving or sending anything in code. When shown the photo of the scar across the back of her thigh, she fidgets uncomfortably.

"That was your fault, Hanora," she says. "You're the one who dared me to climb the tree. You're the one who made me fall."

But that isn't the way Hanora remembers the accident. Not at all.

At that moment, afternoon tea is brought out on a wheeled trolley. Staff members carry cups of tea and coffee around to the tables. Snacks are served: small squares of pizza, and fresh fruit chopped into small, manageable chunks.

A man and woman wander over and ask if they might sit at their table. Hanora hasn't seen either of them before. They tell her they are new to the place, a married couple, and have moved into a suite on the second floor. They introduce themselves as Claire and Marcel.

Billie looks them over and sips at her tea. She's had enough of the boxes and pushes them across the table to Hanora. She addresses the new residents who have joined them. "You're Marcel," she says, as if to clarify and remember. "And you are Claire."

She looks across the table at Hanora, and says, "You are Hanora."

And then, looking anxious, she asks in a faltering voice, almost a whisper, as if speaking confidentially and only to Hanora: "Who did you say I am?"

"AIR CONDITIONED JUNGLE"

H ANORA RETURNS TO HER APARTMENT, GOES directly to Duke's music and selects "Air Conditioned Jungle." She stretches out on the chesterfield to listen.

The music has an unusual title, but contains a powerful solo voice. At first, it's as if a bird has been spotted in the sky, a new life bursting with dazzle from the blue. The music slows because it can, because it has shown what it can be. Now it drifts, lilting, changing direction as mood and currents change.

Someone knows something. Clarinet leads, clarinet has the inside story. Jimmy Hamilton. Up and down the notes the story goes. Insistent, eager to share the news.

Excitement, now. Follow the main thread, punctuate. Someone adds darker bits with growly undertones. Bass all

343

the way through. Low brass. Scuttlebutt. All-out, down-and-dirty news. Followed by comment, running notes up and down, conversation jumping lip to lip, ear to ear.

And finally, the word sails on past because everyone is ready for a new topic. The music blares to a finale. In slightly more than two minutes.

Imagine.

Imagine sending news that fast. Receiving because you are part of the message. Belonging to the larger scene. Owning what everyone owns. Knowing what everyone knows. Knowing what it feels like to belong.

Listen to the beauty of this man's clarinet, and weep.

Hanora does not weep. Not now.

If she weeps, it will be because of the wonder of Jimmy Hamilton's brilliance. The music, the clarinet, each of the other instruments. Together, they convey what they know to be complex and true.

𝄢

MARIAH'S diaries are stacked in her office, every one of them read. The book's first chapter is complete. The sketchpads and drawings are laid out in rows on the living-room rug. One of these depicts Maggie and her horse, the day of the auction, August 2, 1902. Maggie was twenty-six years old when she and her husband sold their farm and moved to town. Thankfully, Mariah did return to the drawing, having been moved by Maggie's reluctance to sell the horse.

In the finished drawing, Maggie wears her hair down long. There is beauty and tenderness in her face as she leans into the horse. One arm is hooked over the horse's neck. The other droops at her side. There is a sadness about the way the arm droops. This is a parting, and Mariah has captured that parting.

Maggie resembles Hanora. Hanora resembles Maggie. She plans to ask the Bindle descendants if she will be allowed to purchase the drawing. She is almost certain they will agree after she explains her relationship to the woman.

Hanora closes her eyes. There is a pause. She holds that pause. She holds it because she is waiting now, for the music to change.

ACKNOWLEDGEMENTS

───────

My sincere thanks go to the adoptees who generously shared personal, intimate and moving stories, all of which helped in important ways while I created the character of Hanora.

Among many books consulted for research, I acknowledge *Let's Dance! A Celebration of Ontario's Dance Halls and Summer Dance Pavilions* by Peter Young; Jack F. De Long's *Summer Dance Pavilions: Bay of Quinte Area*; Michael Macklem's translation of *Samuel de Champlain: Voyages to New France 1599–1603*; *Champlain's Dream* by David Hackett Fischer; *Picture History of the French Line* by William H. Miller, Jr.; the very helpful biography *Beyond Category: The Life and Genius of Duke Ellington* by John Edward Hasse; *Duke Ellington* by James Lincoln Collier; *Boy Meets Horn* by Rex Stewart; *The Log of*

Christopher Columbus, translated by Robert H. Fuson; and Barbara Mitchell's new book, *Mapmaker: Philip Turnor in Rupert's Land in the Age of Enlightenment*. For an account of the Hastings and Prince Edward Regiment (the Hasty Ps) in Italy, I relied on Farley Mowat's *The Regiment* (introduction by Lee Windsor). The film *Sizzle* is a 1981 Aaron Spelling production. "Fame and Friendship" is by Henry Austin Dobson (1840–1924). Websites consulted include canadianwarbrides.com and flickr.com/photos/deserontoarchives. For Duke's music, I draw attention to *Duke Ellington Masterpieces 1926–1949*, Proper Records Ltd.

Love and thanks to my (musician) son, Russell Satoshi Itani, for discussions of Ellington's compositions. Thank you, Charles Magill, for sharing childhood memories of the Blitz; for your memoir, *A Very British Boyhood*; and for bringing to my attention *Balanced Menus for School Canteen Dinners* by K. Magill and F.E. Morkam. Thank you, Dr. Antoine Hakim, Neurologist and Patient Advocate, for discussions about dementia and concussion, and for your book *Save Your Mind: Seven Rules to Avoid Dementia*. My gratitude goes to Amanda Hill, archivist for Community Archives of Belleville and Hastings County; Jeffrey Atwood for finding the film; Frances Cherry; Jane Anderson; Carol Reid at the Canadian War Museum; Evan Morton, curator at the Tweed and Area Heritage Centre;

Bill Summers for giving me a grand tour of the renovated Tweed Dance Pavilion, constructed in 1929 (now operated by the Kiwanis Club of Tweed); Jack Granatstein for responding so willingly to my questions; Frances Hill for memories of the Depression years; Carrie Oliver; Al Stoliker; Joel Oliver for tracking down period magazines and terrible cats; Edward and Amy Shubert, owners and hosts of the beautiful Merrill Inn in Picton, where I stay while doing research in Prince Edward County; Alexander Gates, manager and curator, Canadian Automotive Museum in Oshawa, for permitting close inspection of the wonderful 1934 McLaughlin Buick. I thank my agent, Jackie Kaiser, and my editor, Jennifer Lambert, for their wisdom, and Janice Weaver for her excellent input as copy editor. Thank you, Noelle Zitzer, at HarperCollins—how could I do this without you? Love to my daughter, Samantha Leiko Itani; you know what you do. And to Frances Michiko Itani, who sings with the birds. Finally, a very special thanks to Marilyn (Cowie) Lambourne, Russell Hansson, Raylene Lang-Dion, Jos Cleary, Natasha Hollywood, Beth Jackson . . . and the others, equally appreciated.